FOUR-ALARM
HOMICIDE

FOUR-ALARM HOMICIDE

DIANE KELLY

St. Martin's Paperbacks

This is a work of fiction. All of the characters, organizations, and events portrayed in this novel are either products of the author's imagination or are used fictitiously.

First published in the United States by St. Martin's Paperbacks, an imprint of St. Martin's Publishing Group.

FOUR-ALARM HOMICIDE

For information, address St. Martin's Publishing Group, 120 Broadway, New York, NY 10271.

www.stmartins.com

ISBN: 978-1-250-81608-5

Our books may be purchased in bulk for promotional, educational, or business use. Please contact your local bookseller or the Macmillan Corporate and Premium Sales Department at 1-800-221-7945, ext. 5442, or by email at MacmillanSpecialMarkets@macmillan.com.

Printed in the United States of America

St. Martin's Paperbacks edition / May 2024

10 9 8 7 6 5 4 3 2 1

To all who serve as firefighters,
with special appreciation to those who responded
when my son suffered a concussion
and when my mother needed help.
Thanks for keeping us safe.

ACKNOWLEDGMENTS

It takes oodles of people to produce a book, and I appreciate every one of you! Thanks to my editors, Nettie Finn and Claire Cheek, for your insightful suggestions on my stories. Thanks to Executive Managing Editor John Rounds for leading the charge. To Sara Beth Haring, Sarah Haeckel, Sara La Cotti, and Allison Ziegler for all your hard work on marketing and publicity. Thanks, also, to artists Danielle Christopher and Mary Anne Lasher for another cute book cover. Thanks to my agent, Helen Breitwieser, for keeping me in the storytelling business. Thanks to Paula Highfill for giving me the suggestion of a house flipper series. Thanks to my author friends for your support, encouragement, and camaraderie, especially author Melissa Bourbon/Winnie Archer for all of the meaningful and helpful conversations. It's wonderful to have a friend and colleague so close!

Finally, thanks to all of you wonderful readers who

chose to spend your precious reading time with this story. I'm honored you picked my book, and I hope you enjoy every second of your time with Whitney, Sawdust, and the gang.

CHAPTER I

A HOT PROPERTY

WHITNEY

I reached out a hand and clutched the cold metal pole, giving it a firm shake. It felt sturdy enough. *Still . . .* I glanced up at the bolts on the ceiling above. All four remained in place, though the plate they were attached to showed signs of rust. I hadn't slid down a pole since the playground in elementary school. Of course, that pole had been six or eight feet high, at most. This one was much longer. The garage floor below seemed miles away. I turned to my cousin Buck. "I dare you to slide down the pole."

He stroked his full blond beard and narrowed his blue eyes. Crossing his muscular arms over his chest, he stared me down. "Darers go first."

He has me there. I can't back down now! Taking a deep breath, I clutched the fireman's pole with both hands and leapt into the void, grabbing the pole between my thighs. I was strong enough to dangle for only a second or two before gravity claimed me and my descent began. "Whee!" The well-worn fabric of my cotton coveralls produced little friction as I slid down from the upper story of the 1930s-era fire station to the concrete floor below. I bent my knees to absorb the impact as my steel-toed, rubber-soled work boots hit the cement with a thud.

Buck gazed down at me through the hole. "It sure is a long way down there."

I cupped my hands around my mouth and hollered up at him. "Chicken!" I crooked my arms into wings and flapped them. "Bawk-bawk!"

"Chicken?" He scoffed and grabbed the pole with his hands and legs, looking as if he were riding an invisible carousel horse. Wasting no time, he slid down at warp speed. I barely had time to back away lest I take a hit from his size-thirteen boots. Releasing one hand, he spun around the pole in a showy manner. "Who you calling a chicken now?"

"Not you, cousin. That's for sure."

Our childish competition completed, we turned from teasing each other to the business at hand. I glanced around the space. While no fire trucks were currently housed in the old building, the oil stains their leaky engines had left behind told a story of a once-bustling firehouse. Several years ago, however, the outdated building had been replaced by a modern facility a few blocks south. The building had been saved from the wrecking ball by a historic preservation group that purchased it from the city at market value. That group had since put the station up for sale with the provision that it would be sold only to someone who'd maintain as much of the original exterior as possible.

Buck and I were in the house-flipping business. So far, we'd remodeled two houses, a motel, a country church, and, most recently, a houseboat. We'd turned the motel into luxury condominiums, and the church into a live music and theater venue. The church's parsonage had been remade into a restaurant, which was operated by Buck's wife Colette, a professional chef.

In search of our next project, Buck and I came to take a look at the old fire station after Wanda Hartley called me to tell me about it. Wanda and her husband Marv ran a real estate brokerage and property management company called Home & Hearth Realty. I'd worked part-time for them for several years as a property manager, while also helping my uncle in his carpentry business. When the house-flipping gigs became profitable enough that I could support myself, I resigned with their blessing. Their niece had needed a job and took over for me. At any rate, when this unusual property popped up as a new listing in the Multiple Listing Service, Wanda knew that Buck and I might be interested and had called to tell me about the open house.

Glancing around, I imagined the possibilities. "What do you think? We could turn this place into a boutique hotel, or a theme restaurant where everything on the menu is a flambé."

"It's already got a stripper pole." Keeping one hand on the pole, Buck hooked a knee around it and swung in a circle, arching his back in a poor imitation of an exotic dancer. "Maybe we should lean in and turn it into a gentlemen's club. It could be called Hooker and Ladder."

I rolled my eyes. "You get a hard no from me on that. But I agree with the leaning in."

Rather than transform the fire station into something entirely new and unrecognizable, it would be far more fun to embrace its history and incorporate interior design elements that celebrated its past. Besides, it would be even more fun to turn it into a private residence than a commercial property, which buyers generally customized to their own particular needs and specifications anyway. I'd hate for all of our remodeling work to be undone by the next owner.

I motioned Buck to come closer and whispered, "The more of the original architecture we agree to preserve, the greater chance we have of landing this property." I pointed up through the hole. "The station already has a kitchen, living area, two bedrooms, and a complete bathroom." Firefighters lived at the station during their twenty-four-hour shifts, after all, so the place had been designed to serve as a home of sorts. "Let's update the cabinets, appliances, and fixtures and sell it as a single-family home."

A rich hipster would snatch up the place in a heartbeat, especially if we added a rooftop patio and upgraded the large bathroom into a spa-like space. From this site north of downtown, the buyers would have a fantastic view of the capitol building and the long, wide green of the Bicentennial Capitol Mall. They could also see the limestone towers of the carillon bells. The towers surrounded a court with three stars symbolizing the three regions of the state—eastern, middle, and western—and anchored the north end of the park. The bells played state classics such as the "Tennessee Waltz" and "Rocky Top" at the top of each hour. The sound of the bells would add even more charm. What's more, the popular Germantown location meant we'd get top dollar for the property when we sold it.

Germantown included eighteen city blocks, bounded by Hume Street on the north, Rosa Parks Boulevard on the west, Jefferson Street on the south, and 2nd Avenue North on the east. One of the neighborhood's most famous former residents was distiller George Dickel, maker of Tennessee whiskey. An early Nashville suburb established by European immigrants, much of Germantown had fallen into disrepair prior to the district's designation on the National Register of Historic Places in the late 1970s. Rediscovered and reborn in recent decades, the neighborhood contained a number of re-purposed historic properties. The Elliott School was a former educational institution turned into luxury condominiums. The Neuhoff Project transformed a former slaughterhouse along the Cumberland River into a mixed-use property.

Of course, the great location close to downtown and Nashville nightlife meant we were not the only rehabbers with eyes on the property. The woman from the historical preservation group was currently upstairs with two other potential buyers, showing them around. One of those buyers was Thad Gentry, a local real estate magnate known for unscrupulous business practices. He and I had crossed paths before, and let's just say it hadn't been pleasant.

Buck sauntered over to a metal box mounted on the wall. A green button at the top read start, while the red button under it read stop. "Is this the alarm?" He reached out a finger, hovering it over the start button. "I wonder if it still works." Before I could stop him, he'd pressed the button. A deafening alarm rang out, echoing in the bay. He quickly jabbed the stop button. "Damn, that's loud!"

"Duh," I said. "It's supposed to be." Back in the day, the bells of the firehouse had been rung to summon fire-fighters. In more recent years, the alarm had served a warning to those in the vicinity to steer clear so the fire trucks could get quickly on their way after exiting the bay. "Let's go back upstairs," I suggested. "See what the other potential buyers are saying."

Buck returned to the pole and made a show of attempting to climb it to the second floor. I rolled my eyes once more. "Go that way if you'd like, monkey man. I'm taking the stairs."

I headed over to an ugly but functional metal staircase on the left side of the garage and made my way upstairs, moving as quietly as I could in my boots. Buck gave up on the pole and followed me. We stepped through the open door and stopped in the empty living area. The president of the historical society had a name that, befittingly, sounded as if it came from an earlier era—Betsy Peabody. She leaned against the kitchen counter, her lips pursed as she listened to Thad Gentry expound on his plans for the property.

Gentry was short and stocky, as solidly built as this old building. His hair and goatee were dark with gray streaks like the fur of a wolf. Like his lupine looka-likes, the man was a skilled predator, though he preyed on property owners rather than deer or rodents. He'd bought out older Nashville neighborhoods for next to nothing, razing family homes and building McMansions, office buildings, or high-dollar residential high-rises on the land with little regard for any concerns other than profits. The former homeowners were left feeling exploited, and the neighborhoods lost their unique personalities and appeal. I believed in progress, but I also believed in preservation.

Gentry shared his plans with Peabody. "With the large bay downstairs, this building would make a perfect auto parts store and repair shop, or maybe one of those express oil change places. All I'd have to do is in-

stall a couple of lifts. The upstairs would be used for re-
tail, storage, and administrative offices. We'd leave the
exterior as is, other than adding a sign."

Though I was no fan of Thad Gentry, I had to admit
he'd come up with a reasonable, if unexciting, plan for the
building. Even so, I could tell the woman wasn't thrilled
by the thought of this historic treasure being turned into a
place that smelled of stale coffee and petroleum.

Gentry seemed to sense her unease. He cast a glance
at my cousin and me, frowned, and returned his attention to Peabody. "I'll beat any other bid you receive by
ten percent. That'll put more money in your group's cof-
fers for buying other historic properties."

Her pursed lips shifted, pointing to one side then the
other as she pondered his offer. "We could definitely use
some new funding . . ."

"No!" The word was out of my mouth before I could
choke it back. "Don't sell to him. At least not until we
tell you our plans for the place."

She turned to look at me, her expression annoyed.
"And what are *your* plans?"

Buck and I exchanged a glance. We didn't want
Gentry using our ideas.

I turned back to her. "May we discuss them in private?"

Gentry scoffed. "As if I'd steal ideas from two amateurs like you."

The first time I'd gone head-to-head with the guy was
when I'd bought the stone cottage where I now lived. I'd
purchased it from one of his competitors, and he'd been
none too happy to lose the sale to me.

"We're not amateurs," I snapped. *Not anymore, anyway.* "Surely, you've heard what we did with the Music
City Motor Court? And the Joyful Noise Playhouse?"

Gentry scowled, but Peabody's mouth formed an inquisitive O and her eyes gleamed with excitement. She looked from me to my cousin. "You two were behind those projects?"

"Yep." Buck held up his hands. "Got the calluses to prove it."

I raised my equally callused hands. As I did, the diamond on my engagement ring caught the light and sparkled. It was a small stone, all my fiancé Collin Flynn could afford on a police detective's salary, but its modest size made it no less beautiful to me.

Her mouth curled up in a smile. "You're gaining quite a reputation for your creative projects."

Gentry snorted, drawing our attention back to him. "I was wondering if this property was too small potatoes for Gentry Real Estate Development, and this conversation has convinced me it is." He flapped a dismissive hand at Buck and me. "You two can have this old heap."

As if it's his decision to make. Sheesh.

The sour look on Peabody's face said she, too, was put off by Gentry's arrogance. Without bothering to bid the woman goodbye, he turned and headed for the stairs.

Is it wrong of me to hope he trips and tumbles down them?

There was no telltale sound of the man somersaulting down the steps but, seconds later, we heard the downstairs door slam. With the entitled developer gone, the three of us resumed our discussion. My cousin held out a hand, deferring to me. "Whitney's the brains behind our business. I'm just the muscle. She's in charge of design. She tells me what to do and how to do it."

Peabody chuckled. "If only all men were so willing

to take direction." She eyed me, waiting to hear what I had in store.

Before coming here today, Buck and I had driven around Nashville and taken a look at some of the older fire stations, including the Holly Street Fire Hall, which had been completed in 1914 by the first city architect, James B. Yeaman. It was the first fire station in the city built to accommodate motorized fire trucks and was designed to blend with the surrounding neighborhood. The station was still in use. When I told Peabody that we'd toured other stations, she appeared impressed. "You've certainly done your due diligence." She cocked her head and arched her brows. "What might you do here?"

I shared my thoughts. "The exterior could be retained almost completely, though it would be a good idea to replace the windows with similar-looking, energy-efficient double-paned models." The current windows were single-paned and drafty. "Buck can get the dents out of the existing roll-up bay door." Some of the stone quoins on the edges of the building were chipped or cracked, as were some in the stringcourse that ran underneath the windows on the upper story, delineating the juncture of the two floors. I assured her we could repair them. "We'll find matching stone at a quarry or stone supply. Buck can use his sander to shape them as needed. Matching masonry could be used to cover the cracks." I gestured to the pole. "We'll replace the pole with a spiral staircase. Or maybe we could install the staircase around it and leave the pole in place."

She let out a little squeal and clutched her fists to her chest. "That would be absolutely charming!" She lowered her arms. "Of course, it's not just up to me. The plans and bids will have to be run by our committee. As soon as you have them drafted, e-mail me. We've received four other proposals already, and we'll be voting at our meeting next Monday."

"Then I'd better get right to work."

CHAPTER 2

HOUSE PLANS AND WEDDING PLANS

WHITNEY

After taking careful measurements of the fire station, Buck and I thanked Betsy Peabody for allowing us to tour the property, took the stairs down to the first floor, and exited the building. The intense August sun beat down on the pavement, and the pavement deflected the heat right back up. If we stood here too long, the soles of our boots might melt. I made a mental note to include flowering dogwood trees in my design. The small trees would provide pretty pink blooms in the spring and light shade in the summer, without overpowering the building. Forsythia bushes would make nice accents closer to the road. They produced striking yellow blooms early each spring and lush foliage through the fall.

As we stopped next to our vehicles in the front parking lot, Buck turned to me. "How much do you think we should offer for this place?"

I chewed my lip, excited about this project but worried we might not be the winning bidders if we offered only asking price or below. Germantown properties, even ones in need of major rehab, went for top dollar. I'd hate to lose this unique opportunity. I performed some quick mental math. By my rough estimate, the cost of materials would be in the range of forty to fifty grand. We'd supply the labor, so there'd be no outlay of cash for workers but, if we bid too high, we wouldn't make enough profit for the project to be worth our time and effort. The remodel would take at least three months, and Buck and I would split any profit fifty-fifty, so the profit margin had to be twice the amount of a reasonable salary for that time period. Still, I thought we could go fifteen thousand over asking price and still make a nice chunk of change when we resold it. Both Buck and I had good credit, and we'd been pre-approved for a loan that would cover the amount we'd need. "What do you think about fifteen over?"

"Let's do it," Buck said.

We parted ways in the fire station parking lot. While he headed out to help his father with a carpentry job, I drove home to work on the design for the firehouse. I had no formal design training, but I was addicted to rehab shows, magazines, and websites. Not to brag on myself, but I might have a little natural talent, too. I'd worked carpentry jobs with my uncle and cousins for years, so I knew how to blend form and function.

As I pulled into the driveway of my home, the stone cottage in the Belmont-Hillsboro neighborhood of Nashville, my buff-colored cat Sawdust stood atop the cat tree in the front window, arching his back in a deep stretch. He put a paw to the window in greeting, happy to see me. I was happy to see the sweet little guy, too.

Before I'd fallen in love with Detective Collin Flynn, Sawdust had been my number-one guy. Now, the two shared my affections.

Sawdust hopped down and met me at the door as I walked in. His partner-in-crime, a cute calico kitty named Cleo, came skittering out of the kitchen. The adorable kitten belonged to my roommate Emmalee. After tossing my purse onto the couch and treating both the cats to an ear rub, I went to the kitchen. There, I found Emmalee warming up a mug of the morning's leftover coffee in the microwave. She wore her chef's uniform, her long mahogany hair pulled into a tight bun at the nape of her neck. She worked as the assistant manager of Colette's eatery, the Collection Plate Café.

"Off to work?" I asked.

She downed the coffee in three quick gulps. "The playhouse is sold out tonight," she said as she rinsed the mug and placed it in the dishwasher. "The café is going to be busy."

"I hope it'll be filled with big tippers."

"You and me both." She cocked her head. "How'd the firehouse tour go?"

"We're planning to make an offer, but we're not the only ones in the running. It's going to be competitive."

She raised her hands and crossed her fingers. "Good luck!" She grabbed her purse, bade me and the cats goodbye, and headed out the door.

For two people who lived together, Emmalee and I rarely saw each other. We both had busy careers. My work started early, and I was often gone before she climbed out of bed in the mornings. She worked late most nights, and regularly arrived home after I'd gone to sleep. I hoped it wouldn't be the same for me and Collin once we were married.

I plopped myself down on a stool at the breakfast bar with my computer, a pencil, and a pad of graph paper. Sawdust hopped up to lie on my lap, while Cleo sat on the counter, batting at my pencil as I moved it across the pad, sketching designs for the firehouse. As I worked, I consulted the pics I'd taken earlier.

Large metal lockers stood along the back wall of the garage bay for the firefighters' turnout gear. The lockers would make great storage spaces, so we'd leave them in place and coat them with bright yellow paint akin to the stripes on firefighter gear. Red paint would be fun for the exterior door. I'd use the same color on the kitchen and bathroom cabinets. New black countertops and appliances would look great in the kitchen. An online search led me to a site that sold cabinet knobs in the shape of fire hydrants. *Perfect.* The wood flooring on the second story was worn down in the high-traffic areas, evidencing decades of firefighter feet having traversed the building. But while some might see the uneven flooring as a flaw, I saw it as character. We'd leave the floors in place, though we'd sand them and apply fresh stain. A soft yellow paint would work well on the walls. Or maybe a pale gray? I'd get samples of each and see how they looked once the other work was completed. *This place is going to look so cute when we're done with it!*

The living area and kitchen planned, I turned my attention to the bedrooms and bathroom. Because the rooms were designed to be used by multiple firefighters at once, all were especially spacious. I flipped to the next page of the pad, sketched the current bedroom and bathroom layout, and stared at the draft, considering our options. *Hmm.* One of the bedrooms could remain as is to serve as the master. We'd put up a wall to divide the other bedroom in two, turning the place into a three-bedroom home. The ugly, utilitarian bathroom could likewise be divided in two. We'd add an entry from the master into a spa-style bath, with a walk-in shower, freestanding soaking tub, and toilet with a bidet attachment and heated seat, which were all the rage. In the secondary bath, it could be cute to leave one of the metal toilet stalls in place, and paint it red. The other stall would be replaced by a standard tub and shower. Hexagonal white tile would look great in both baths.

Now, for the rooftop patio. A perimeter railing of sturdy metal posts with black cables would provide safety without obstructing the view. A propane-powered firepit would make a nice focal point, and provide warmth and ambiance on cool evenings. A slatted cover would provide respite from the sun on hot summer days. Outdoor curtains could be added to soften the look and provide privacy.

I proceeded to sketch the designs and typed up a detailed description of our plans. When I was done, I e-mailed a copy to Betsy Peabody along with the amount of our bid, and cc'd Buck. I crossed my fingers and looked to the heavens. *Please let them accept our proposal!*

As the deities pondered our fate and that of the old fire station, I turned to a matter that I could control—my wedding. I'd always been a homebody and an introvert, preferring a small handful of close, trusted friends to a large roster of gal pals. Though I wasn't lacking in confidence, I didn't generally relish being the center of attention. My heart sang at the thought of becoming Collin's wife, but we'd agreed to keep the ceremony short and sweet, and the celebration fun but simple. Even so, there still seemed to be a million and one details to sort out for the celebration. Making a guest list. Selecting invitations. Registering for gifts. Making a wedding website. Finding a deejay and drafting a playlist. And of course, we needed a place to host the event, so choosing a venue was at the top of the list. In fact, Collin and I planned to tour several venues over the next week.

For now, I could work on my part of the guest list and the registry. The only gift Collin wanted for our wedding was a GPS attachment for his computerized telescope. We planned to spend our honeymoon in North Carolina, stargazing in Hominy Valley and various spots along the Blue Ridge Parkway, before continuing on to the Outer Banks, home to lighthouses, the tallest sand dunes on the east coast, and a herd of wild horses, not to mention the Lost Colony of Roanoke and the site of the Wright Brothers' famous first flight. I could hardly wait!

I spent the next quarter hour making a list of family and friends I wanted to invite to the wedding, knowing my mother would add some names, as well. Collin was making a list, too, and I'd asked his mother to provide me with names and addresses for those she'd like us to invite. Her list had been provided promptly, and was quite long. We'd need a sizable venue to accommodate everyone.

Once I'd completed the guest list, I began searching for things online that we could add to our registry. Having both lived on our own for several years, there was little we lacked. We had plenty of dishes and cookware, bedding and towels, and decorative items. In fact, we'd probably be getting rid of duplicate items when we merged our households. *Would it be weird to register for a new drill press?* I figured it was no less weird than the GPS thingamabob that Collin wanted, so I started a gift registry at Ace Hardware, adding an electric dust collector, too.

These tasks completed, I took a shower and headed to bed. I plugged in my phone to charge and sent a text to Collin, checking in. *How was your day?*

It was a half hour later when his reply finally arrived. By then, I was two chapters into a new murder mystery novel. *Busy. Working a double homicide. Appears to be drug related.*

The duties of a homicide detective were hardly nine to five. Of course, the same went for a house flipper. Buck and I often worked evenings and weekends, though I had so much fun seeing my visions come to life that I didn't much mind so long as it wasn't keeping me from time with Collin.

Knowing my fiancé was busy, I simply sent him a kissy face emoji along with *We'll catch up later.* Sighing, I set my phone down on the night table. It was a good thing Collin and I would be moving in together after the wedding. Cohabitation was the only chance we had of seeing each other on a regular basis.

I turned out the light. Sawdust shifted into position next to me, and I draped an arm over him. I gave him a soft kiss on the head. "Good night, boy."

He revved up his purr and settled his face on the blanket.

CHAPTER 3

OPPORTUNITY KNOCKS TWICE

WHITNEY

The following Tuesday morning, Collin and I met up at the fifth potential wedding venue on our list. With his dark hair, green eyes, and lean, athletic build, Collin was much more attractive than the gruff, swarthy detectives often depicted in television shows and movies. However, he was just as clever as those weathered investigators. What's more, he was smart enough to listen to me when I speculated about his cases. More than once, a hunch I'd had paid off.

After I slid out of my red SUV, he greeted me with a smile and a soft, warm kiss on the cheek. I gladly accepted his kiss before turning to the building and exhaling sharply. "Let's hope this place works out. We're running out of options."

While any of the four proceeding venues would have been wonderful places to hold a wedding, none had available dates that would work for us. Prior to Collin's proposal, my parents had booked a two-week cruise on the Italian Riviera between Thanksgiving and Christmas. Collin had a training conference in Chicago in late October. Buck, Colette, Collin, and I had tickets to see Kacey Musgraves in concert on a Friday in early November, which meant that weekend was out. We'd need to have a rehearsal and rehearsal dinner the evening before our wedding ceremony, after all. That didn't leave us many dates in the near future to work with, and Collin and I didn't want to wait until next year to tie the knot. Even the Joyful Noise Playhouse was fully booked on weekends through the end of this year and well into the next.

We took the stairs up to the wraparound porch, entered the beautiful Victorian home through beveled glass doors, and checked in with the manager, who took us on a tour.

When the tour ended, Collin turned to me and took my hand, a hopeful gleam in his eyes. "What do you think, Whitney?"

I gave his hand a squeeze. "I love it."

The house had sprawling grounds, a picturesque pond, and plenty of space to invite everyone on our list. It was also booked until kingdom come. "Our next available Saturday is in August of twenty twenty-six," the woman said. "Would you like to reserve it?"

My jaw dropped. "I was told on the phone that you had an available Saturday this fall."

"We did," she said, "but that date was booked this morning."

I put my hands over my face and groaned.

Collin exhaled sharply. "August twenty twenty-six is over two years from now."

She shrugged. "It takes nearly that long to properly plan a wedding."

I certainly hoped not. Collin and I had just three months to pull ours together.

Before we could respond, she said, "If you're willing to have a mid-week ceremony, we can get you in much sooner. There's a Wednesday open in mid-October."

Collin and I exchanged an exasperated glance. There was no way we'd hold our wedding on a weeknight. Had we known it would be so hard to get a wedding venue, we might have just eloped and been done with it. Our mothers would have thrown a hissy fit, of course. They both wanted to see us walk down the aisle and have a proper ceremony, be a part of our big day. I couldn't blame them. I'd feel the same way if I had a child one day. We declined the offer of a Wednesday evening wedding, thanked the woman for her time, and walked back outside.

"What are we going to do?" I asked Collin.

He pulled me to him and held me tight, stroking my hair to calm me. "There's dozens of chapels in Vegas. We could treat our guests to an all-you-can-eat buffet and a show."

I put a hand on his chest and pushed him back. "That's not happening."

"I know." He heaved a sigh. "But it was worth a shot."

A backyard wedding wasn't an option. None of our family members owned a house that was big enough. *What are we going to do?*

I'd silenced my phone during the tour, and it now jiggled in the pocket of my overalls, letting me know someone was trying to reach me. According to my screen, that someone was Betsy Peabody. Buzzing with anticipation, I raised a finger to let Collin know I'd be quick, and accepted the call. "I hope you've got good news for me," I said without preamble. "I could use some right now."

Peabody laughed. "I do. Another buyer outbid you by five grand, but they planned to turn the firehouse into a gym with an outdoor rock-climbing wall. The committee didn't like that it would cover the building's façade."

I pumped a victorious fist and grinned at Collin. "We got the fire station!" He held up his hand for a high five. Meanwhile, Peabody said they could close on Friday afternoon. "Great!" I said. "I'll let our mortgage company know." I was glad things were moving rapidly. I didn't like to lose momentum on a project.

I thanked Peabody and we disconnected. As I slid my phone back into my pocket, an idea occurred to me. The truck bay on the bottom floor of the firehouse could easily hold a hundred and forty chairs. Rather than proceed down an aisle, my father could escort me down the spiral staircase we planned to install. Tables could be set up along the sides of the bay and, while guests ascended to the rooftop patio for pre-dinner cocktails after the ceremony, the tables could be moved onto the garage floor for dinner. The upstairs kitchen would provide an on-site base for Colette's team to cater the event. The living room could serve as a dance floor, while a few tables and chairs could be set up in the bedrooms for those who preferred a quieter place to engage in conversation. There was room for about twenty cars to park at the fire station, but the café next door served only breakfast and lunch, and closed at three o'clock in the afternoon. For the right price, surely the owner would allow us to use their parking lot after hours.

I took Collin's hands in mine and looked into his

eyes. "What if we got married at the fire station?" I ran through my thoughts. "It has everything we've been looking for in a venue, and it would cost us nothing."

His shoulders relaxed in relief and he gave my hands a squeeze. "It's a perfect plan. But forget coming down the spiral staircase. You should slide down the pole in your wedding dress. It would make for a spectacular entrance."

I slid him a grin. "I'll think about it."

Friday afternoon, after Buck and I signed our way through a virtual mountain of paperwork, the fire station was ours. We drove straight over to start the demolition. Collin and I had decided to get married on the Saturday before Thanksgiving, which meant Buck and I had three months to complete the rehab. It could be done, but only if we worked diligently.

Buck pulled his toolbox out of the back of his van and set it on the fire station's front drive. He reached into the bay again and pulled out a metal yard sign that read WHITAKER WOODWORKING. He carried it over and jammed the support posts into a narrow swath of soil between the sidewalk and the curb.

I had no problem giving Whitaker Woodworking some credit for this job. After all, it was Buck's father—my uncle Roger—who'd taught us carpentry and employed us for years. But with five projects under our tool belts, maybe it was time for Buck and me to come up with a name for our house-flipping business. When I mentioned the idea, he asked, "What would you want to call it?"

I raised my shoulders. "I don't know. I haven't had time to think it through."

His eyes narrowed as he pondered. "What about Two Tools Renovations?"

"That name would get people's attention for sure, but I'd prefer a name that's less self-deprecating." I chewed my lip as I thought. "Two Cousins Transformations?"

Buck snorted. "That makes it sound like we turn into werewolves on a full moon."

He had a point. When no other name immediately came to mind, we decided to shelve the discussion for later and headed inside with our toolboxes. While I worked in the kitchen, removing the cabinet doors to be sanded and painted, Buck toiled in the bathroom. His voice echoed in the space as he sang along to Tim McGraw playing on his phone.

I was working to remove a stubborn screw when a finger came out of nowhere and tapped me on the shoulder. Gasping, I spun around, my screwdriver raised in an instinctual act of self-preservation. With Buck's caterwauling, I hadn't heard the two strangers walk up behind me. Fortunately, the woman who'd tapped me on the shoulder whipped her head back in time to avoid losing an eye. I lowered my tool and put a hand to my chest in a vain attempt to still my pounding heart. "I didn't hear you come in."

With their arms hanging loose by their sides and mild-mannered expressions on their faces, the two appeared harmless. The woman held a shiny green and white rectangle in her left hand. My first thought was cell phone, but when my nose detected a slight smell of smoke, I realized it was a pack of Newport cigarettes. Her thumb held a white disposable lighter tight against the pack. The woman's hair had probably once been blonde, but she'd let it go natural and now it was the same gray shade as sun-bleached driftwood. Her hair and the crow's feet around her hazel eyes put her in her mid to late sixties. She wore minimal makeup, just enough to give her face a touch of color but no glamour. She was likely retired, in light of her age and the fact that she wore a green V-neck T-shirt, denim shorts, and a pair of wedge flip-flops on what for most folks was a workday. In addition to the scent of cigarette smoke, she'd brought the gangly man along with her. He was best described as a gargoyle come to life. His hair was the color of concrete, his skin pale, his facial features oversized. His deep-set pewter eyes gazed out from under a protruding browbone. The man looked to be about her same age, pushing seventy.

Evidently, Buck and I had forgotten to lock the door. While I didn't appreciate people wandering into the place, I supposed the fact that it was a former firehouse made it seem like a public building. I made a mental note to post signs that read Private Property—No Trespassing.

"Sorry," the woman said. "We didn't mean to startle you." Her accent was all Mississippi, with elongated vowels, a playful lilt, and an "aah" sound replacing the letter *r* in her words. She offered me her hand. "I'm Joanna Hartzell."

I slid my screwdriver into my tool belt, tugged off my work glove, and gave her hand a shake. "Whitney Whitaker." At least that was my name for now. Once Collin and I married, I'd become Whitney Flynn. I'd debated keeping my maiden name or hyphenating Whitaker-Flynn. We'd even discussed combining surnames, but we didn't want to be known as the Flakers or the Whitlynns, and could only imagine the red tape that would be required. In the end, I decided to share the last name of the man I'd chosen to share my life with.

After I'd shaken hands with Joanna, the gargoyle offered his hand, as well. "Gideon Koppelman."

"We live in the neighborhood." Joanna gestured in the general direction of the back wall, which I took to mean they lived in the residential area behind the fire station. "We saw your sign and the van out front. Are you rehabbing this place?"

"Yes. My cousin and I plan to turn the station into a residence."

"Oh, yeah?" Gideon's thick gray brows lifted. "Can't wait to see how it turns out."

"You and me both." There was nothing more satisfying than stepping back once a project was finished and feeling proud of what my cousin and I had accomplished.

Joanna cocked her head. "Any chance you can take a look at a townhouse around the corner? It could use some work and I'd love to get some professional input."

At work less than half an hour, and already my progress had been derailed. It could be seen as a bad omen, but I preferred to think of it as an opportunity to help someone. I didn't mind doling out some free remodeling advice now and then so long as people weren't cheapskates looking for free repair work. "I'd be happy to take a look." I returned my screwdriver to my toolbox. "I just need to tell my cousin that I'm stepping out."

Gideon grinned. "He the one singing in the shower? Good thing he knows a trade. He'd have starved to death as a performer."

A total stranger insulting my cousin didn't sit well with me, but the man wasn't wrong. Buck could benefit from a voice lesson or two.

The two followed me out of the kitchen and into the hall, where I stopped at the open door of the large bathroom. Buck danced a little two-step as he made his way across the floor of the shower. "Hey, Buck!" I called over his music. After he turned around and turned down the volume on his phone, I held out my hand to indicate our visitors. "Joanna and Gideon are from the neighborhood. They want me to take a look at a townhouse around the corner."

Buck tossed his wrench into his toolbox. "I'll go with y'all. Give you my two cents, too."

We followed Joanna and Gideon down the stairs. This time, I remembered to lock the door of the fire station behind us so no one else could venture inside. We took to the sidewalk and circled around the end of the block, turning left onto a residential street lined with the townhouses Germantown was known for. Though some of the construction in the district was new, most of the townhouses on this street were in structures built in the early 1900s and originally designed to house multiple families, each on a separate floor. Back then, the residences been filled almost exclusively by European immigrants. These days, the diverse neighborhood was home to people from all sorts of backgrounds.

The first house on the left sat perpendicular behind the fire station. Parked at the curb in front was a bright green tow truck with a yellow light bar atop the cab. A crumpled silver sedan was hiked up behind it, an old model from the early 2000s. The tow truck faced away from us, against traffic. Brake lights flashed as the driver started the motor.

Joanna cupped her hands around her mouth and hollered. "Lane! Wait up!" But it was too late. The loud putter of the engine drowned out her cry and the tow truck pulled away from the curb. Joanna's hands fisted in frustration at her chest and she stomped her right foot on the sidewalk. "I wish he'd tell me when he plans to come by so I don't miss him."

"There might be a reason he didn't tell you." Gideon cut her a sour look. "You'd better check and see if anything is missing."

Joanna lowered her hands and watched as the truck disappeared down the block. Her chest heaved in resignation before she tossed her friend a glance of equal parts shame and irritation. "He can't get in. I changed the door code after what happened last time."

Who's Lane? And what happened last time? I wanted to ask, but it was none of my business. I'd only been asked to take a look at the property.

Joanna stopped in front of the house. The towering three-story structure was painted fern green with ivory trim and shutters. It was split directly down the middle to form two townhouses with identical covered porches on each half of the first floor. But the paint and porches were where the similarities ended. The half on the right was well kept, the porch adorned with a welcome mat, a hanging basket of pink petunias, and two wooden rocking chairs with a small table between them. Yellow lantana filled the flowerbed. Bumblebees buzzed around the tiny blooms. The small lawn in front of the townhome on the right side was filled with lush green grass, the kind that felt wonderfully soft when you stood on it barefoot, making you want to dig your toes into it. The left side looked like its evil twin. The flowerbed was likewise filled with yellow flowers—dandelions. What grass remained in the front yard was overgrown, while the rest of the patch was bare dirt. Three shutters on the upper floors hung askew. One of the front windows on the second floor was covered with a large piece of plywood. The porch steps were rotting, the edges uneven, one stair tread broken through.

Joanna pointed to the right side of the house. "That's my side."

I pointed to the dilapidated left half. "Is this one vacant?"

"Vacant and abandoned." Joanna said a couple called the Bottiglieris had lived there for decades, even before Joanna and her late husband bought the adjoining townhouse, but they'd since passed away. "Mrs. Bottiglieri went first. Kidney disease. Her husband lived here by himself another two years before he moved to a nursing home. He passed on three years back."

"Who owns the place now?" I asked. "Did he have any heirs?"

"He left the house to his children," Joanna said. "All seven of them."

"Seven?" As an only child, I could hardly imagine what it would be like to grow up in a house with six siblings. I supposed it would be awfully crowded, and they'd likely had little privacy. But it could have been a lot of fun, too. There'd always be someone around to play with.

"Seven kids," Gideon confirmed, frowning. "And not one of them willing to lift a finger to help their father maintain the place. The grandchildren wouldn't help, either. They're just as useless as their parents. The house declined nearly as fast as Mr. Bottiglieri did. He couldn't keep up with it himself. Us neighbors did what we could, which wasn't much. He was on a fixed income and didn't have the money to pay for the bigger repairs it needed."

"Damn shame." Joanna frowned and shook her

head. "Anyway, shortly after their father died, the oldest daughter rented it out. The other kids got in a dither about Mary Ruth leasing it without getting their okay first, but she offered to split the income with them and that shut 'em up. Problem was, everyone wanted a share of the revenue, but nobody wanted to fork out any cash to keep up the place. One thing after another went wrong, nobody would take responsibility for fixing anything, and the tenants got fed up. They moved out before the end of their lease."

A townhome like this would sell in an instant if it were in good condition. Heck, at the right price, it would sell quickly despite the sorry shape it was in. "Why didn't the Bottiglieri children just sell the place? Get it off their hands?"

Gideon snorted. "'Cause they're idiots. All they do is bicker, bicker, bicker."

Joanna sighed. "I keep my side looking nice and in good repair. It's the neighborly thing to do. But with the Bottiglieri kids not keeping up their half of the house, it puts my half at risk, too. Mold could spread. Wood rot, too. Not to mention the negative effect on my property value." She gestured to Gideon. "He and I put that plywood in the window after a limb fell off their tree and broke the glass. If it wasn't for us, the place would be in even worse shape than it is."

The situation was horribly unfair to Joanna. "Have you reported the issue to the city's code enforcement office?"

"I did," Joanna said. "But the house is still in Lorenzo's and Giorgia's names. The citation was issued to *them*, even though they're deceased. The code office said that's all they can do since they're legally required to go by the names on the deed."

Buck hooked his thumbs in his tool belt. "You thought about suing their children?"

"I sure have," Joanna said. "I even talked to an attorney about it. He said it would be difficult for me to prove an amount for damages since my house is still in good shape now. He also told me that just because somebody leaves property to a person in their will doesn't mean it automatically passes to the heir. The children could disclaim ownership and walk away without paying me a cent. I might be able to get a judgment and file it as a lien against the property, but trying to foreclose on the lien would be a heap of trouble since there's no living owner of record. Dragging the kids into court would cost a small fortune and Lord only knows how much time."

What a mess. Buck and I had bought the roadside motel we'd rehabbed at a tax sale. I wondered if this place might eventually go on the auction block. "Have the taxes been paid?"

Joanna raised her hands, palms up. "Who knows?"

Buck's gaze had roamed the front of the townhouse since we'd arrived, taking in the foundation, roof, and siding. He turned to Joanna. "Any chance you've got a key to the place?"

She shook her head. "They left one with me a few times over the years so I could feed their dogs while they went on vacation, but I always returned the key when they got home."

Buck walked over and stepped up onto the porch, stretching his long legs to bypass the broken step. He tried the front door and found it locked. Same for the windows.

Curious, I asked, "What are you doing?"

"Just thought we'd take a look," he said. "If the Botticelli kids don't want this place—"

"It's Bottiglieri," Joanna corrected.

Gideon added, "Botticelli was a Renaissance painter."

"Whatever," Buck said. "My point is, if the heirs don't want this place, maybe someone else might. Especially if it's fixed up nice." He raised his brows and sent me a look—a look that said this property might be worth considering for a flip project.

It's a good idea, isn't it? With the fire station and townhouse on adjoining properties, we could use the dumpster we'd rented for the firehouse job to dispose of the townhouse debris, too. We'd also save time by working on similar projects in each property in succession, while we had the appropriate tools and materials already rounded up and ready for use. I raised my brows, too, and sent a message back to him. *I'm willing to consider it.* But before we made a commitment, we needed to figure out exactly what we'd be getting ourselves into.

CHAPTER 4

QUITTING TIME

WHITNEY

Buck scurried back to the fire station, returning a short minute later with an extension ladder. He leaned it up against the front of the townhome, climbed up to the boarded window, and used the claw end of his hammer to pry the nails out of the plywood Gideon and Joanna had hung. After tucking his hammer into his tool belt, he carefully handed the plywood down to me.

"Be careful!" I called up to him. "That broken glass looks sharp."

Buck pulled his hammer back out of his belt and knocked the pointed shards of glass out of the bottom pane of the window. They made a soft tinkling sound as they shattered. Now that the glass was out the way, he climbed through the opening. He disappeared into the townhouse and was gone for a minute or two before the front door swung open. "Come on in."

I hesitated. "Won't we be trespassing?"

Buck snorted. "Who's going to mind?"

He had a point. Avoiding the broken step, I ascended to the porch and stepped inside. Joanna and Gideon carefully followed me. The door opened directly into the living room, with only a three-by-three-foot square of parquet flooring forming an entryway. A closet with folding doors took up six feet of the wall along the right side of the room. Many of the slats on the doors were missing. A built-in bookshelf took up the rest of the wall. The shelves rested at odd angles, support brackets missing. The beige, builders-grade carpeting was stained, the telltale signs of grape juice spills and popsicle drips. The once-white walls were dingy, scuffed, and full of holes where pictures had hung. The plastic covers over the electric sockets and light switches had yellowed with time. Most of the furniture had been removed, probably pilfered by the Bottiglieri offspring.

It was dim, thanks to the accumulation of grime on the windows, and out of habit I reached for the light switch. Nothing happened when I flipped it. The electricity was turned off.

I followed Buck into the kitchen. The peeling wallpaper, blue Formica countertops, and scarred linoleum told me the place had last been updated in the 1980s. The kitchen cabinets were scratched, but nothing sandpaper and a fresh coat of paint couldn't improve on. A door led from the kitchen to the side yard. Sunlight peeked through gaps where weather-stripping was missing around the door. Beyond the kitchen was a half bath and laundry room, followed by the master bedroom. The green faux-marble tile in the master bathroom was a little loud for the space, but at least the tile in the shower and on the counters was serviceable. The floor tiles were cracked and dissolving into dust. Like the kitchen, the bathroom featured gaudy wallpaper, golden roses with greenery climbing on a latticework background.

Buck blew a long breath out of his mouth. "Whoa. This must be what a person sees after taking psychedelic mushrooms."

As we returned to the living room, I noticed a bright white spot of paint in the shape of a cross over the front door where a crucifix had evidently once hung. We continued up the stairs. The second floor comprised three bedrooms, a bathroom, and an open loft area that could be used as a playroom, home office, or den. The bath needed new fixtures and tile, and all of the bedrooms would require new flooring and fresh paint, as well as new closet doors, outlet covers, and light fixtures. The stairwell to the third floor was narrower, stopping at a door that had been left ajar. Buck pushed it open to reveal an attic space. Lest he fall through the floor, he activated the flashlight app on his phone and shined the light around before stepping inside. I stood at the door, looking in. Joanna and Gideon had opted to wait in the second-floor hallway.

"There's a bucket in here," Buck called. "It's half full of water." The flashlight's beam circled upward as he shined it on the ceiling. A dark stain on the plywood indicated where the roof had leaked. He turned the flashlight downward to reveal assorted scat scattered about. Mice, squirrels, and who knows what else had traipsed about in the attic at one time or another.

Our tour complete, we walked back downstairs and out the door, leaving it open. As we gathered on the concrete walkway that led from the porch to the sidewalk, a thirtyish couple came around the corner across the street. The woman pushed a toddler in a stroller, the small but unmistakable bump on her abdomen telling me another bundle of joy was on the way. The man walked two mismatched mutts, a variety pack. One dog was enormous, solid red, and as fluffy as a bathroom rug, some type of chow-chow mix. The other was tiny, silver, and sleek, with a skinny waist, mostly Italian greyhound if I wasn't mistaken. They looked our way, slowing their steps. The woman said something to the man, and he said something back, but they were too far away for me to hear. They were clearly curious, their heads angled, their eyes remaining on us.

Joanna raised a hand to the couple and they waved back, continuing to watch us with interest. Joanna turned back to me and Buck. "What do you think? Is my place at risk?"

Buck told her about the bucket he'd seen. "The roof has a leak, but I saw no signs of mold. Good thing someone put a bucket up there or things would've been much worse. The water could've seeped all the way down to the first floor, caused all sorts of damage."

Joanna frowned. "I bet the tenants put the bucket there. I can't imagine the Bottiglieris going to even that tiny bit of trouble."

When Buck and I had purchased the old country church as a rehab project, we'd been forced into a legal battle with the owner of the adjacent property, who claimed he owned the property through an obscure legal maneuver called adverse possession. We'd consulted a real estate attorney, who'd assured us he was as full of crap as the stalls in his horse barn. "This place could be saved," I said. "It *should* be saved." If not for Joanna's sake, for its own. The house had stood for more than a hundred years, and it could stand another century with some tender loving care. "I'll check with our attorney, see what it would take for us to get ownership of the place."

Joanna's face brightened. "You will? Thank you!"

I raised a palm. "There's no guarantee we'll be able to do anything. Even if our attorney can find a legal way for us to get the property, I'm not sure we can scrape the funds together. We just got a loan for the firehouse, so we'd have to convince our mortgage banker to give us the additional funds, assure them the townhouse would be a moneymaker. I'd hate to see you get your hopes up if there's nothing we can do."

"Understood," Joanna said. "I appreciate y'all taking the time to look things over. Let me know what you find out."

Gideon raised his index finger. "If y'all fix this place and put it up for sale, I call dibs!"

Joanna cut him an irritated look. "Dibs? I don't think so! If anyone should have the right of first refusal, it's me. I own the other half of the house, after all."

Gideon frowned and gestured to Buck and me. "But I'm the one who noticed them working at the fire station and suggested you talk to them. You hadn't even thought about buying the property until I just mentioned it."

In light of the deterioration that had occurred to the adjacent townhouse, I could understand why Joanna would want to own it—to protect her investment in her own home. But why would Gideon be interested? "Why would you want this place?" I asked. "I thought you already lived in the neighborhood."

"I do." He pointed to a three-story house that sat catty-corner across the street. It was painted dark blue with crisp white shutters and trim. Judging from the four mailboxes at the curb with the letters A, B, C, and D on them, the house had been divided into four units. The fact that there were two doors on the first-floor porch plus two more on the second-floor balcony confirmed my conclusion. "I moved there with my partner in the early nineties. He and I bought the whole building. I live in unit A on the bottom left."

Ah. He's an investor. I took a closer look at the outside of his unit. Gideon had placed flower boxes along the porch railing and filled them with bright orange impatiens and trailing deep purple sweet potato vine. On the wall beside the front doors hung a large kitschy aluminum sign with an outdoor thermometer built into it. The sign had a mustard yellow background with a bottle of brown soda depicted on it, a promotional item for Dad's Old Fashioned Root Beer. The sign must have been at least two feet tall, and eight to ten inches wide. Judging from the rust around the edges, it was probably decades old, a bit of nostalgic Americana. I wondered if the thermometer still worked.

Gideon continued. "I rent out the other units. In fact, Joanna's daughter and son-in-law rent from me. They live in unit B with their own daughter. It's a two-bedroom like mine."

Joanna nodded. "It's been nice having them close, especially since my granddaughter will be heading off to the University of Memphis in a year. It's been such a blessing watching her grow up. Alyssa will be the first person in our family to attend college. It should've been her mother, but that's a whole 'nother story." She shook her head and issued a sigh before resuming her praise of her granddaughter. "Alyssa is smart as a whip. She gets it from her mother." She cupped a hand around her mouth and leaned toward me as if to share a secret.

"Her daddy's not the sharpest tool in the shed." She barked a laugh as she pulled back.

With that, the two neighbors bade us goodbye. As Gideon headed back to his home across the street, I noticed the couple with the toddler and the dogs had stopped at the bottom of an exterior staircase that led up to the second-floor balcony. The woman bent over the stroller and unbuckled the baby, lifting him out. The man walked up the stairs with the dogs and unlocked the door on the right side of the balcony. The woman followed, carrying the child into the unit before coming back out to round up the stroller. With the dogs and a child—and another on the way—living on the second floor appeared to be less than convenient for them, but I knew from my experience managing properties that few landlords allowed pets, and tenants with animals often had to take what they could get. With my wedding scheduled to take place in a few months, I couldn't help but wonder whether Collin and I would have children someday, how many we might have, and who they would look like—me, him, or a blend of the two of us. I hadn't realized I was staring at the woman until she looked my way and caught me watching her. My cheeks warmed with an embarrassed blush, and I offered her a smile. She offered a smile in return before collapsing the stroller and lugging it up the stairs.

"Suppose I'd better lock this place up." Buck turned to walk back into the townhouse, closed the door, and locked the deadbolt from the inside. Seconds later, he climbed out the broken second-floor window. I handed the plywood up to him and he nailed it back in place. Done here for now, he gathered his ladder and we returned to the fire station.

Buck resumed his demo work in the bathroom, while

I placed a call to the real estate attorney. After giving her the information, she said, "Assuming everything you've told me is correct, that Lorenzo Bottiglieri died without a will, his children would be the default heirs, and there's a fairly simple procedure you could use to become owners of the property. In return for your payment, you'd need each of his children to sign what's called a quitclaim deed. Essentially, it's a way for them to transfer whatever interest they might own to you." She went on to say that, unlike the usual general warranty deed or special warranty deed, a quitclaim deed came with no guarantees. "It's possible a superior ownership interest could be claimed by a third party, like a lienholder or an unknown heir if a will is discovered later. But I can have my legal assistant run a search for you in both the probate and property records and give you some assurance you won't have trouble. The fact that the property has sat there for three years with nobody stepping up to seize it tells me the risk is low."

"Could we get a title insurance policy?" I asked. The last thing we wanted was a deed problem preventing us from reselling the property after we fixed it up.

"Shouldn't be a problem, so long as nothing unexpected shows up in the filings." She said she'd get back to me once her legal assistant had completed the research.

I thanked her and ended the call. After making a quick mental estimate, ballparking what we'd have to spend to fix up the place, we decided $25,000 was a fair price for each of the seven interests in the townhouse, for a total of $175,000. I immediately called our mortgage banker. In light of the unusual situation, it was going to be problematic getting a mortgage loan on the property. Given the fact that Buck and I had a steady stream of income from the Joyful Noise Playhouse, they were willing to extend us a personal loan, but only for a hundred grand. We needed more money if we were going to offer each of the Bottiglieri heirs twenty-five grand for their interests. I believed in this project. To come up with the remaining funds, I'd be willing to dip into my retirement account and suffer the tax penalty. The profit would be worth it.

I'd done what I could for the time being, and resumed the kitchen demo. Despite the fact that the townhome was not yet ours, I found myself mulling over design ideas for the place. We could replace the exterior kitchen door with a glass one to give the space a more open feel and let in natural light. Vinyl plank flooring would be a good option for the living room and kitchen. Not only would it tie the two spaces together, it would also be durable. The intact marble could remain in the master bath, so long as we toned it down with a subtle, solid wall color.

By six o'clock, both Buck and I were tuckered out. Demolition work was exhausting. We locked up the fire station, climbed into our vehicles, and headed home.

My hair was still damp from the shower when Collin knocked on my door at seven Friday evening. I opened it to find him in shorts and a T-shirt, smelling fresh from the shower himself. He'd probably taken a quick run after work. Standing in a carrier at his feet were his two cats—Copernicus, a solid gray kitty with green eyes, and Galileo, a debonair tuxedo with gold eyes. He'd brought them along so they could have a playdate with Sawdust. Might as well get the three used to each other before they officially became family. Of course, Cleo would join in the fun, too.

"I brought dinner." Collin held up a large white take-out bag.

I lifted my nose and inhaled the delicious aroma. "Thai?"

He confirmed that my nose was correct. "Got an order of pad see ew and green curry. Spring rolls, too."

"Yum!" I gave him a warm kiss in welcome and gratitude before relieving him of the bag and stepping back to allow him to carry his cats inside. As Copernicus and Galileo strode out of their carrier, Sawdust and Cleo greeted them by sniffing their faces. Once they'd reacquainted themselves, Sawdust literally got the ball rolling on their playdate by using his paw to send one of his jingle balls rolling down the hallway. The four cats made chase, sending the ball ricocheting off the walls like a game of improvised pinball.

Collin and I ate dinner on my couch while looking through wedding invitation options online. There were so many to choose from! Fortunately, we shared similar tastes and it was an easy decision. We opted for basic white invitations with silver ink and a calligraphy font. That task complete, we set about renting tables and chairs. We compared prices from local vendors and read their customer reviews before e-mailing one to check availability on our wedding date.

These items checked off our to-do list, we sat back to relax and watch a movie, the four cats lounging about on the sofa with us. Throughout the show, my mind kept going back to the townhouse. A lot of things would have to fall into place for the deal to go through, and there was no sense wasting mental energy on it until I knew for certain the place would be ours. Still, I couldn't help pondering the possibilities. I'd told Collin about the place while we'd fixed our plates earlier, and several times during the show he cast glances over at me. When the movie concluded, he picked up the remote and turned off the television. "You've been thinking about that townhouse all this time, haven't you?"

"Busted." I sighed. "It would make a perfect flip project. I just can't get my mind off it."

A sexy grin slid across his lips. "Maybe I can help with that." He leaned over, nuzzled my neck, and any conscious thought disappeared. *Townhouse? What townhouse?*

Come Saturday morning, my mind was back to wedding matters. Today, my mother, Emmalee, and Colette would accompany me on my quest to find the perfect wedding dress.

Emmalee followed me to my parents' house in the Green Hills neighborhood of Nashville, where we met up with my mom and Colette. Mom was a petite woman whose hairdresser ensured that, no matter her age, she remained as blonde as ever. Colette's dark curls bobbed about her face as she approached me and gave me a hug. She and I had been best friends since we'd met in college. The fact that she'd married my cousin and we were now not just friends but also family was a wonderful bonus. The four of us piled into my mother's car and set off to visit the city's bridal shops.

As we entered the first store, a sixtyish saleswoman greeted us at the door with flutes of champagne. "Welcome, ladies." After determining that I was the bride, she asked, "What style of dress are you looking for?"

I had no idea what type I wanted, or what options would be best for my body shape, so I went with, "A pretty one?"

She laughed. "All wedding dresses are pretty, hon." She looked me up and down as if mentally taking my measurements. "Why don't I choose a few different looks for you to try? It might help you narrow things down."

The woman moved about the store, selecting several dresses for me. Meanwhile, my mother, Colette, and Emmalee flitted about the store, doing the same. A quarter hour later, the saleswoman and I were in a large dressing room, while the others waited in chairs by a three-way mirror outside. The saleswoman helped me into the first dress, a flashy, fitted model with a plunging neckline, a thigh-high slit on the side, and more sequins than a Vegas showgirl costume. Though the dress was stunning, it would be far more appropriate on an actress walking the red carpet in Hollywood than a bride walking down the aisle.

I stepped out of the dressing room. My mother took one look at me and choked on her champagne. When she could catch her breath, she rasped, "Absolutely not!"

The saleslady's lips pursed. "We've sold quite a few in this style to tall brides. It allows them to show off their legs."

"And everything else!" Mom cried, fluttering her hand all about.

Colette attempted to smooth things over by saying, "It's a bit showy for Whitney."

The saleswoman nodded. "We'll try something more traditional, then."

Back we went into the dressing room. Once she'd freed me from the revealing dress, she sorted through the others hanging on the garment rack, sliding aside another that featured more beads than a Mardi Gras parade. She pulled out a gown that was ruffled from neck to ankles, and helped me into it. The dress was actually more retro than traditional, like something a girl would have worn to a high school prom in 1985. Again, I stepped out in front of my mother and friends, twirling to give them a three-hundred-and-sixty-degree look at me.

Colette cringed. "That's not the one."

"No," my mother agreed, but at least she offered the saleswoman some encouragement. "We're getting closer, though."

I tried a third dress that was all ivory lace and bustles. It rustled as I moved.

"It's pretty," Emmalee said, "but it sure is noisy."

Lest I sound like an approaching hurricane coming down the aisle, we moved on to the next dress. This one was bright white brocade and featured an abundance of three-dimensional fabric roses across the neckline, waist, and hem.

When Colette saw me in it, she had to bite her lip to keep from laughing. "You can't wear that. You'll be mistaken for the wedding cake!"

By this point, the saleswoman didn't bother to hide her frustration. She grabbed the bottle of champagne, poured what was left into a flute for herself, and tossed it back.

The next dress I tried was a mermaid style. It was immediately clear the design would look far better on a curvier woman than on one whose chest and behind were only slightly less flat than a pancake. Though the next few gowns I tried on were undeniably gorgeous, none felt quite right to me. In light of the hefty price tag that came with a wedding dress, I wanted to be completely happy with my choice.

We thanked the woman for her time and, after a quick stop for lunch, hit two more bridal shops. We had no more luck there. The dresses were beautiful, but they simply weren't *me*.

We drove back to my parents' house, where Colette and Emmalee climbed into their cars and set off for the dinner shift at Colette's café. After mooching an early meal from my parents' fridge, I drove back home, feeling defeated and stressed. With the wedding only three months off, time was of the essence. I'd tried on dozens of dresses today. *Did the right wedding gown even exist?*

After giving Sawdust and Cleo some attention, I grabbed my laptop and plunked down on the couch. The stores could carry only so many dresses in their inventory, but the internet would offer virtually unlimited options. Surely, I could find the perfect wedding dress online, couldn't I?

I spent the next hour perusing various bridal websites. Sawdust sat on my lap, purring and kneading my coveralls with his paws, scratching the skin on my thigh and leaving pinprick holes in the fabric. Flinching occasionally, I endured the pain for my sweet kitty's sake. I knew the kneading meant he was happy and that, despite the agony it caused me, he saw it as a sign of affection. No way could I reject his expression of love, no matter how much it hurt.

I went from site to site to site to site, having the same experience as I'd had at the brick-and-mortar stores. Every gown was gorgeous, but each caused me concern. Some contained intricate beading I feared would snag and leave a trail of tiny beads in my wake. Others were so flashy I'd feel more like a Broadway performer than a bride. A simple fitted chiffon dress caught my eye, but the back was trimmed with two dozen tiny fabric-covered buttons that would be difficult to fasten and unfasten. There was also the question of cost. While

my father was an otolaryngologist and my parents had
plenty of money to pay for a fancy dress, I was simply
too practical a person to blow thousands of dollars on
a designer gown when others were available at much
more reasonable prices. *Hmm . . .*

I continued on through several more websites, filtering the dresses by price and available sizes. I was about
to give up when a thumbnail image caught my eye. I
clicked on it and gasped. *That's it. That's my dress!* The
cap-sleeved white satin dress had a square neckline, a
pale blue sash at the waist, and an A-line skirt that hung
to the floor. No train to trip me up. No teeny tiny buttons. No beads or sequins. Simple yet elegant, classically
feminine. With a flourish, I added the dress to my cart
and placed the order.

Things were really moving along now, as far as the
fire station rehab and wedding were concerned. I could
only hope we'd have as much luck with the townhouse.

CHAPTER 5

CLAWS FOR CONCERN

SAWDUST

Sawdust could tell that Whitney had been distressed earlier. He could sense the tension by her rigid posture. He could smell her emotions, too. The pheromones said it all. Something had her anxious.

He'd done his best to relieve her anxiety by kneading his paws on her skin. It's what he'd done as a kitten to help his mother relax and release more milk, and it's what instinct told him to do now to calm both himself and his human. It worked. Whitney had closed her computer and was cuddling him in her arms, scratching under his chin. He looked up at her and stretched his face up to swipe at her cheek with his tongue.

She smiled down at him. "Thanks for the kiss, sweet boy."

Being held in her warm arms was pure bliss. His purr activated on its own accord as he closed his eyes. *Aaaaaah . . .*

CHAPTER 6

QUIT COMPLAINING

WHITNEY

At noon the following Wednesday, the real estate attorney called with both bad news and good news. "The bad news is the property taxes are several years in arrears. The good news is that Lorenzo and Giorgia Bottiglieri took advantage of the tax freeze program for senior citizens, so the amount due isn't as high as it could be. The city hasn't started the foreclosure process on the place yet. At any rate, you'll have to pay the delinquent taxes before you sell the place."

If we sold the fire station first, we could use the proceeds to pay the past-due property taxes on the townhouse.

"The good news," continued the attorney, "is that the title looks clear up to the point that the Bottiglieris bought the place. My assistant has prepared quitclaim deeds for each of their children to sign. I'll email them to you. You'll need to have them notarized."

Fortunately, I knew a licensed notary public—Presley Pearson, the manager of the Joyful Noise Playhouse.

We'd met a while back, when she still worked for Rick Dunaway, a local real estate mogul who'd ended up dead in the flowerbed at the cottage Buck and I had bought from him to flip. While my relationship with Presley had gotten off to a rocky start, we'd since made amends. She'd even partnered with Buck and me on the motel rehab, chipping in the funds we'd needed to nab the place at the tax sale. She'd been more than happy to be a silent partner. She was in the real estate game for the profits, not because she had an interest in remodeling or design. The three of us owed our success to each other. Buck and I never would have landed the motel property without Presley, and she could never have afforded it or remodeled it on her own. The place had made a significant profit, been our big break. This townhouse could be another big break—assuming the Bottiglieri children were willing to sell. *What if they aren't? Or what if some are willing to sell, but not others?* I posed the question to the attorney.

"If you can get at least one to sign a quitclaim deed," she said, "you'd be part owner and thus have legal standing to sue for a partition."

A what *now?* "Meaning . . . ?"

"Meaning that, if the others won't sell you their interests, you could force a sale of the property and bid on it yourself. But it would be up to the court to approve the sale."

"So, we could end up having to buy the others out for more than we're hoping to pay for the quitclaim deeds, or the judge could decide it should be sold to someone else entirely."

"That's the risk," the attorney said. "You have to decide if it's a risk worth taking."

Thus far, the risks Buck and I had taken had mostly

paid off. I figured this was a risk worth taking, too. I thanked the attorney, ended the call, and immediately placed another.

"Hey, Whitney," Presley said, identifying me via caller ID. "What's up?"

"Any chance you and your notary seal are available this evening?" I told her about the townhouse, and our plan to buy it from the Bottiglieri children. "I'm hoping we can get signatures from at least half of them tonight. We can try the rest tomorrow evening."

"I'll make the rounds with you," she said, "*if* you give me a piece of the action."

"We'd be happy to cut you in." I knew I could speak for both myself and my cousin. Besides, if she could chip in the shortfall, I wouldn't have to dip into my retirement account.

We quickly worked out the details, and she transferred her funds into a joint account we'd set up earlier when working on the motel project. We arranged to meet at my house early that evening so we could visit the Bottiglieris together.

Once I got off the phone with Presley, I ventured up to the roof, where Buck was measuring the perimeter to determine how much we'd need in materials to complete the rooftop patio. "Good news," I said. "The lawyer said the title looks clear. Presley said she'd come with us tonight to notarize the deeds if we'd cut her in on the deal."

"You told her yes, right?"

"Of course." I mentioned my concerns about the Bottiglieri heirs, whether one or more of them might be holdouts. "If any of them refuses to sign, we'd have to go to court and force a sale. We'd get our portion of the proceeds, but there's no guarantee we'd get the property."

"We need to be strategic, then." Buck returned his measuring tape to his belt. "Let's go talk to Joanna, see which of the heirs she thinks will be easiest to deal with."

Buck and I headed out of the fire station and around the corner. As we stepped up onto Joanna's porch, Buck's toe caught a board that had come loose and stuck up a quarter inch higher than the others. He stumbled but quickly caught himself, and glared down at the board. "That board needs to be nailed down."

It would be easy to do. All that was needed was a hammer and a nail. Unfortunately, our hammers and nails were all back at the fire station.

We rapped on Joanna's door. To my surprise, Gideon answered. After greeting him, I said, "Is Joanna around?"

He jerked his head. "She's in the kitchen fixing lemonade. Come on in." He stepped back and allowed Buck and me to enter before calling to Joanna. "The fixer-upper folks are here!"

As we stepped inside, my nose detected the faint scents of cigarettes, the morning's coffee, and the seafood Joanna and Gideon evidently planned to have for lunch. Two shrimp cocktails sat on the coffee table, served in glass bowls with red sauce for dipping. An ashtray with three butts in it sat next to them, along with a crystal candy dish filled with strawberry hard candies in cellophane wrappers. The TV was on, playing the theme song from the popular soap opera *The Young and the Restless*.

Gideon glanced at the screen. "Joanna and I watch this soap every day. Some of the stars have been in their roles for decades. At some point, they'll need to rename it *The Old and the Arthritic*."

We shared a chuckle. As he took a seat on the sofa, Joanna came out of the kitchen with two glasses in her hands. "Hey, you two." She raised the glasses. "Care for some lemonade?"

We only planned to be here a brief time, but the cold drink looked wonderfully refreshing, especially for two people who'd been sweating it out in a warm fire station all morning. The building's air conditioner definitely needed some work. "I'd love a glass."

"Me too," Buck said.

Joanna handed us the glasses she'd already prepared and scurried back to the kitchen to get two more for Gideon and herself. When she returned, she handed one to her neighbor, set the other on the coffee table, and turned to me. "Did you hear from your lawyer? Is it good news?"

I gave her an update, letting her know what the attorney had told us and that we'd found a third investor who'd helped us raise the funds to make the offers. "We need to be strategic in our approach. Which of the Bottiglieris do you think would be the most agreeable to signing?"

Before Joanna could respond, Gideon said, "Benedict. That boy was always looking to make a quick buck." He picked up one of the bowls from the coffee table, took a shrimp by the tail, and dunked it into the red sauce before tearing off the meat with his teeth.

"That's right." Joanna's head bobbed. "But only if that quick buck was also an easy buck. Benny was always asking the neighbors if we had any odd jobs he could do for cash. He never wanted to work hard, though. He'd get tired or bored, quit halfway through a job and expect to be paid a portion of what had been agreed on. He mowed half my lawn one time, then quit because he said it was too hot. This is Nashville. Of course, it's hot! I had to go out there and finish the mowing myself. I refused to hire him after that." Joanna leaned to the left and looked past me, out her front window, her face clouding in concern. "What are Macy and Holden doing home this time of day?"

Gideon glanced out the window, too, and shrugged. "Looks like we're about to find out."

I turned and looked through the glass to see a white pickup truck parked at the curb in front of Gideon's building. A couple headed our way from across the street. A blonde teen in form-fitting black spandex shorts and a striped tank top trailed after them, looking down at her phone, her thumbs working the screen. Also with them was a small, scruffy mutt, as much mop as dog. The man and woman appeared to be in their mid to late thirties, just a few years older than Buck and me. Holden had brown hair and the type of thick mustache that had been popular decades ago, especially with police officers and porn stars, and that had recently come back in vogue. He wore navy pants and a long-sleeved ice-blue shirt with some sort of logo on the left side of his chest, what appeared to be a work uniform. Macy wore tan wedges and a bright red dress with a ruffled skirt that ended just above her knees, casually stylish. As they ascended the steps onto the porch, I could see that her blonde hair hung in perfect loose curls over her shoulders and her makeup was impeccable, though not overdone. The girl and the dog scampered up after them.

Joanna went to the door and opened it as the family stepped up onto the porch. Gideon stood and followed her over, the two of them effectively blocking the doorway.

"Is everything okay?" Joanna asked. "Why aren't y'all at work?"

Though Joanna and Gideon now blocked my view of Macy, her voice came through loud and clear. "We've got some exciting news!"

Gideon gestured back into the townhouse. "Want to come in and tell us over shrimp cocktails? We've got plenty."

"No, thanks," Macy said, a teasing lilt in her voice. "Women are supposed to limit seafood intake . . . *when they're pregnant*."

The pause following her big reveal was as pregnant as Macy. After hearing Joanna express affection for Alyssa the day before, it seemed she'd be thrilled to learn she'd have another grandchild. Instead, she tossed up her hands and let out a wail. "No! You can't be pregnant!"

"I know!" cried the teen, the only one of the three I could see through the window. "The thought of my parents having sex is totally disgusting." She shuddered. "Ew! Ew! Ew!"

Macy judiciously ignored her daughter. "I *can* be pregnant," she told her mother slowly and firmly. "And I *am*."

Joanna's head shook in denial. "But you had so many problems last time! Preeclampsia. Gestational diabetes. High blood pressure. We nearly lost both you and the baby! You were only eighteen then, too. The risks will be much worse at the age you are now!"

Macy groaned. "Every pregnancy is different, Mom. Just because I had trouble last time doesn't mean I will again. Besides, thirty-five is not that old. You were only three years younger than I am when you gave birth to Lane, remember? Lots of women have babies in their forties now. But in an abundance of caution, the doctor put me on bed rest until we see how things go."

"Bed rest?" Joanna put a hand to her forehead, as if suffering an intense headache. "If you'd listened to me and gone to college, you'd have a cushy office job where you could sit down and you wouldn't need to go on bed rest. Instead, you're on your feet all day in the salon!"

Macy sighed. "How many times do I have to tell you? I love my job, Mom. I help women feel good about themselves. And need I remind you that I have never been out of work? Some of my friends who went to college have been laid off and had to go on unemployment. That's never happened to me."

"You'll lose your clients! They'll find a new hairdresser and where will y'all be then?"

"Relax, Mom," Macy said. "You're blowing this out of proportion. We can get by on Holden's salary for a few months until the baby comes and I go back to work. We're fine."

"That's what you think," Joanna muttered.

Macy huffed a frustrated breath. "What's that supposed to mean?"

Rather than answer her daughter, Joanna turned her head to focus her tirade on her son-in-law. "How could you be so stupid, Holden? Why didn't you take precautions?"

A timid male voice responded. "We took precautions, ma'am. They don't always work."

Macy came to her husband's defense. "Don't blame Holden, Mom. It takes two to tango."

"Ew! Ew! Ew!" Alyssa cried again.

"Besides," Macy continued to address her mother, undeterred by her daughter, "you're one to talk about health risks. I've been begging you for years to quit smoking!"

"I have quit!" Joanna insisted, though she then contradicted herself in a quieter voice. "More or less, anyway. I'm down to just two cigarettes a day."

Gideon cocked his head, looking askance at Joanna, his expression skeptical.

Buck and I exchanged a glance. It felt awkward to overhear what should have been a private family conversation. Then again, Gideon hadn't excused himself, and *he* wasn't family. He seemed to be a close friend of Joanna's, though. Having received the information we'd come for, I quickly downed the lemonade and set my glass on the coffee table. Buck followed suit. We stepped up behind Joanna and Gideon. "We'll head out now," I said. "Give y'all some privacy."

Gideon stepped back to allow us to exit. As we did, I cast a surreptitious and supportive smile at the couple on the porch. Though I could understand Joanna's concerns under the circumstances, the last thing her daughter and son-in-law needed now was her causing them more stress. Besides, medicine was constantly evolving. There might be new techniques that could lower Macy's health risks. I hoped her pregnancy would go smoothly.

Up close like this, I could see that the logo on Holden's shirt featured a smiling snowman. One of the snowman's twig arms curved over the top of a blue dolly from which hung several pointed icicles. I could also see that Macy had her mother's hazel eyes, and the skin around them crinkled as they narrowed, taking in me and Buck. Clearly, she hadn't realized that we had been in Joanna's home. Her dog wagged his fluffy tail and sniffed our boots as her cheeks pinked with embarrassment. "Mom!" she snapped. "You should have told us you had company!"

Macy and Holden's daughter took advantage of our departure as an excuse to skedaddle, too. "I'm out. Later!"

At seven o'clock that evening, I turned into a decades-old apartment complex in an Antioch neighborhood. Buck, still in his coveralls like me, sat in my passenger seat. Presley sat in the back, stylishly dressed, as always, tonight in a fitted sleeveless dress and heels, perfectly accessorized with shiny gold jewelry. She looked like a TV news anchor.

I glanced around the place. The buildings suffered from poor maintenance, the metal railings rusting and the wood trim rotting. Likewise, the cars in the parking lot were older models, many with dings or scrapes or missing hubcaps. The few people milling about looked down on their luck, too, their expressions vacant or scowling.

Buck ducked his head to better see the numbers on the buildings. He pointed to a unit ahead. "There it is."

I pulled my SUV to a stop in front of Benedict Bottiglieri's place and cut the engine. Like many Catholics, Lorenzo and Giorgia had named each of their children after saints or people from the bible. Benedict. Matthew. John. Peter. Judith. Tabitha. Mary Ruth.

Presley sat in the back seat, sorting through the file folder on her lap, looking for the deed with Benedict's name on it. She fished one out and held it up. "Here we go."

We climbed out of the van and walked up to Benedict's unit on the second floor. The sound of a television came through the door. Judging from the squealing tires and gunfire, the program was an action movie or cop show. I raised a hand and rapped three times. A male voice from inside called, "Whatever you're selling, I ain't buying! Go away!"

I leaned into the frame and called, "We're not selling anything, Mr. Bottiglieri! We're here to make an offer on your parents' house."

The door jerked open so fast I nearly fell through it. Benedict Bottiglieri stood there in a too-tight T-shirt and a pair of loose-knit shorts, the elastic waistline of which curved under his basketball-shaped belly. His salt-and-pepper hair was washed but messy, as if he hadn't bothered to comb it after taking his shower today, but had merely run his fingers through it. The smell of pizza emanated from his apartment, along with the odor of garbage funk. A look over his shoulder revealed a living room decorated with a cheap end table and a recliner, the faux-leather seat stretched and worn. The walls were bare. A bottle of Pepto Bismol sat on the kitchen counter, along with a bottle of vitamins designed for the fifty-plus consumer. The place was clearly a bachelor pad for an aged bachelor. Though Joanna and Gideon had referred to Benedict and his siblings as the Bottiglieri "children," this man was anything but a child. He appeared to be in his late sixties. His eyes gleamed. "What's this about buying my parents' house?"

Buck said, "We'd like to make an offer for your one-seventh interest."

Benedict snorted. "You've seen the place, right? It's a dump."

Buck, Presley, and I exchanged glances. His parents' place might need some repairs and updating but, if anything was a dump, it was this apartment.

Fortunately, Benedict had given me an opening. "The townhouse needs a lot of work," I agreed. "Paint. Carpeting. New fixtures and appliances. Landscaping. The whole nine yards. But we think we can get it back in shape."

"We fix up houses for a living," Buck elaborated. "In fact, we've bought the old fire station right around the corner from your parents' place. We're gonna remodel it into a single-family home."

I reached into the breast pocket of my coveralls, removed the check I'd tucked there, and unfolded it. "We're willing to pay you twenty-five thousand for your share in the townhouse."

"Sold!" He reached for the check.

I pulled it back, just out of reach. "We'll need your signature on a legal document first."

Benedict motioned for us to come inside, and led us to the kitchen. He pushed aside a pile of fast-food wrappers and dirty dishes to clear a space. Presley lay the deed on the counter and held out a pen. Benedict grabbed it in a flash and signed the deed with a flourish. When Presley asked for his ID, he scrounged up his wallet from the pocket of a pair of rumpled pants hanging over the back of a kitchen chair and handed her his driver's license. She filled in the requisite information in her notary notebook, brandished her seal, and worked her notary public magic, making everything official.

Benedict's signature obtained, I handed him the check. "Thanks."

"Thank *you*." He chuckled and shook his head. He walked us to the door, closing and locking it quickly behind us, as if expecting us to change our minds and demand he return the check. Either he was simply happy to have someone hand him thousands of dollars with no effort required on his part, or he knew something about the house we didn't. I hoped it wasn't the latter. Because we hadn't obtained a traditional mortgage, we hadn't bothered with a professional inspection, instead relying on the once-over we'd given the place. Even so, we'd assumed there could be unexpected expenses beyond the repair needs we'd noted, and the price we were offering the siblings reflected this uncertainty. I chose to consider our encounter with Benedict as a good omen. With this one-seventh ownership interest, we now had legal rights with respect to the townhouse and could force our hand if the other siblings didn't cooperate. I certainly hoped it wouldn't come to that.

Our next stop was at Judith's house, a small, older ranch model on an acre south of the city, in the town of Thompson's Station. With deep lines etched on her face, Judith appeared a few years older than Benedict. Unlike her brother, who couldn't sign the quitclaim deed fast enough, the thin platinum blonde said, "I'm not signing until you show me your appraisal."

"We didn't get one," I explained. A mortgage company would have required an appraisal before making a loan, but since we didn't get a mortgage, we hadn't sought an appraisal. "Appraisals cost several hundred dollars, and it seemed like an unnecessary expense. But I looked at comparable real estate listings in the area and deducted the expected cost of the rehab to come up with our offer price."

"No appraisal, huh?" Her eyes narrowed. "I'll take a look for myself." She whipped out her phone and searched for Germantown listings. After scrolling through them, she snorted. "There's not a three-bedroom townhouse in Germantown under six hundred grand. You think you can buy me and my siblings out for less than a third of that? What do you take us for, morons?" She went to close her door, but I stuck my steel-toed boot inside the frame to stop her. She looked down at my foot, then up at me, her eyes burning in outrage.

"We don't take you for morons," I said, which was true. "We take you for people who are stuck with an asset they can't afford to maintain and can't agree what to do with. We're offering you a reasonable price and a solution for your impasse. Hear us out." I gestured to the folder Presley was holding. She riffled through the folder and pulled out the cost estimate I'd prepared. I handed it over to Judith, pointing out the numerous items on the list. "It's going to cost us over a hundred grand to fix the place up. What's more, there's tens of thousands of property taxes in arrears that we'll pay off for you."

Judith's rigid stance softened. She appeared to be wavering, but not entirely convinced.

Buck took a more direct approach. "Look, Judith. This is a fair deal for you and your siblings. If y'all aren't willing or able to pay the taxes and remodeling costs yourselves, your only other option is put the place on the market as is. Once the taxes were deducted from the proceeds, you'd probably end up with less in your pocket than what we're offering you right now. You'd have to pay a real estate commission, too. And that's if someone is even willing to buy the place. Not many people are willing to take on a project this big."

Judith sucked her lower lip into her mouth and gnawed on it, her head cocked.

Presley also weighed in. "If you do nothing, the townhouse will continue to deteriorate, and the tax office will eventually foreclose and sell it for peanuts. If that happens, you're likely to get nothing at all. It would be foolish not to accept our offer."

Judith took a second look at my estimate. "You've built in a big profit for yourselves."

Buck shrugged. "It's comparable to what you'd pay in labor costs if you hired someone to do the work. We've got to earn a living. We've got bills to pay, same as you."

Judith called back over her shoulder. "Hey, hon? Come here a minute."

A moment later, a tall man in boots, jeans, and a Western shirt joined her in the doorway. He lifted his chin in greeting. "What's going on here?"

She told him who we were and showed him the cost projection I'd prepared and the listings she'd found online. "Bennie's already accepted a check from them for his share."

Her husband mulled things over for a brief moment before saying, "I don't see the harm. The house is just sitting there not doing any good for anyone. We don't want to deal with it. Our plate is full keeping up our own place."

Her head bobbed. With her husband on board, she was now, too. "All right. I'll sign."

Judith signed the deed, Presley notarized it, and I handed over her check.

As we headed back to Buck's van, he said, "Two down, five to go."

We aimed for Peter's house in Mount Juliet. At around fifty, Peter was the baby of the family. He and his wife invited us to join them at their kitchen table while their two sons, both in their late teens, played a video game on a large screen television nearby, the sound turned up to a deafening volume.

Peter looked over the paperwork before shouting over

the music and sounds of the game coming from the TV. "How much did you pay Benny and Judy?"

"Twenty-five thousand!" I hollered. "Same as we're offering you!"

Peter's wife shouted at the boys to turn the volume down. Once we could hear ourselves think, Peter lay the pen on the table and crossed his arms over his chest. "I want thirty grand."

Buck snorted. "That wouldn't be fair to your brothers and sisters now, would it?"

"I don't care," Peter said. "I'm not signing unless you pay me more than you paid them."

Obviously, some sort of sibling rivalry was going on here. Buck rolled his eyes, opened his wallet, and pulled out the bills, thirty-eight dollars in total. "Does thirty-eight bucks sweeten the deal enough for you?"

Apparently, it did. All he wanted was to best his siblings. It didn't matter by how much. Peter picked up the bills, folded them, and tucked them into his pocket. "Where do I sign?"

After obtaining his signature, we returned to my SUV. It was late by then, so we gave up our mission for the night. It had been a long day, and I was glad to get home to Sawdust. After I climbed into bed, he curled up on my pillow and licked my cheek, giving me sweet, sandpapery kitty kisses as I stroked him. I looked forward to marrying Collin and coming home to him and his kisses at night, too.

The following evening, Buck, Presley, and I went on to obtain signatures from Matthew, Mary Ruth, and Tabitha. We had a much easier time with these three. Each seemed relieved to be rid of what they considered a burden rather than an asset, and they were thrilled to have the unexpected windfall fall into their lap. Twenty-five grand would go a long way toward their own mortgages. Tabitha said she might even spend her share on a backyard pool.

"Six down." Presley brandished her notary seal. "One more and it's ours."

Our final visit was to John. The stocky septuagenarian crossed his arms over his chest, just like Peter had. "I'm not signing. That place was my childhood home. I've got a lot of happy memories there. You can't expect me to just hand over my ownership share for next to nothing."

Twenty-five grand was hardly next to nothing. Given what I'd heard about the Bottiglieri family, I suspected he didn't truly have a meaningful attachment to the place, but was instead using emotional blackmail in an attempt to get us to raise our offer.

He cocked his head. "I might be persuaded to part with my share if you doubled your offer."

"That's not gonna happen," Buck snapped, his patience gone after a long evening traipsing all over Nashville and the surrounding areas. "We already own six of the seven shares. We can force a sale. You'd never get fifty grand for your interest in its current condition. If we move ahead and fix it up, we'll ask the court to make you reimburse a portion of our costs."

John snorted, indignant. "You can't make me pay to improve a house I don't own!"

"If you don't own the house," Buck said, "then why should we pay you anything at all? We'll tell the court you disclaimed ownership, and you won't get anything."

"You can't cut me out!" John shrieked. "Part of that house is mine!"

"Make up your mind," Buck snapped. "Do you own

an interest in the house or not? You're contradicting yourself, talking out of your a—"

"Out of both sides of your mouth," I interjected, sending Buck a disapproving glance. I turned back to John. "Excuse us just a moment." I waved for Buck and Presley to follow me over to a tree. Once there, I whispered, "If we have to go to court, we'll end up with several thousand dollars in legal fees." John was worse than Peter with his juvenile sibling rivalry, and I hated to feed that ugly monster, but it would be more efficient to pay him a bit more and get on with things than go to court. "Let's offer him another five hundred and see if he bites."

Presley nodded in agreement with the plan. Buck frowned, but nodded, too. We walked back to the door. "We'll offer you another five hundred dollars. Final offer. Take it or leave it."

He jerked a shoulder in a shrug. "I'll leave it."

"All right," Buck said. "We'll let the judge decide."

Buck turned and strode back to his van. Presley and I followed. We'd all climbed in, taken our seats, and fastened our belts when John eased down his steps as if his feet were in control. Buck started the engine. He'd begun to pull away from the curb when John threw himself in front of the van, putting his palms on the hood as if he could stop it.

Buck snorted. "Who's this guy think he is, Superman? I've half a mind to punch the gas."

We remained in our seats while Buck unrolled his window. John circled around to it. "Okay. If you give me another five hundred, I'll sign. Can't say I appreciate your aggressive tactics, though. I feel coerced."

"What you feel is disappointment," Buck said. "If anyone is guilty of coercion, it's you."

"No sense arguing," I said. "It's a moot point now. Let's just get his signature on the deed, give him his check, and get out of here."

We did just that and, finally, with the sweep of the pen, the townhouse was all ours.

CHAPTER 7
A HOUSE DIVIDED

WHITNEY

First thing Friday morning, I dropped the quitclaim deeds at our attorney's office so that her assistant could get them filed in the county records. I parked my SUV at the fire station but, rather than going inside, I circled around the corner to Joanna's townhouse to give her the good news. When she opened her door, a haze of cigarette smoke hung in the air. Looked like she'd been smoking. Judging from the thickness of the cloud, she might've fudged when she told Macy and Holden that she was down to two cigarettes a day. As before, she held her pack of cigarettes and her lighter in her left hand. They seemed to function as a security blanket of sorts.

"Good news!" I told her. "We got all seven of the Bottiglieris to sign. The place is ours."

"Wonderful!" She put her right hand to her chest, and released a long breath. "I can't even begin to tell you what a relief this is. My husband and I worked hard to afford this place. I feared I'd see it fall into ruin."

She lowered her hand. "When will you get started on the rehab?"

"The fire station is our number-one priority," I said. "It has to be completed by mid-November. But Buck and I will be working on the townhouse simultaneously. My guess is we'll have it done by year end, January at the latest."

She stuck her head farther out the door and looked around before whispering, "Don't forget I want first crack at the place. Macy, Holden, and Alyssa don't have much space in the two-bedroom they're in now. It'll only get worse after the baby comes and, even with Alyssa heading off to college next year, she'll still need a bedroom when she comes home on school breaks. I'd love to buy it and lease it to them on a rent-to-own arrangement."

Her request made me a little uncomfortable. "I can't make any promises," I said. "Buck and I have a silent partner who's invested quite a bit of money, too, so it won't be entirely our decision. We'll have to put it on the market and go with the best offer."

She frowned. "You'll at least give me a chance to match it, won't you? I can pay cash."

It was a reasonable request, one I knew Buck and Presley would agree with. A cash buyer was always preferable to one who'd need to secure financing. Much less paperwork was involved and there was less chance of the deal falling through. "Sure. If you match the highest offer and pay cash, the townhouse is yours."

She gave me a thumbs-up with her empty hand. "Thanks, Whitney."

After leaving Joanna's, I returned to the fire station. Buck and I spent the rest of the day finishing up the demo work. Buck had already gone for the day, and I was using a dolly to transport an old, cracked toilet to the dumpster when Collin pulled up to the fire station at half past six. My hair and coveralls were coated in dust, and my skin was dewy with sweat.

A grin tugged at Collin's lips as he climbed out of his car, dressed in faded jeans and an old T-shirt. "You've never looked prettier."

I rolled my eyes and lifted my chin to indicate the dumpster. "Give a girl a hand?"

He helped me heave the heavy porcelain toilet over the edge. It fell into the metal bin with a clunk. The task complete, we went into the station. While a Friday night date spent sweeping and vacuuming was hardly romantic under normal circumstances, the fact that Collin and I were readying our wedding venue added a touch of romance to our chores, nonetheless. We ordered a pizza for dinner and ate it sitting atop overturned five-gallon plastic buckets.

"You know," he said, finagling a second piece of pizza from the box, "we haven't decided where we're going to live after we get married."

I circled my finger in the air to indicate the fire station. "We won't be able to afford this place once it's fixed up." *There's an irony for you. I can build it, but I can't buy it.* It would cost too much to buy out Buck's and Presley's shares of the fire station at market price. Besides, as unique and trendy as the firehouse would be once it was finished, my personal tastes tended to be more traditional. I wanted a backyard and flowerbeds.

We briefly debated our options. Collin had a small, older house that he'd bought a few years back and I, of course, had the cottage—half of which technically belonged to Buck. I also had a roommate—two if you counted Emmalee's cat Cleo. The cottage was in a better neighborhood than Collin's place, and more centrally located. Though it was worth quite a bit, its value would be significantly less than the remodeled fire station. "What would you think about the cottage? I could get an appraisal and we could buy Buck out. And Emmalee would probably be fine with moving out."

Collin cocked his head. "Would you be willing to give up half your closet space?"

"Heck, no! But the master bedroom is big enough that I could build you your own closet along the front wall." The additional closet space would help with resale value further down the line, should we ever choose to move. "I can customize it any way you'd like."

"Works for me," Collin said.

"I'll call the Hartleys," I said. "They'll list your house for you and get you top dollar."

We finished our pizza and got back to work. By the end of the evening, the floors and surfaces were dust free. We parted ways in the parking lot with a warm kiss.

Colette had given herself the day off on Saturday and, naturally, Buck wanted to spend time with his wife. Collin had been an avid jogger since junior high, when he'd joined the cross-country team where he'd met his best friend—soon to be his best man—Ren Fujita. The exercise relieved the stress of his job, and he'd recently decided to up his game to trail running. He'd joined a local running club, and he and Ren were off to complete the 5.3-mile Mossy Ridge Trail at Percy Warner Park. In other words, I was on my own today.

I slept in, enjoying some extra snuggle time with Sawdust. At ten, I slid out of bed, started the coffee, and took a quick shower. The aroma of the warm brew had roused Emmalee, who I found curled up in her papasan chair with a steaming mug and her cat.

After pouring myself a cup, I sat down on the couch and broached the subject of our living arrangements. "Collin and I talked last night about where we'll live once we're married."

Emmalee pointed downward to indicate the cottage. "He's moving in here, isn't he?"

"That's the plan. We hate to put you and Cleo out on the streets, though."

"No worries. I saw this coming since he proposed. I wouldn't mind living closer to the café anyway. With the restaurant doing so well, I can finally afford a place of my own."

Seemed life was moving along for all of us. "Sawdust sure is going to miss Cleo."

She ran a hand over the calico's head. "We'll get them together for playdates."

"Perfect." I finished my coffee, kissed my sweet boy on the cheek, and bade my roommate goodbye before heading out.

The electricity and water had been turned on at the townhouse late Friday afternoon. I decided to go by and take another look at the place Saturday morning, determine what else might need repair. I used a ladder to get inside the same way Buck had, by climbing in the second-story window. I'd expected there to be additional items, and my expectations were met. Although the water heater had been turned on for well over twelve hours, the water that came out of the faucets was tepid at best. The dishwasher worked, though it was an older, low-efficiency model. What's more, the racks were bent and the silverware basket was missing. We'd replace both appliances with new energy-efficient models. Same for the oven and refrigerator. The washer and dryer still worked fine and, though older models, were in decent shape. I'd list them online as a free giveaway. Someone would want them and come take them away, saving us the trouble.

After donning my gloves, I pulled the electric oven out from the wall, wrestled it onto a dolly, and rolled it out the front door. I was easing the appliance down the intact side of the front steps, hoping they wouldn't collapse under me, when a female voice came from behind me.

"Excuse me. Are you cleaning the townhouse?"

I turned to see the couple from earlier in the week. As before, they were walking their baby and their mismatched dogs, both of whom wagged their tails as they, too, stared my way. The baby banged a hand on the plastic tray on the front of the stroller, like a judge banging a gavel to call for order in the court. "Ba-ba-ba!"

I couldn't help but smile at the adorable tyke.

Before I could answer the woman, the man strode over. "Can I help?"

"That would be great."

He helped me carefully maneuver the oven off the steps and onto the sidewalk, where I parked it and thanked him for his help. I turned to his wife and answered her question. "My cousin and I plan to fix the townhouse up for resale. I'm working by myself today, but I figured I could remove some of the smaller appliances that we need to replace."

Her brow furrowed in confusion. "You own this house? How? I thought there was a legal fight among the heirs, that several people claimed to own it."

As was typical, the rumor mill hadn't quite gotten things right. I explained the situation, and told them how Buck and I had acquired the property through the quitclaim deeds.

The two exchanged a look and conversed briefly in another language—Hindi, maybe? Bengali?—before turning back to me.

The woman sighed. "I wish we had known such a thing was possible. May I ask how much you paid for the townhouse?"

I saw no harm in sharing the information. I looked up and mentally calculated. "One hundred seventy-five thousand five hundred and thirty-eight dollars."

The two exchanged another look, and the man's brow furrowed now, too. "That is a strange number."

"A couple of them were holdouts. We had to sweeten the deal with another check and what we had in our wallets."

"Ah." The man and his wife exchanged another glance before he held out his hand. "I'm Dhananjay, but I go by D-Jay." He angled his head toward the woman. "My wife, Samira."

As I shook D-Jay's hand, Samira smiled and reached down to stroke her chubby son's cheek. "This is our son Kavish."

I bent down, putting my hands on my knees. "Hello, Kavish. You're a cutie."

He slammed his hand on the tray a second time and repeated his mantra. "Ba-ba-ba!"

I couldn't help but laugh at his enthusiasm. "Ba-ba-ba to you, too!"

Their dogs wanted in on the action, and came over to sniff my coveralls, probably scenting Sawdust and Cleo on my clothing. It was clear they were well-socialized, so I gave them each a few pats, their fur soft under my fingers.

When I stood again, D-Jay asked, "What will be your asking price for the townhouse when you sell it?"

"I'm not sure. We haven't gotten that far yet. We just turned the paperwork over to our attorney for filing yesterday."

Samira's grip tightened on the handle of the stroller. "We are wanting to buy a place in Germantown. Would you consider owner finance?"

In light of the question, I assumed the couple must have less-than-perfect credit. "Sorry, but we're not in a position to accept installment payments. We need to get our money back out of this property so we can invest it in our next flip project."

Samira seemed to feel the need to explain her request, or maybe she hoped she could win me over. "We are very responsible people. We both work in government. Dhananjay is the chief of staff for a state senator. I work for the Department of Veterans Services. We are not wealthy, but we earn a good income. We owned a condominium not long ago. It was a one-bedroom we bought when we married. We had a fifteen-year mortgage, and we made an extra principal payment each month, so we paid down the loan quickly. We had only seventeen payments left when my father in Bangladesh got injured on the job and could not work for several months. We had to send money to help my family. We were late on three mortgage payments in a row, but we made up the past-due amount in only four months' time. We learned right after that that I was pregnant. We put our condo up for sale so that we could buy a bigger home. We did not realize until that time that the banks would not give us a new mortgage with the late payments on our credit reports. By then, it was too late. We had already sold our condo."

Their situation was similar to Macy and Holden's, a growing family needing more room.

"We are stuck," D-Jay added. "Without a loan, we can only rent. We are throwing our money away."

I felt for them. One of my duties as a property manager had been running applicants' credit reports to evaluate their creditworthiness. Property owners were reluctant to rent to those with bad credit, especially if they'd defaulted on rent or a mortgage. That said, I'd learned that defaults rolled off a credit report after seven years, giving people a chance at a fresh start.

When I mentioned this to the couple, Samira said, "That does not help us. It was only two years ago when my father was sick and we failed to pay our mortgage on time."

In other words, it would be five more years before they could obtain a traditional mortgage. "I'm very sorry," I said. "I would be very frustrated, too, if I were in your shoes." They were lucky Gideon had taken a chance on them and allowed them to rent one of his units.

They exchanged another look and more words, before D-Jay turned back to me. "We will try to work something out so that we can make an offer when you put the house up for sale."

Short of robbing a bank or winning the lottery, I had no idea what options they might have for coming up with the funds, but I wished them luck. Even if they could somehow obtain financing, it was unlikely they'd be the highest bidders on the property. Joanna had already implied she'd match or beat any other bid, and she had a big motivation to buy the townhouse. She also had ready cash to buy the property outright, no pesky mortgage to deal with. I felt it was only right to let them know their odds were slim. "I don't want you to get your hopes up for nothing. Joanna Hartzell has expressed an interest in buying the property. So has your landlord."

"Gideon?" Samira frowned. "But he already owns a home. Three others as well." She gestured to the house behind her. "The entire building belongs to him."

D-Jay added his two cents. "The rich snatch up all the properties and leave no homes for anyone else to buy. Housing becomes too expensive. The average person can't afford it."

He had a valid point. It was happening everywhere. Corporations and the wealthy were buying up residential properties and driving up the prices, making it more difficult for others to become homeowners. Homeownership was one of the best ways to amass wealth, and when people were kept out of the market, they couldn't advance economically.

A voice came from the street. Gideon's. "Did I hear my name?"

Samira and D-Jay glanced back at the man none of us had heard coming, then exchanged a frantic look. Gideon was their landlord, after all, and would be none too pleased if he thought his tenants had disparaged him.

I covered for them. "I just met your tenants," I called as he approached, carrying a foil-covered baking dish. "I told them that you and Joanna came over to the firehouse to see what could be done about this place." I hiked a thumb over my shoulder to indicate the townhouse behind me. "D-Jay helped me move the oven down the front steps. We're lucky they held up."

D-Jay and Samira slipped me soft, surreptitious smiles, a subtle way of thanking me for not telling their landlord what they'd been implying about him. That he was greedy.

Gideon stepped up, bringing the smell of fish with

him. He grinned a gargoyle-like grin. "Glad to see you're already at work on my townhouse."

He was looking at me, and failed to see the irritated looks D-Jay and Samira traded behind him. I told him the same thing I'd told the couple. "I've told Joanna that as long as she matches our best offer, the place is hers. It only seems right."

Gideon waved a dismissive hand. "I've got more money than I know what to do with. She won't be able to match my bid."

Looks like friendship only goes so far when a hot property is up for sale. Rather than continue to discuss the sale of the townhouse, which wouldn't take place for months, I turned the topic to the food in his hands. "Whatever that is smells delicious."

He raised the dish. "My mama's tuna casserole," he said. "I loved it as a boy, and I served it to the troops when I was a cook in the army. It's what made my partner fall in love with me." He chuckled. "'Course that was back in the 'don't ask, don't tell' days, but we had our ways. I'd slip him an extra cookie in the chow line, and he'd polish my boots. He died before we had the right to marry, or he'd have been my husband." A pained look crossed his face before he brightened again. "Anyway, Joanna loves it, too. Thought I'd bring some over for her lunch."

How sweet and thoughtful. "If I'd known you provided meal delivery service to your neighbors, I wouldn't have planned to sell the townhouse. I'd move in myself."

He chuckled. "You want to learn how to cook? Come on over sometime and I'll show you the ropes."

I didn't mention that Colette, my best friend/cousin-in-law, was a professional chef. I didn't want to sound like I was one-upping him. She'd offered to teach me how to cook, too, but I'd declined. I preferred power tools to kitchen tools, and was happy to stay in my lane. Still, no sense in insulting the man's interest in the hobby. "I just might take you up on that."

With that, I bade them all goodbye and set off down the sidewalk with the oven, feeling uneasy. I'd hoped that remodeling the townhouse would be a positive mission, but it seemed the project was pitting neighbor against neighbor.

CHAPTER 8

HEADACHE AFTER HEADACHE

WHITNEY

I'd nearly reached the corner when a maroon Saturn sedan screeched to a stop on the perpendicular street. Before GM discontinued the brand about fifteen years ago, Saturns had been very popular in the area. They were manufactured in the town of Spring Hill, which sat just south of Nashville, and many of the carmaker's employees drove them. The rosary hanging from the rearview mirror swung forward and smacked against the inside of the windshield before swinging back. Judith Bottiglieri sat at the wheel, her face puckered in rage. It appeared that she'd been headed to the fire station, but jammed on the brakes when she saw me coming up the side street. The pickup truck behind her slammed into her back bumper with a *BAM*, rocking her car forward. Matthew sat at the wheel of the truck. *What in the world?*

Both of them rolled down their windows and began screaming at me. With them hollering over each other,

I couldn't make out what they were saying. But I didn't have to hear their words to know they were angry as hornets, and that the target of their anger was yours truly. I turned toward the firehouse with the oven. Judith pulled her car into the fire station and again braked to a quick stop. As before, Matthew was too close and ran his front bumper into the back of her car, but with less force this time. Thank goodness both vehicles were older models that already sported assorted dents and scrapes. A fender bender wouldn't make things much worse.

As the two climbed out of their cars, four more vehicles came up the road and turned into the parking lot. Tabitha, Benedict, Peter, and Mary Ruth slammed their doors as they, too, exited their vehicles. All six yelled at me now. Neck veins throbbed. Eyes bulged. Spittle flew. I looked from one to another to another, trying to figure out what had them so agitated. Finally, I threw up a hand in a stop gesture. Once they quieted, I turned to Benny, "What's got all of you so upset?"

He jabbed an accusing finger at me. "You gave John five hundred dollars more than you gave the rest of us!"

Sheesh. "John was holding out. We only paid him more because it was late, we were tired, and we wanted to get the deal done without having to resort to legal action."

Peter scoffed. "That doesn't make it fair!"

He wasn't wrong, and I might have felt the same way in their situation, but we'd paid them a fair amount and I didn't at all appreciate the aggressive way they'd approached me here. I was alone, one against six. Not exactly a fair fight, should one break out. I hoped it wouldn't come to that, but I didn't trust these folks. My body warmed with a fast, nervous pulse.

Judith virtually snarled. "You'd better pay each of us another five hundred dollars or we're calling things off!"

"Calling things off?" I repeated. "What do you mean?"

She crossed her arms over her chest in what seemed to be a Bottiglieri family habit. "We'll rescind the contracts."

"The deeds were properly signed and notarized," I said. "They've been filed in the county records. It's all done. There's nothing to rescind. We legally own the townhouse now."

"Well . . ." She looked up in thought, evidently hoping to find a viable argument written in the clouds. She brought her eyes back down to look at me. "We won't cash our checks, then. If we don't cash them, that means you haven't paid us and there's no deal."

Benny looked sheepish. "I already deposited mine."

"Me too," said Tabitha.

The others concurred, though it didn't matter one way or another. I'd tendered payment, kept up my end of the bargain. As far as I knew, failing to cash a check wouldn't negate the deed.

Peter stepped up close to me. I was taller than him, but he had a good hundred pounds on me. I turned the dolly and eased behind it so the oven now stood between me and this pushy jerk.

He gripped the edges of the stovetop and leaned over it, his face so close I could tell he'd eaten something with onions for lunch. "You refusing to pay us? 'Cause you'd regret it. Trust me."

I wished I had my big wrench in my pocket, my defensive weapon of choice. *But a cell phone is a weapon of sorts, too, isn't it?* I pulled my phone from my pocket and hit the button to record a video. I aimed the lens at him. "Are you threatening me?"

My ploy worked. He backed away, a fake smile plastered on his face. "We're not threatening you. We're just asking you to pay us equal amounts for our equal shares, that's all."

"Really?" I said, sarcastically drawing out the word. "I'm surprised at you, Peter. You were nearly as stubborn as John. You demanded more than your siblings received. We gave you thirty-eight dollars in cash. Remember?"

My tactic worked. The other five turned their ire on Peter now, yelling at him. Benny even gave him a small shove toward Judith. Judith shoved her brother right back toward Benny. He put his arms over his head to protect himself as Mary Ruth clobbered him with her purse. I'd never seen middle-aged people act so childish. *Grow up, for Pete's sake!*

Lest the situation devolve into fratricide, I drew their attention back to me. "I don't have the checkbook with me, so I can't pay you today. Besides, I have to get an okay from my partners." I doubted Buck and Presley would balk at paying the additional amount, but I still had to run it by them. Though I knew I'd have an answer sooner, I said, "I'll get back to you on Monday." The Bottiglieris had given me unnecessary flack today. They deserved to sweat a little.

"You'd better!" Judith growled.

Ugh. Ten o'clock in the morning and already my patience had been exhausted.

The six got into their automobiles, and more bumpers met as each one tried to be the first to exit the parking lot. These people took sibling rivalry to a whole new level.

Once they'd gone, I set up two sawhorses across the entrance to the parking lot. If any of them tried to come back to make more demands, I wanted it made clear they were not welcome.

I rolled the oven over by the dumpster and tilted it left and right, walking it off the dolly. For safety's sake, I removed the door. Didn't want a child or animal getting trapped inside. I returned to the townhouse to remove the rest of the smaller appliances that would need to be replaced. I'd leave the refrigerator for Buck to handle. By the time I was done it was early afternoon, and I decided to call it a day. I had grocery shopping and housecleaning to do at home, and I wanted to spend some quality time with my cat. I hadn't seen much of the sweet little guy lately. I attached a padlock to the front door so that we wouldn't have to climb through the upstairs window next time, and headed out.

At the break of dawn Sunday morning, Sawdust followed me to the door. Colette would be working at her restaurant today, and Buck and I planned to meet at the building supply store that afternoon to buy materials and supplies for the fire station rehab. For now, I simply needed to complete some measurements to make sure we bought the appropriate amounts of framing materials, sheetrock, drywall tape, and joint compound to build the wall that would divide the current large secondary bedroom into two smaller rooms. *Might as well get an early start.*

I looked down at my cat as he peered up at me. "Want to go to work with me?"

My beautiful buff-colored boy issued a definitive *mew.* I took it as a yes. I rounded up his carrier and opened the door, and he sashayed in, swishing his bushy tail. Cleo watched from her comfy spot atop the papasan chair. She opened her mouth and yawned. She obviously preferred to stay right here and continue her nap than get into a carrier. I could understand why. For her, a carrier usually meant a trip to the vet. Not so for Sawdust, who often accompanied me to work, so long as we weren't performing tasks that might pose a danger to him.

I carried Sawdust out to my SUV, stashed him in the back seat, and ran the belt buckle through the carrier's handle to secure it in place. As we drove to the fire station, I told Sawdust all about our plans. He meowed on occasion, letting me know he approved. As we drew near the station, my nose detected the scent of smoke. I sniffed the air. *Is someone grilling?* I quickly dismissed the idea. It was only half past seven, much too early to barbecue. *But smoke is definitely coming from somewhere . . .* The air was cloudy with it, increasingly so as I neared our destination. I gasped as the firehouse came into view, reflexively hitting the brake. Thank goodness nobody was behind me. Smoke billowed from a second-story window and flames shot out, doing their best to evade the stream of water a firefighter had aimed at it. *Could there be anything more ironic than a fire station on fire?*

My heart banged in my chest and my head spun. *What happened here?* Unfortunately, I was no stranger to fires. Old, defective wiring in the cottage had caused a fire there, and for a few moments I thought I'd lost Sawdust. And I'd recently watched helplessly as a boat burned on the lake after exploding with a man inside. I'd tried to force the memories from my mind, but seeing the flames here brought that same feeling of horror back to the surface.

I pulled into the parking lot of the café next door,

where a crowd of patrons stood, watching the excitement. I parked my car, unrolled the windows so Sawdust wouldn't get overheated, and scurried over to the station. A female firefighter held up a hand to stop me, much as I'd held up a hand to silence the Bottiglieris when they'd accosted me here the day before. "Stay back, ma'am."

I took a few steps back, gesturing at the firehouse. "I own the building."

She ran her gaze over my coveralls and boots. "You're with the historical society? We've been trying to get in touch with you."

My guess was she'd envisioned someone in Victorian-era dress, not a woman dressed like a grease monkey. "No," I explained, "I'm not from the historical society. My cousin and I just bought the station from them." My guess was the property records hadn't yet been updated to reflect the change in ownership. Thank goodness we had an insurance policy in place. "Can you tell me what happened?"

"We don't know the details yet," she said. "Was anyone in the building?"

"No," I said. "At least nobody should have been." *Could a homeless person or reckless teenagers have found their way into the station and accidentally caused the conflagration?*

"Was there anything flammable inside?" the firefighter asked.

"Not that I know of." I fanned the smoke out of my face, but it was too late. The air infiltrated my lungs, making me cough. When I could get my breath, I said, "We just completed the demolition. All the debris was removed and put in that bin." I gestured to the dumpster.

"Any building materials inside? Paint? Thinner? Lumber?"

"No. I was coming here to measure. I planned to pick up supplies and materials today."

She nodded and collected my contact information. "We'll be in touch once we know more and to let you know whether it's safe enough for you to go inside."

I thanked her and returned to my car, where I promptly phoned Presley, waking her up.

"How bad is it?" she asked, her voice still gravelly from sleep.

"Hard to say. It's still burning so we won't know until we can get inside."

As a silent partner who'd have no responsibility for repairing the mess here, Presley was pragmatic. "Well, this is why we paid for insurance."

Buck, on the other hand, spat a string of curses when I informed him about the fire. "First the Bottiglieris give us grief, and now this. Maybe we should bail on these projects and get the hell out of Germantown. These properties have been nothing but headaches."

After working out all the design details, I was too mentally invested in these projects to give up on them now. I told Buck I'd be in touch once I knew more. I started the motor, exited the parking lot, and drove around the block the long way to avoid the firetrucks in the street. Gideon, Joanna, and Holden stood on the opposite sidewalk from the townhouse, where they could watch the goings on without being in the way. D-Jay, Samira, and Kavish stood nearby. Macy, presumably, was in bed, per doctor's orders. I hoped the fire engine sirens hadn't startled her. A trio of older men had even brought canvas lawn chairs along so they could sit while they watched the activity, apparently considering the event to be first-class entertainment. I assumed it was the sirens that had drawn everyone outside, but perhaps they'd smelled the smoke first. Maybe one of them had been the person to call in the report and summon help.

I parked in the narrow driveway of the townhouse, carried Sawdust up to the porch, and left him there temporarily before walking over to speak with the neighbors.

Not bothering with a greeting, Samira jumped right in. "What happened? How did the station catch fire?"

I raised my shoulders and palms. "No idea. I'm hoping the firefighters will be able to tell us once they've put the fire out."

Joanna glanced upward. "It's a good thing it's not windy, or the fire might have spread to our homes." She put a hand to her head. "All this smoke is giving me a headache."

Gideon cast a glance at Joanna before turning to me, his face tight with concern. "You think it could be arson?"

My mind hadn't gone there yet but, now that he'd brought it up, I realized it was possible. The Bottiglieris hadn't been at all happy with me yesterday. Maybe Peter had made good on his threat to make me regret not paying them the additional $500 each, or at least not paying them right away. Maybe he'd started the fire to show me what he was capable of if we didn't fork over the additional funds. Then again, maybe it was only a homeless person or delinquents who'd caused the fire, like I'd wondered earlier. Or maybe there'd been some type of freak accident, a piece of equipment that had short-circuited or something. But Buck and I always ensured everything was unplugged when we left a worksite. *Hmm.*

The only thing I knew for certain was that I didn't want the day to be a total waste. To that end, I decided to do some demo work on the townhouse. I'd already driven over. Might as well make good use of my time.

I bid adieu to the neighbors, returned to the town-house, and carried Sawdust into the place. Though I'd expected to smell some smoke inside, the scent was much stronger than I'd anticipated, and a haze hung in the air. When I turned around, I sucked air for the second time that morning. *What the—?!* Someone had written THEIVES in bright red spray paint on the living room wall. They'd misspelled the word by putting the *e* before the *i*. The letters were enormous, spanning from floor to ceiling, though they were relatively narrow. The paint had dripped, looking like blood running down the wall. As if we wouldn't get the message, they'd painted the word across the kitchen cabinets, too. The exterior kitchen door had been left open, which explained how the house had filled with smoke. I bumped the door closed with my hip in the hopes of preserving any fin-gerprints that might be on the knob. I continued on to discover they'd spray-painted the sentiment on the master bedroom walls as well. They'd started to paint it across the bathroom mirror, but the can must've run out partway through. They'd only gotten so far as theiv.

It must have been one of the Bottiglieris. Each of them likely had keys to the townhouse. After all, they'd all lived here at one point, as had their parents until their deaths not too long ago. Besides, they'd be the only ones who'd write a word like *thieves*—or should I say *theives*?—on the wall. Only the Bottiglieris had a rea-son to believe, however unfounded, that Buck, Presley, and I had stolen from them. I found myself putting a hand to my head, just like Joanna had earlier. This juvenile vengeance was enough to give anyone a migraine.

Mentally chastising myself for not immediately changing the locks on the place, I snapped photos of the vandalized walls and texted them to Collin before dialing his number. He answered the phone sounding incredulous. "Someone vandalized the townhouse?"

"Looks that way," I said. "But that's not all. The fire station is burning as we speak."

"What the—?" His mind shifted from fiancé mode to detective mode. "Stay put, so long as it's safe. I'm on my way."

CHAPTER 9

CURIOUS AND FURIOUS

SAWDUST

Sawdust smelled the smoke, heard the commotion, and sensed that these things had upset Whitney. She sat cross-legged in the middle of the floor, her face in her hands. Sawdust hated to see her feeling so defeated, and was angry at whoever had caused this. He rubbed himself across her back and down her thigh, mewing to let her know he was concerned about her.

She removed her hands from her face and picked him up, gently laying him in her lap. She ran a hand across his back over and over. Though he couldn't hear her thoughts, of course, he could sense her mind working. Her body remained rigid. He rolled over onto his back, looking up at her, hoping to distract her from her worries. Though she scratched his chest and murmured to him, she remained stiff with tension. Eventually, she placed him on the floor and stood. He'd done what he could to console her, and she was heading to her toolbox now. He decided to explore the place. He'd never been here before, and there might be some interesting things to discover.

He wandered the downstairs, stopping twice to dig his claws into the carpet. It wasn't particularly lush or satisfying, worn too thin to be much fun. He chased a small spider around the bathtub before it escaped into the drain. He trotted upstairs and checked out the bedrooms. Not much to see here. Once he'd been through the entire place, he settled on a second-floor windowsill to watch the firefighters work on the building next door, his cat curiosity causing him to wonder. *What happened over there?*

CHAPTER 10

SMOKE AND SMOKES

WHITNEY

When Collin arrived, I showed him the cell phone footage I'd recorded the day before, when Peter had gotten in my face, demanding more money for the deeds. Collin took the phone from my hand, forwarded the video to his own phone, then returned my cell to me.

I gestured around at the spray-painted walls. "Do you think Peter did this?"

"He sure seemed angry enough in the video."

Collin photographed the damage at the townhouse. I suspected the fire and vandalism were related, and that the fire wasn't an accident. It would be an awfully big coincidence for both of the new properties Buck and I owned to have suffered damage on the same night if it wasn't the same culprit—or culprits. Collin agreed.

I went along with him as he made a quick sweep of the neighborhood. Samira and D-Jay weren't home, but we spoke with Joanna, Gideon, and Holden. None had seen or heard anything at the townhouse the night before, nor had they spotted any unusual cars parked nearby. Whoever had spray-painted the walls had been quiet and sneaky. We were nearly certain it was a Bottiglieri, but which one? We had six to choose from, seven if Johnny'd had second thoughts about the $25,500 we'd paid him for his share. If the rest thought they'd see another five hundred dollars, they were sorely mistaken. I'd planned to deliver their checks tomorrow, but no way would we pay them any more for their interests now.

When Collin had done what he could here, he said, "I'll share your video and the photos I've taken here with the fire investigator. We'll see what they come back with. In the meantime, I'll go speak with the Bottiglieris."

An hour later, a knock sounded at the front door. Sawdust followed me as I went to answer it. Through the peephole, I could see Samira and D-Jay on the porch, Kavish perched on Samira's hip. The stroller next to her told me they'd just returned from a walk. That explained why they hadn't answered their door when we'd gone by.

When I opened the door, Kavish pointed down at Sawdust. "Kee-kee!" The cat mewed up at him, to the boy's delight.

I groaned inwardly. After battling the Bottiglieris, and dealing with the fire and vandalism, the last thing I wanted to do right now was debate who I should sell the townhouse to. I decided to be frank. "I hope you're not here to try to change my mind about giving Joanna the right of first refusal. I've already made a promise to her, and I won't go back on my word."

"No-no-no," Samira assured me. "We are not here to argue with you."

D-Jay said, "I am here to offer my help. Are there more things that need to be moved?"

I bit my lip, feeling sheepish. "Buck's going to move the fridge, and I've finished removing the smaller appliances, but thanks for the offer. I'm going to start the demolition now."

"May I assist?" D-Jay asked. "I do not expect to be paid, of course. When Samira and I are able to buy our next house, it is likely to be a fixer-upper. It would be good for me to learn how such things are done."

I debated for a moment. *I'd be a fool to turn down free labor, wouldn't I?* If it got to the point that teaching him the ropes was slowing me down more than his help was speeding things along, I could end the arrangement. "I'd be glad to have your help. But be forewarned. You will be very tired and your back will hurt by the end of the day."

Samira slid him a look. "Do not cry to me." She angled her head to indicate their son. "I hear enough crying each day." The grin playing about her lips said she was teasing her husband.

I opened the door wider to allow D-Jay inside. He'd taken two steps in when he stopped in his tracks, his jaw slack as he stared at the spray-painted wall. "Who did that?"

"I don't know. Someone got in last night. The police are looking into it."

Samira poked her head inside now, too. When she saw the paint, her eyes went wide. She squeezed past her husband to come into the living room. Even Kavish seemed to realize the paint wasn't normal. He stared at the wall, mouth agape, drooling. "Ga-ga-ba-ya!"

D-Jay appeared wary, his face tightening. "Someone broke in?"

"Not as far as we can tell," I said. "No windows or doors were damaged. But if you're concerned, it's okay if you leave. I won't hold you to your offer to help."

He stared at the wall another beat or two, considering, before saying, "I'll stay."

I looked from one of them to the other. "Any chance you saw something last night? A suspicious person walking around? Maybe a car you didn't recognize?"

Both shook their heads. "Sorry," said D-Jay. "We go to bed early."

Samira reached out to put a hand on my forearm. "May I look around?"

I supposed there was no harm in it, though I feared she might get her hopes up of one day owning the place. "Just don't go in the attic. The floor is unstable."

While she carried Kavish about, taking a look at the place, I handed D-Jay a screwdriver. "Let's start with removing the outlet and light switch covers, and the light fixtures. Then we'll move on to the cabinet hardware."

We were still in the living room ten minutes later, when Samira carried Kavish down the stairs. "See you later!" she called sweetly to her husband before heading out the door.

The tasks I'd given D-Jay were mostly busy work, though I did show him how to safely detach the wires from a light fixture by turning off the electricity, then replacing the wire nuts right away to prevent electricity from arcing when it was turned back on. "The final step is removing the mounting plate."

We chatted as we worked. D-Jay told me that he and Samira enjoyed the ethnic diversity of the Germantown neighborhood. "Samira found a nice playgroup here for Kavish. Our favorite coffee shop and Indian restaurant are here, also. And it is only a short commute to our jobs."

It was easy to see why they wanted to stay in the area. Too bad they couldn't get a loan to buy their own place, one where they wouldn't have to lug dogs and a stroller upstairs.

By the time we finished removing the items, it was the middle of the afternoon. We carried the first load of light fixtures to the dumpster at the fire station. Dozens of charred wood flooring planks sat atop the demolition debris Buck and I had removed from the fire station in the days before. We'd intended to leave the old wood flooring in place, but it looked like we'd have to replace it, after all. The installation of new flooring would add several days' time to our estimated completion date. *Sigh*.

"Miss Whitaker!" The firefighter I'd spoken with earlier waved me over. She held a flooring board in her arms. Next to her stood another woman, this one with thick, flaming red hair. She wore rubber-soled shoes, khaki pants, and a short-sleeved blue golf shirt with the fire department logo emblazoned on the chest. I recognized her right away as Melanie Landreth, the fire investigator who'd looked into the boat explosion. Realizing I'd likely be tied up here for a bit, I thanked D-Jay for helping me out. "I'll move the rest of the stuff to the dumpster later."

As he left to return home to his wife and son, I walked over to Landreth. She remembered me, too. "We meet again."

I gave her a feeble smile. "Let's stop doing this. Shall we?"

She issued a mirthless chuckle and got right down

to brass tacks, using her pen to point to the board in the firefighter's hands. A black line zigzagged across it. "See that?" She moved her pen back and forth to indicate the line. "That burn mark tells me someone poured an accelerant on the wood. Given the narrow width of the line, I'm thinking lighter fluid. This board was directly under a sprinkler head in the kitchen and was extinguished quickly. We found some charred bits of crumpled newspaper, too. It was probably used to get the fire going."

In other words, the blaze had been intentionally set. *But by who? And how'd they get in?*

She went on to answer the latter question. "A second-floor window on the back of the building was broken. That's likely how the arsonist or arsonists gained access. Detective Flynn sent me the video you recorded here yesterday, as well as the photos from your townhouse." She lifted her pen to point to a security camera on the café next door. "I'm hoping that camera caught something. It might tell us whether the folks you bought the townhouse from are involved in what happened here. I'll let you know what I find out. Stay out of the station until we give you the all-clear. Okay?"

"Sure." I thanked her for her efforts and returned to the townhouse to lock it up. Like Buck, I found my enthusiasm for the two projects had waned. What should have been fun flips had turned into futile frustrations.

With the fire station still off-limits Monday morning, Buck and I met at the townhouse. He cursed at the paint on the wall. "Did Collin figure out which of the Butt-uglies did this?"

"Not yet." I repeated what Collin had told me the

evening before. "Judith didn't answer her door and Peter's wife claimed he wasn't home. Collin thinks she was lying. He'll go by again soon, set up camp out front if he has to."

Buck tore up the carpet downstairs, while I did the same in the smaller bedrooms upstairs. I was kneeling by a window that faced the front of the house, working the edge of the carpet free from the baseboard, when movement on the street below caught my eye. Gideon was heading diagonally across the street to Joanna's place. He held something in his hand. It was white and green, rectangular. *Is that a pack of Newports?* It sure looked like it. Joanna must have left them at his place. He disappeared from sight under the porch roof. I figured he'd knock on her door to return them, maybe even go inside for a bit. But a mere three seconds later he emerged from the porch, looked both ways before crossing the street, and returned to his townhouse, going inside. Joanna must have met him at the door.

The carpet was stubborn, and I had to use a blade to loosen it from the wall. Finally, it came free. I rolled the old, stained carpet up. It would be much too heavy for me, but Buck would be able to carry it down the stairs. Around ten o'clock, I went down to the first floor to check the status of his work. He had just a little way to go in the master closet. I decided to take a break on the porch where I could get some fresh air. Carpet removal stirred up all kinds of dust.

I went out to the porch, closing the door behind me. It was a partly cloudy day, not too hot, with a light, refreshing breeze. After pulling down my dust mask, I took a swig from my water bottle. Though the fire had been out for hours, a faint scent of residual smoke still hung in the air. As I went to take a second sip, I glanced over at Joanna's porch. The pack of Newports sat on the small table between her rockers. Looked like Joanna hadn't met Gideon at the door, after all.

My cell phone came to life in my breast pocket, and I pulled it out to see it was Landreth calling. "Got some news for you," she said. "Care to meet me at the firehouse?"

"We'll be right there."

I rounded up Buck and we headed over, relieved to see the cordon tape had been removed.

"Y'all are free to go back inside the station," Landreth said. "The subflooring seems stable enough to support weight and there's no major structural damage."

Buck issued a *phew*. "That's good news."

"We've got a person of interest, too—at least we will once we can identify them." She pulled her tablet from under her arm and brought up some video footage. The angle told us it had been recorded by the camera on the café next door, and the time stamp said it had been recorded at 2:57 A.M. While the lights in the restaurant's parking lot provided dim illumination, the station was dark. Headlights flashed as a large vehicle pulled slowly into the fire station's lot. My heartrate amped up. *Could that be Matthew Bottiglieri's pickup?* I was quickly disavowed of the notion when the shadow that formed against the streetlights behind it made it clear what kind of truck it was. A long bar rose up at an angle behind the cab, a hook on the end. *A tow truck.*

"Ohhh," I said on a breath.

Landreth's brows raised. "This truck mean something to you?"

"Yes," I said. "I mean, *maybe*. Joanna Hartzell, the

woman who owns the townhouse that adjoins ours,
has a son who drives a tow truck. I believe his name
is Lane, if I'm recalling correctly. Buck and I overheard a conversation between Joanna and her neighbor, Gideon Koppelman, that implied Lane had stolen
from Joanna."

Landreth's brows lowered slightly. "Even if that's the
case, what reason would he have to start a fire here?"

I racked my brain, but couldn't come up with one. "I
don't know."

Buck mused aloud. "If he stole from Joanna, that
would make him a *thief.*"

His emphasizing the word got me thinking, too.
Could the spray-painted word *THEIVES* on our wall be
somehow related to Lane? Might he have taken something from someone who wanted revenge? Maybe
they'd thought he was living with his mother and that
she owned the entire house, and they'd mistakenly
painted the word in our unit by accident. I supposed
it was possible. But there seemed to be a lot of incor-
rect assumptions that would have had to take place for
things to play out that way, and it didn't explain how
someone had accessed the townhouse without breaking in. Then again, maybe Buck and I had forgotten to
lock the kitchen door, or maybe the intruder had picked
the lock. With the weatherstripping missing, someone
could have inserted a putty knife between the door and
frame, and used it to push the deadbolt aside. Heck, I'd
done as much myself when I'd been a property manager
and a key had broken off in a lock.

We continued to watch the video. The image was
grainy and the breeze caused the trees to cast moving
shadows. No light ever came on in the cabin of the tow
truck and, as far as I could tell, nobody had exited the

vehicle. When I mentioned this to Landreth, she said, "They could have turned off the interior lights. With the truck being parked sideways, there's no way of telling whether a door opened. They might have slid out and snuck around in the shadows."

As we continued to watch, a small dot of light lit up inside the cab for just a second or two. An even smaller dot of light appeared, like a tiny firefly, moving back and forth on a lateral trajectory. "What's that?" I asked. It seemed too small to be the screen of a cell phone. *Could it be a penlight?*

"Can't say for sure," Landreth said, "but my guess would be a cigarette."

The little light eventually disappeared. The tow truck sat there for just under half an hour before the headlights came on again. The driver circled slowly around and exited the lot. I shifted my focus to the upper windows of the station, waiting to see the light of the fire starting inside, but I saw nothing. Landreth fast-forwarded to daybreak when, in the dim light of dawn, we saw glass burst out of an upstairs window and smoke pour out. I supposed I'd been naïve to think it would be obvious when the newspaper went up in flames inside. After all, it was a spacious place and, from what Landreth had told me earlier and the flooring she'd shown me, it appeared the fire had been started in the kitchen area, away from a window.

On the security camera feed, we saw a driver pull their car to the curb in front of the firehouse. They must have been the one to summon firefighters to the scene.

"When did the fire start?" I asked. "Is there any way to tell?"

"Not precisely," Landreth said. "There's too many variables."

"So, we don't know how soon it started after the tow truck left?"

"No, but at least you've given me a place to start."

While she set off to Joanna's townhouse to get contact information for Lane, Buck and I ventured carefully into the fire station. The place reeked of smoke, and the walls were dark and sooty. Plywood would have to be placed over the broken window until a new one could be installed, and some of the drywall was scorched and would have to be replaced along with the damaged flooring. But, all in all, it wasn't nearly as bad as it could have been.

When we returned to the townhouse to finish removing the carpet, I noticed the cigarettes were no longer on Joanna's porch. She must have rounded up the pack when Landreth went by to see about getting in touch with Lane. I hoped she wasn't too upset that the fire investigator wanted to speak with him. We weren't even sure it had been him in the tow truck.

Colette had sent provisions with Buck, gourmet sandwiches with a protein-packed garlic-lemon chickpea spread and sides of fruit for lunch, much better than the pre-packaged peanut butter crackers I kept in my toolbox to snack on. We enjoyed a late lunch around two in the afternoon, sitting on the top step of the porch to eat. I'd assumed Joanna and Gideon had been inside her place, watching *The Young and the Restless* as usual, so it surprised me when a blue VW Beetle convertible pulled into Joanna's driveway with Gideon at the wheel. Joanna sat slumped in the passenger seat. Gideon climbed out and scurried around to open the door for Joanna. He helped her out, and she clung to his shoulder as they made their way to the door.

Reflexively, I stood. "Everything okay?"

Gideon looked up, his expression pensive. "We've been at urgent care. When I came over to watch our soaps, Joanna could barely walk. She was dizzy and shaking. Had a headache, too."

"Worst of my life," she said weakly, shuffling along beside him.

"Her vitals were normal," Gideon said. "They gave her some migraine medicine. It's seemed to help some. I'm going to get her inside and put her to bed. I'll stick around awhile, make sure she's okay before heading back home."

In light of the fact that Joanna's daughter was on bed rest and her son-in-law was at work, she was lucky to have such a good friend close by to look out for her.

Gideon scowled. "It didn't help that the fire marshal came by, asking about Lane. That got Joanna upset. Lane's caused her many a headache, too, over the years."

Joanna turned a weak, unfocused glare on her friend. Even if what Gideon said was true, no parent appreciated someone criticizing their child. I felt a twinge of guilt in my gut, but what was I supposed to have done? Keep mum about Joanna's son and his tow truck? If Lane was innocent of setting the fire, it seemed he could easily prove it. All he had to do was account for his whereabouts in the wee hours Sunday morning.

I stepped down from the porch, careful to avoid the broken step. "Can I help you get her inside?"

Gideon stopped me with a raised hand. "No need. I got her."

At that point, all I could offer was well wishes. "I hope you feel better real soon, Joanna."

Gideon helped her up the steps, punched in the code on her door's keypad, and led her inside. The door swung closed behind them, followed by the sound of the deadbolt sliding home.

CHAPTER 11
ALARMED

WHITNEY

On Tuesday, Buck and I spent the morning at the firehouse. We removed the damaged flooring and sheetrock the firefighters hadn't already pulled out, and completed the measurements I'd intended to make on Sunday, before I'd been thwarted by the fire. I revised my list of materials needed, and we set off for the building supply store.

The first thing I put in my cart were two sets of hardware for the exterior doors at the townhouse, the front door and the kitchen door. I bought the type with a numeric keypad, like Joanna had. Physical keys were slowly becoming obsolete. They were easy to lose, they could break, and if one got into the wrong hands the only solution was to install a whole new lock. With a keypad, all a homeowner had to do was change the code to prevent anyone with a previous code from gaining access.

This easy task complete, we headed to the flooring department.

"Sorry," said the clerk. "There's kinks up and down the supply chain. Hardwood floor planks are on back order. We've got engineered wood if that'll work for you."

Engineered wood, while still relatively durable, had only a thin layer of hardwood atop a plywood base, and thus could not be repeatedly refinished. We'd much prefer real hardwood. I'd see about getting some elsewhere. We declined, but thanked the clerk for the information.

We bought sandpaper and enough stain to refinish the floors in the bedrooms. Several sheets of drywall along with multiple gallons of primer went onto our carts, as well. I bought small paint samples in shades of red, yellow, and gray. Once I determined what combination looked best in the firehouse, I'd be back to buy more to complete the painting. We also bought a doorbell with a built-in security camera for the townhouse, and five wide-angle security cameras, one for each side of the fire station and one for the back of the townhouse.

Our last stop was in the lumber department. While I counted out lengths of trim and quarter round, Buck meandered down the aisle. He returned with a number of raw pinewood slats and a heavy-duty piece of plywood.

"What's all that for?" I asked.

He said nothing, but a slow grin spread across his face. I took a second look at the materials. *What could he make out of them? A lattice for climbing roses? A ventilated bin for compost?* "It's for a crib!" I shouted, matching Kavish in my excitement and volume. "Colette's pregnant!"

Men passed by, casting looks in our direction, some of them smiling. One patted Buck on the back, chuckled, and said, "God help ya, son. Your life will never be the same."

Buck confirmed my suspicion with a proud grin. "The baby's due in late January."

"Why didn't y'all tell me?!"

"We didn't want to jinx things by telling anyone too soon. Besides, I'm telling you now."

My mind reeled. I was thrilled for my cousin and my best friend, and myself as well. *I'm going to have a baby cousin!* A baby cousin once removed, officially, but whatever the relationship would technically be, I was over the moon.

We took our items to the checkout. While the cashier rang us up, I texted Colette a photo of my face with a huge smile on it. *Buck just told me the news!*

She texted me a photo right back. It was a picture of her in her chef's uniform, a hand over her mouth as if she were about to succumb to morning sickness. She accompanied the photo with a message. *My pregnancy's been real fun so far.* She followed it with the green sick-face emoji.

Buck read the message over my shoulder. "It's been hard for her to go to work, what with all that heat in the kitchen and the food smells."

"Maybe it'll pass soon. I've heard morning sickness gets better as things move along."

"I sure hope so. She's miserable."

Between Joanna's daughter, Macy, being sentenced to bed rest and Colette's nausea, I began to think maybe Collin and I should just adopt some shelter cats to complete our family when the time was right.

We loaded the large materials onto the flatbed trailer attached to Buck's van, and stowed the smaller supplies in his van and my SUV. After a quick lunch of fast-food burritos, we drove back to the fire station, arriving at a quarter to two. Buck opened the rolling door of the big garage bay and started unloading.

We were about halfway through when he left the bay to carry some of the drywall upstairs. No sooner had he disappeared through the upstairs door than Joanna came veering around the corner, teetering on her feet. She held a hand to her forehead. A lit cigarette dangled from her lips, smoked down to a nub. With my arms full, I couldn't reach out immediately to steady her. By the time I set the cans of paint down, she'd grabbed the metal fireman's pole and appeared to be hanging on for dear life. Her mouth opened and the cigarette fell to the concrete floor, smoldering as she turned vacant eyes on me and muttered gibberish that sounded like Kavish's nonsense words.

I rushed over and ground out the butt with the toe of my boot. "Are you okay, Joanna?"

Her head circled on her neck. *Is that a yes or a no?* She crooked her elbow around the pole to hold herself upright while shaking another cigarette from her pack. It took three tries before she managed to get it between her lips. When she did, a few stray pieces of tobacco fell out of the end. She went to light the cigarette with her plastic butane lighter, but was off-kilter again. She nearly set her hair and collar on fire before I was able to take it from her. The cigarette dropped from her lips and hit the floor near the butt of the other before rolling a few feet away.

My heart pounding like a hammer, I tucked the lighter in my pocket, cupped my hands around my mouth, and shouted up through the hole in the ceiling. "Buck! Buck, come quick! Something's wrong with Joanna!"

Buck's face appeared, peering down through the void.

Seeing Joanna, he set aside the pieces of sheetrock in his hands and ran for the stairs, his footfalls thundering overhead. It would have been quicker to slide down the pole but, with Joanna hanging onto it for dear life, that wasn't an option. He clambered down the steps and dashed over. "Is she having a stroke?"

I didn't know whether Joanna was suffering a stroke, a heart attack, or something else entirely but, no matter what was happening, it was clear the woman needed medical attention ASAP. My first reflex was to run for the alarm button on the wall, but I realized that was a misguided impulse. Joanna's eyes rolled back in her head and she began to slide down the pole. *Oh, my gosh!* "Call nine-one-one!" I shrieked. While Buck whipped out his cell phone, I grabbed at Joanna, claiming two handfuls of her blouse and a bra strap, enough to slow her descent but not stop it. At least I'd broken her fall. I went down with her, falling to my knees on the hard concrete. *Damn, that hurts!* Too bad I wasn't wearing my knee pads. I was able to get my arms under Joanna to prevent her head from slamming to the concrete. I maneuvered to a sitting position on the floor. As gently as I could, I crooked a knee under her and positioned her so that her head rested on my thigh.

Meanwhile, Buck was on the phone with the dispatcher. He turned to look at me. "What's the address here?"

As I rattled it off, he repeated it into the phone. The dispatcher kept him on the line while we waited for the ambulance to arrive. It felt as if we were stuck in time, each second an eternity. I was aware of each of my breaths, as well as Joanna's, as I kept watch to make sure she continued to breathe. Looking down at her, I contemplated the irony of having to wait for EMTs when an ambulance had once made its home right here in this very bay. Tremors shook her body as she lay in my lap, staring at nothing, her eyelids at half-mast.

An eerie sensation slithered up my spine as I realized her breaths were coming slower, the time between each inhale increasing bit by bit by bit. I put a hand under her chin, feeling for a pulse point. Her heartbeat, too, seemed to be slowing down. Perhaps her respiration and pulse had slowed because she was no longer moving around, much as these vitals slowed when someone slept. *But maybe they'd slowed because her life is slowly slipping away . . .*

Buck and I waited in silent panic, the only sounds coming from the rustling trees and the occasional street traffic outside the open bay. A soft *whush* sounded as a car drove past. A bird chirped. The wind blew a dry leaf into the bay, where it whirled in a circle along with some flecks of dust. Finally, a siren sounded in the distance, the woo-woo-woo telling us that Joanna would soon be in the hands of people who would know how to help her—*if she could be helped.*

As the siren grew louder, Buck stepped out to the parking lot to wave down the ambulance. A minute later, two paramedics—one male and one female— scrambled around me. They gingerly transferred Joanna from my lap to a gurney, all the while peppering me with questions to try to help them determine what had happened.

I had little information to offer. "She just wobbled into the bay and collapsed. She had a hand to her head when she came in. Her neighbor took her to urgent care for a migraine yesterday. They gave her medication for it." *Could what is happening to Joanna now be an allergic reaction to the migraine pills?*

Buck held out a hand and pulled me to my feet as the female EMT affixed the straps around Joanna. "Any idea what medication they gave her?"

I shook my head, but realized the medic's focus was on her patient, not me, and said aloud, "No. I might be able to find out, though. I can check with the neighbor."

"Please do. Call dispatch if you find out. They'll relay the information to us. Give her family a heads-up, too, please."

They raised the gurney and rolled it over to the ambulance, then slid Joanna inside. Seconds later, the doors closed and the ambulance turned out of the parking lot, on its way to the emergency room.

"I'll be back," I told Buck. "I'm going to check with Gideon, see if he knows what medication she took." If nothing else, he might know her door code and be able to get inside to check the bottle. He might also know how to get in touch with Holden. With Macy on bed rest, I wasn't sure it was wise to rouse her and shock her with the news.

I sprinted down the sidewalk and across the street, my boots pounding loudly on the asphalt and concrete. I took the two stairs up to Gideon's porch in one step, noting the Dad's Old Fashioned Root Beer sign hung slightly crooked. I might have straightened it were this a social visit, but in light of current events a crooked sign was entirely unimportant. I banged on Gideon's door, willing him to make haste.

A few seconds later, he pulled the door open and gave me his gargoyle grin. "Hello, Whit—"

"Joanna collapsed at the fire station," I said, interrupting him. There was no time for niceties. "The paramedics need to know what medications she's on. Do you know what the doctor at urgent care prescribed her?"

Gideon simply stared at me for a second or two as he processed what I'd told him, then he shook his head once and said, "Lasmiditan. It's also called Reyvow."

I pulled out my cell phone and dialed 9-1-1, putting the call on speaker in case they asked for more information that Gideon would be in a better position to provide. After explaining why I was calling, I gave the dispatcher the name of the drug.

"What dosage?" she asked.

Gideon gave her the answer. "One hundred milligrams."

The dispatcher asked, "When did she take her most recent dose?"

Gideon said, "Probably right before she collapsed. They gave her a dose at urgent care around this time yesterday. She was only supposed to take one pill every twenty-four hours." He eyed me. "The doctor warned her it could cause dizziness. He told her not to drive for eight full hours after taking a pill."

The information brought me a small measure of relief. As scary as Joanna's condition had seemed, maybe it was nothing more than the side effect of the drug. Maybe they needed to reduce her dosage.

The dispatcher asked, "Is she on any other meds?"

"Lipitor," Gideon replied. "She has high cholesterol. I don't know the dosage, but she takes it in the morning with her breakfast."

"Got it." The dispatcher wrapped things up and terminated the call, promising to pass the information along to the EMTs.

As I slid the phone back into my pocket, Gideon put a hand on the doorframe as if he needed to steady himself. He was not a young man, and the news about his friend had to be upsetting. "I'd better get in touch with Holden," he said. "I'll let him notify Macy."

My guess was he didn't want to risk upsetting Macy in her fragile condition. It was too much responsibility. He motioned for me to follow him into his place, and once we were inside he shut the door behind me. His cell phone was charging atop the end table. He unplugged it, pulled up Holden's name in his contacts list, and placed the call. He stared at the carpeting while waiting for Holden to answer. Gideon had the volume turned up high, and I heard Holden's phone ringing on the other end of the line. One ring. Two rings. Three. After four rings, Gideon was transferred to voicemail. He left a message. "We've got an emergency with Joanna. I haven't said anything to Macy. I figured that was best left to you. Call me as soon as you get this."

He jabbed the button to end the call and frowned. "Holden mentioned they don't like the warehouse workers taking personal calls on their cell phones when they're on duty."

"Call the main number," I suggested. "They can track him down."

"I don't know it."

While he could dial 4-1-1 for the information, it would probably be faster to find the number on the internet. "I'll search online." I whipped out my cell phone and brought up the browser. "Who does he work for?"

"Frozen Freight Carriers."

Holden's employer explained the ice-blue shirt he'd been wearing at Joanna's when he and Macy had come to share the news that Macy was expecting. I'd seen the company's trucks on the roadways. They, too, were ice blue, and likewise featured a large image of the

company's mascot, a smiling snowman with a twig arm
crooked over the top of a blue dolly laden with icicles. I
typed the company's name into my browser, clicked on
the link to their website, then clicked on the contact tab.

As I rattled off the number, Gideon typed it into his
phone. He held for a few seconds before his call went
through. "I need to speak with Holden Griffin. He works
in the warehouse. We're having a family emergency and
he's not answering his cell phone." He paused a second or two. "Yes, I can hold. But y'all need to find him
quick. It's urgent."

We waited for a couple of excruciatingly long minutes before someone came on the line. Gideon put a hand
to his head in exasperation, much like Joanna had put a
hand to her forehead in apparent pain earlier. "What do
you mean he's not there?" He paused a second or two.
"I've already tried his cell! He's not answering." Another
pause. "All right. I'll do that." He hung up without a
goodbye and looked up at me. "He must've stepped out
for a break. They suggested I send him a text. They said
he might be more responsive if he can see right away
what's going on." Gideon proceeded to send Holden a
text, dictating it out loud as he typed in all caps. *JOANNA
ON WAY TO ER! CALL ME NOW!*

The strategy worked. Fifteen seconds later, Gideon's
cell phone buzzed with an incoming call from Holden.
Gideon poked a crooked finger at the screen to accept
the call and put the phone on speaker. "Something's
wrong with Joanna. That builder girl is here and she said
Joanna collapsed at the fire station. They took her away
in an ambulance."

Like Gideon, it took Holden a second or two to di-
gest the news, but then his cry came through loud and
clear. "Is Macy with her?"

"No," said Gideon. "Macy doesn't know. We thought you should be the one to tell her."

"Thanks, Gid. The last thing Macy needs right now is stress. I hope Joanna will be all right, for her sake and for Macy's."

Gideon said, "Could be a reaction to that migraine medicine they gave her." He repeated what he'd told the dispatcher, that feeling dizzy was a potential side effect of the pills she'd been prescribed at urgent care. "The doctor told her not to drive and to be careful."

Having heard this, Holden sounded more optimistic. "I hope that's the case and that they can get her feeling better fast. I don't want Macy getting worked up if this could all be for nothing."

"Agreed," Gideon said. "Joanna would never forgive herself if she caused Macy so much worry that it hurt the baby. But I don't like this one bit. I'm going to head over to the hospital." He looked my way and addressed me now. "Do you know which one they took her to?"

The EMTs had made sure I knew where they were headed when they drove off. "Nashville General."

"I'll head over to the hospital, too," Holden said. "I'll see you there."

They ended their call and Gideon snatched his car keys from a peg inside the door. "I'd better get going."

"Will you let me know how things turn out?"

"All right." He turned back, fished a pen out of a coffee mug atop the table, and handed me a pad of yellow sticky notes. "Jot your number down there for me."

I hurriedly wrote my name and number on the pad and handed it back to him. I opened the door to go and nearly ran smack dab into a teenage girl with long blonde hair. The strap of a lightweight nylon backpack in a pink polka-dot print was hiked up over one shoulder. I

recognized her as the girl I'd seen before through Joanna's window, when Macy and Holden had gone over
to tell Joanna about the pregnancy.

"Hey, Alyssa," Gideon said quickly. He gestured to
me. "This is Whitney. She's fixing up the other side of
your grandmother's house, the one the Bottiglieris used
to live in."

"Cool," she said, her head bobbing.

Alyssa hadn't asked why I was at Gideon's place,
and probably didn't care. In my experience, teens didn't
think anything adults did was at all interesting. I'd felt
the same way at her age. Gideon, however, felt obligated
to give her an explanation for my presence. "Whitney
came to borrow a tool."

Another "Cool." Another head bob.

I gave her a smile and a nod, afraid to open my mouth.

Turning her attention back to Gideon, she gestured
across the street behind her. "I was just over at Grammy's place. Her car's in the driveway, but she's not in
her house or backyard. You have any idea where she
went?"

"Nope," Gideon lied, attempting to sound casual. "I
suppose one of her lady friends might have picked her
up. Or maybe she went for a walk."

"Grammy? Take a walk?" Alyssa snorted. "Giddy-up
you know that woman don't exercise."

Gideon forced a laugh that sounded more like he was
choking. "I'm sure she'll turn up."

Alyssa eyed him closely, seeming to sense his unease.
"You okay?"

"Never better." He'd have been more convincing if
his voice wasn't two octaves higher than usual. Fortunately, he managed to deflect attention from himself.

"You said you were looking for your grandmother. You need something?"

She cocked her head, put the backs of her fingers under her chin, and batted her eyes. "Ten bucks to get a smoothie with my friends later?"

"Don't you have your own money?" His eyes narrowed. "I thought you earned good money babysitting Kavish."

"I do," she said. "Samira and D-Jay are very generous. But I spent all I had on these new kicks." She angled her ankle to show off her new pair of fancy sneakers. "I just had to have them or my life would not be complete, and I would have spiraled into utter despair."

Chuckling and shaking his head, Gideon reached into his back pocket, removed his wallet, and pulled out a twenty-dollar bill. "Here you go. My treat."

Alyssa snatched the bill out of his hand and held it up. "This is why I love you."

Gideon scoffed in jest. "I hope that's not the only reason."

"Just one of many." She stood on her tiptoes and gave him a smooch on the cheek before turning and walking across the porch to enter the adjoining unit her parents rented from Gideon.

I might think the girl was an entitled brat, but I'd seen real affection in both her eyes and Gideon's. He seemed to be a surrogate grandfather for her. It was sweet. I wondered then about her actual grandfather, Joanna's husband and Macy's father. I knew he'd passed away and thus was no longer in the picture, though I didn't know the details of his death. "If you don't mind me asking," I said as I stepped out onto the porch, "what happened to Joanna's husband?" I gestured in the direction Alyssa had gone. "Did he ever get a chance to meet his grand-daughter?"

"Billy Roy?" Gideon, too, stepped out, turning to lock his door behind him. "He died of a massive heart attack at work. He was a warden in the Riverbend Maximum Security Prison. Fell flat on his face in the exercise yard while trying to break up a fight. Happened about fifteen years back, when Alyssa was a toddler. Billy Roy was only in his late fifties at the time. Damn shame."

It certainly was. Joanna's husband should have had a lot more years left. So should Joanna. But I feared that might not be the case. I'd held the woman in my arms, felt her body shutting down. But I was no medical expert, and I'd certainly heard of doctors bringing people back from the brink of death. *Who am I to say?* Before I left, I basically repeated what Holden had said, though I kept my voice to a whisper. "I hope Joanna will be okay."

"Me too, girl," Gideon said. "Me too."

CHAPTER 12

ANSWERS AND ANEURYSMS

WHITNEY

Wednesday morning, Buck was upstairs at the fire station, cutting and removing the fire-damaged sheetrock for replacement. I was in the open bay downstairs, loading sheets of new drywall onto my dolly, when Gideon walked in. His gargoyle face was softer today, looking more like putty than concrete, and his eyes were puffy and pink from lack of sleep, tears, or both. The news was written on his face.

"Oh no," I said on a breath, my heart sinking. I set down the sheetrock I'd been holding. "Joanna's gone, isn't she?"

Gideon dipped his chin in a somber nod. "We were told she passed away in the ambulance on the way to the hospital yesterday. The EMTs did their best to revive her. The folks in the emergency room, too, but nothing could be done." He choked up for a moment, putting one hand over his face and grabbing the metal pole with the other to hold himself up. It was the same thing Joanna had done the day before, right before she'd fallen into my lap.

Lest he fall, too, I stepped over and put a supportive hand on his back, ready to grab an arm should he go down.

He went on to give me the details. In light of the intense headache Joanna had suffered the day before, the doctors presumed she died of an aneurysm. "'Course, we had to tell Macy, despite her condition. The poor girl is beside herself, riddled with guilt over their argument last week. I hope she can get past that. She and her mother often didn't see eye to eye, and things could get heated between them, but they always came back around to each other in the end. She's angry, too. She thinks the doctor at urgent care didn't take Joanna's situation seriously enough. Macy researched aneurysms online, and she says the doctor should've ordered an MRI or a CT scan to screen for an aneurysm, or done an angiography. She thinks that if he'd done any of that, her mother might still be alive. She's talking about suing him for malpractice."

While Macy might have a valid point, she'd need to know for certain that her mother had died of an aneurysm in order to prove her case. "Will Joanna's medical insurance cover an autopsy?"

"The folks at the hospital said insurance won't pay for it, but with the inheritance she'll get from Joanna, Macy's got plenty of money to pay for an autopsy out of pocket. Holden and I aren't so sure she should pursue it. Even if Macy wins the malpractice case, it's not going to bring Joanna back, and it's going to cause her a lot of anxiety in the meantime. She doesn't need the worry of a lawsuit during her pregnancy." He released a shaky breath. "I suppose it's never a good time to die, but this was a particularly unfortunate time for Joanna to go."

I gave Gideon's shoulder a gentle squeeze. "I'm so sorry, Gideon. This must be so hard for all of you."

His breath hitched. "Joanna's been my best friend since Billy Roy died. I'd already lost my partner a few years earlier and, when I heard her husband had passed, I took a meal over to her. We were just neighbors then, barely knew each other, virtual strangers really. But she invited me in and we bonded over the shared pain of losing our partners. Both of us were sad sacks, alone and lonely. We discovered we had a lot more in common than we could have ever expected. Next thing we knew, we were keeping each other company on a daily basis." He glanced out of the bay, a faraway look in his eyes. "You never know what life has in store for you until it happens." He broke down completely now. "I don't know what I'll do without her!"

Poor Gideon. He's alone again. I circled around to embrace him. He put his head on my shoulder, and I patted his back while he sobbed, soaking my coveralls with his tears. My chest felt tight with emotion and my eyes pricked with moisture I blinked hard to hold back. The door to the upstairs opened and Buck emerged with ragged chunks of drywall in his arms. He'd taken two steps down the metal stairs when he spotted Gideon and me and stopped moving. At the emotional visage, he got the look of a deer in headlights. *Men. Sheesh. So scared of feelings.* Buck tiptoed the rest of the way down, and exited the bay to toss the debris in the bin outside.

Gideon got himself under control and lifted his head. "Thanks, Whitney. I needed that."

"Anytime." I gave him a soft smile. "Please let us know when Joanna's funeral is scheduled. If it's okay with the family, we'd like to attend."

"I'm sure they'd appreciate it."

Buck had reentered the bay and stood behind Gideon. He shook his head, his eyes wide, and moved his arms in a *no* motion. *Tough.* Whether Buck wanted to or not, he'd be attending the funeral with me.

As Gideon turned to go, Buck immediately changed his demeanor. He gave Gideon a somber nod and a supportive pat on the shoulder as he passed. "So sorry, man."

No sooner had Gideon gone than Landreth pulled into the station's parking lot. Buck and I walked out to meet her at her vehicle as she slid out.

She got right down to brass tacks. "It was Lane Hartzell in the tow truck that was parked here early Sunday morning."

"Oh yeah?" Buck said. "How'd you figure that out?"

I was wondering the same thing.

Landreth said, "Lane confirmed it himself. I spoke with him yesterday afternoon. Of course, he said he had nothing to do with the fire. He claimed he didn't even know there'd been a fire here."

I asked the obvious question. "Then why had he been here?"

"He said he was working the night shift for the towing service. Things were slow and he was in the area, so he pulled in to take a smoke break."

"You were right about that tiny dot of light, then. It was a cigarette." *Like mother, like son.*

"He said he had happy memories of the fire station from when he was a kid. His father took him over here a few times, and the firefighters let him sit in the driver's seat of the truck and pretend to drive it. They even let him try on their hats and jackets."

Buck cocked his head. "Do you believe him?"

She jerked one shoulder, uncommitted. "He didn't give me a reason not to. He seemed forthcoming, and I couldn't glean any clear motive for him to have started the fire. Y'all haven't even met him, and he seemed to think it was a good thing that you're planning to fix up the other side of Joanna's building, so it couldn't be personal to the two of you. He doesn't have a history of arson, either, though he does have a record."

"For what?" I asked.

"Opioids. He was caught with drugs he didn't have a prescription for. Twice. He said he became addicted to painkillers after being prescribed oxycodone. He'd wrenched his shoulder when a car he was loading onto the tow truck shifted. The first time he got arrested he was given probation, community service, and mandatory attendance at drug offender school. The second time, he spent a month in jail and was ordered to go into rehab." She exhaled a slow, soft breath. "He seems adrift. He said sometimes he wishes he could go back to being that little boy in the fire truck, start his life over. He said he'd do things different if he had a second chance."

My heart squirmed inside me. While he hadn't known at the time Landreth had talked to him, by now Lane had surely been informed of his mother's death, that she had come to the firehouse and collapsed in the bay before being loaded in the ambulance and driven off to die. He'd probably never have those same warm feelings about the fire station again. I hoped he could at least retain the warm feelings about his father and the firefighters.

"Detective Flynn is still working on the Bottiglieris," Landreth said. "No sense us duplicating efforts. I'm hoping he'll know soon whether one of them might have set the fire here."

After we thanked Landreth for the information, she took off to attend to other fire department business, and Buck and I returned our attention to repairing the drywall.

I was bent over in the bay, butt in the air, when a tsk came from behind me. "You don't want to use that brand of tape."

I turned to find the trio of older men who'd watched the fire Sunday morning from the comfort of their lawn chairs. All three wore easy slip-on shoes with white crew socks, loose-fitting shorts, and knit golf shirts—one in blue, one in green, and one in orange-and-white stripes, the colors of the University of Tennessee Volunteers. Blue Shirt and Stripes wore baseball caps, while Green Shirt's head was bare.

"That's right," agreed Green Shirt. "You go with that cheap tape, you'll be sorry."

I was upset about Joanna's death, and saddened by what I'd learned about Lane. It had been an emotionally taxing day already. I didn't need this irritation on top of it. My ire rose. "Are you, or were you, home builders?" I snapped. "Work in skilled construction trades?"

They looked to one another in surprise at my harsh tone before turning back to me. "Well, no," said Blue Shirt. "I sold insurance." He stood straighter and puffed out his chest. "But I finished out my garage."

Stripes said, "I was a dentist, but I repaired the drywall in my laundry room after it flooded."

Green Shirt gestured to Blue Shirt. "I helped him with the garage job."

In other words, these guys were armchair handymen. While I didn't mind advice from professional contractors who were more experienced than me and, in fact, sought out and appreciated such advice, input from your average Joe, no matter how well-meaning, annoyed me. Coming from these older men, there was likely some sexism underlying their advice. They might have a hard time imagining a woman could be more knowledgeable than them on construction matters.

I held up the roll of tape. "I've been using this brand *for years* without a problem." *For years! Did you hear that?*

Blue Shirt tsked again and shook his head. "I certainly wouldn't use it."

"To each their own." I turned away from them, bent over again, and dug through my toolbox.

Failing to take the hint I hoped my backside would imply, they stepped closer.

Blue Shirt was back at it. "You'll need a putty knife, sweetie."

Sweetie? Oh, it's on now! I found the tool I was looking for, turned around, and held it up, feeling like the Statue of Liberty with her torch. "Actually, this drywall tape knife works much better than a putty knife. It has just the right amount of flexibility."

Green Shirt's face soured. "I wouldn't use one. It's a waste of money to buy a tool for such a specific purpose."

First, they'd implied I was cheap. Now, they'd called me wasteful, a spendthrift. I fought the urge to roll my eyes. This wasn't the first time this type of thing had happened, and it wouldn't be the last. The habit of retired men offering unsolicited advice to construction workers in public places was annoying yet common. The Italians had even coined a word for these critical, self-appointed foreman—*umarell*. The word was derived from a term that meant "little man."

Though I didn't want to encourage further debate, I felt the need to defend myself. "It's not a waste to buy a specialized tool if you use it repeatedly for multiple projects like I have." The tape in one hand and the tool in the other, I stretched my arms out to each side and walked toward them, as if shooing chickens. "You'll need to clear the bay. I've got to close the door."

Grumbling, the umarells reluctantly moved back, stopping just the other side of the threshold. I made a fist and used the side of it to hit the button to lower the garage door. As it came down, the meddling men disappeared inch by inch, until the final thing I saw was a flash of white crew socks. I hoped it was the last I'd see of them.

Over lunch at the café next door, I phoned every lumber outfit I could find in the general vicinity of Nashville, trying to find hardwood flooring. While a few places had some in stock, the prices they demanded were four or five times the usual rate, far surpassing what we wanted to spend, especially since, prior to the fire, we'd planned on maintaining the existing floor and had budgeted only for sandpaper and stain to refinish the boards.

When I gave Buck the last quote I received, he snorted. "Now *that's* thievery."

"Takes a thief to know a thief," I teased.

Last I'd heard from Collin, Peter and Judith were still ghosting law enforcement, refusing to account for their whereabouts the night someone had spray-painted the walls in the townhouse and set a fire in the firehouse. But the two couldn't hide forever. He'd catch up with them eventually.

While Buck's father, my uncle Roger, had the equipment we'd need to mill boards ourselves, it was a time-consuming process to get them cut, processed, and sanded to a perfectly smooth finish. We preferred to let someone else do the heavy lifting when possible.

Having failed in my quest to find affordable new hardwood flooring, I scrolled through my contacts as I nibbled on a salty French fry, searching for folks I knew who worked in reclaimed materials. The remaining wood in the fire station was aged. Seemed we could use aged wood to replace the boards that had burned. Heck, old boards would probably match better than new planks, anyway. On my second call, I hit pay dirt. Someone had bought an old farmhouse in Lynchburg and ripped out the wood floors to replace them with tile. The planks could be mine for a reasonable price. The only catch was I had to pay in advance and drive down to a storage unit in Moore County to pick them up myself. "No problem," I said. "It's a deal."

I promptly sent the agreed-upon amount via Venmo, then finished my fries. I was debating whether to order peach cobbler for dessert when my phone chimed. Collin had texted me a pic. Peter Bottiglieri's mug shot. The man scowled at the camera, none too happy about having his photo and fingerprints taken. *Ha!* The accompanying message read *Booked him for the vandalism at the townhouse.*

I held up my phone so Buck could see the screen. "Looks like Collin made an arrest."

"I hope they throw the book at him."

"Me too. Breaking and entering. Property damage. Failing to put *i* before *e* except after *c.*"

"Or when it sounds like *A,*" Buck added, "as in neighbor and weigh."

"Speaking of neighbors," I said, "are we going to sell the townhouse to Gideon now that Joanna is gone? Assuming he matches the highest offer, of course."

Buck shrugged. "I don't know. Did your agreement with Joanna extend to any owner of her half of the house? I wonder if Macy and Holden would want to buy it. They're going to move into her place, right?"

"I assume so. Gideon would probably let them out of their lease. He seems like a reasonable guy. I don't know whether Macy and Holden would be interested in buying the Bottiglieris' place but, even if they are, I'm not sure they could afford it. Half of what Joanna owned will likely go to Lane. Once the estate is divided, Macy might not inherit enough to buy the townhouse, especially if she has to buy out Lane's share of Joanna's place." Switching topics, I said, "How about a double date for dinner tonight? We can celebrate your and Colette's happy news, and Collin can fill us in on Peter's arrest."

"Sounds like a plan," Buck agreed. "Let me text Colette and see what she's craving today. Yesterday, she sent me to the grocery store for a jar of green curry. The day before that it was garlic hummus and pita bread."

While he texted his wife, I texted Collin. In minutes, Colette had responded that she was craving refried beans and guacamole. We made plans to meet at her favorite Mexican restaurant at seven, then got back to work.

Over pre-dinner margaritas later that day, Collin filled us in on Peter's arrest. "I looked up the sanitation department's pickup schedule for their neighborhood," he said. "Today was garbage day."

"Ew." Colette put a hand over her mouth. "The thought of stinky garbage makes me queasy."

Buck picked up his menu and fanned her with it. "Is that better?"

She nodded and removed her hand from her mouth, picking up her virgin mango margarita. "Much. Thanks."

The crisis resolved, Collin continued. "Putting out the trash is generally a man's job, so I figured Peter would be the one to roll the bin out to the curb. I drove out there bright and early to stake out their house. Sure enough, when daylight rolled around, the garage door went up and out came Peter, rolling the bin. I met him at the curb. He looked like a kid caught with his hand in the cookie jar." Collin sipped his margarita and fished a tortilla chip from the basket on the table. "I handed him a pen and paper, and asked him to print the word *thieves* for me. I told him it was a handwriting analysis to see if his handwriting matched the lettering painted on the walls of the townhouse. He fudged his handwriting, of course. He wrote the letters short and wide so they wouldn't resemble the tall, thin lettering on the walls. But what he didn't know was that I was really just checking his spelling. He misspelled *thieves* by transposing the *e* and the *i*."

"Busted." Buck made a friendly fist and gave Collin a light punch in the arm. "Way to go, bro!"

Collin finished chewing his chip and took another sip of his margarita. "I asked Peter if he also started the fire at the station, but he claimed innocence. I searched his car and house for evidence that he'd set the fire, but I didn't find any. He had a bag of charcoal and a nearly full bottle of lighter fluid in his garage, but who doesn't? When I told him the vandalism could get him up to a year in prison and a twenty-five-hundred-dollar fine, he said he'd be happy to tell me who started the fire if we let him off on the vandalism charge."

"Are you going to do it?" I asked. "Give him a plea deal?"

"I'll have to consult with Landreth and the assistant district attorney assigned to the case. Unless he can give us concrete proof, a recorded confession or some other hard evidence, I'm not sure I'd trust him. He seemed eager to throw his siblings under the bus. He might make a false accusation just to give them some grief. We've got to know he's not just blowing smoke. We're going to set up a meeting in a few days and see how it goes."

The server came by to take our dinner order, and told us about the daily specials. "We've got our ceviche and our shrimp tacos on special for two dollars off tonight." He pointed to the menu. "They're right here, under *mariscos*."

Each of us placed our orders. I noticed Colette went for the spinach enchiladas, and my mind went back to what Macy had said to Gideon when he'd offered her a shrimp cocktail, that pregnant women aren't supposed to eat seafood. We handed the server our menus. As he headed back to the kitchen, I turned to my friend, curious. "What's the deal with seafood? Why can't women eat it when they're pregnant?"

"It's the mercury," she said. "It sticks around in the body, so it builds up in the food chain. Small fish accumulate a little of it, then they're eaten by bigger fish, which are then eaten by even bigger fish. By the time you work your way up the chain, it really mounts up. The process is called biomagnification. Shark and tuna have some of the highest levels of mercury, especially albacore and yellowfin tuna."

I sucked air through my teeth and grimaced. "I give Sawdust tuna!" *Could I be poisoning my cat?*

Colette reassured me. "As long as you're not giving him tuna too often and are feeding him a variety of other foods, too, he should be fine."

That's a relief.

She took a sip of her drink. "Bluefish, orange roughy, and swordfish can be high in mercury, too. I learned about biomagnification back in chef school, but my doctor also mentioned it at my last checkup. Mercury poisoning can affect anyone, but it's especially bad for unborn babies. It causes brain damage. Hearing and vision problems, too."

The mention of brain damage brought my mind back to Joanna, how she'd looked when she'd stumbled into the fire station. The poor woman. At least she hadn't suffered long. As long as I lived, I'd never be able to get the image of her out of my mind.

Colette wasn't done enlightening the rest of us about the dangers of eating fish. "There's other health risks with seafood, too. Two other types of poisoning people can get that can be serious. Ciguatera poisoning and scombroid poisoning. I don't remember a whole lot about them, only that they sounded real nasty."

I jumped onto my phone and, as Colette spelled the words out for me to the best of her recollection, typed them into my browser. My eyes skimmed the information and I summarized it aloud. "Ciguatera poisoning causes head and muscle aches. It makes the skin feel numb, tingly, and itchy." I didn't recall Joanna scratching at her skin but, then again, she could barely keep herself upright. Even if her skin had felt itchy, she'd likely lacked the coordination to scratch herself. "Early signs are numbness in the tongue and lips, and a metallic taste in the mouth." I looked up. "Eep." I pointed to my phone. "It says here that ciguatera poisoning makes a person have difficulty distinguishing between hot and cold temperatures, and that they'll feel like their teeth are coming loose."

Collin cringed. "That's the stuff of nightmares."

"Like I said," Colette noted, "real nasty."

I went on to read that the neurological symptoms caused by ciguatera poisoning could persist, and were sometimes misdiagnosed as multiple sclerosis. Death, though very rare, was not unheard of. *Hmm.*

Per the internet, scombroid poisoning, or a *Vibrio vulnificus* infection, occurred when a person ingested fish contaminated with the bacteria. It was found in oysters and shellfish. A person didn't necessarily have to eat the fish to contract it. If they had an open cut, they could get it merely by handling the fish. The symptoms were typical of other types of food poisoning. Abdominal pain, vomiting, and diarrhea. The symptoms could also include fever, chills, and a reduction in blood pressure, as well as swelling, redness on the skin, and even blisters. Though rare, scombroid poisoning could be life-threatening if it entered through an open cut and infiltrated a person's bloodstream. "With scombroid poisoning, a person—"

"Enough!" Buck barked. "You're going to ruin our

dinner." He looked to Colette and Collin. "Either of you have something better to talk about?"

Colette twirled a finger in the air and turned to Collin. "Speaking of Sawdust, Whitney tells me you have cats?"

"Two," Collin replied. "Copernicus and Galileo."

"Got pics?"

I snorted. "There isn't a cat owner alive who doesn't have a million photos of their cat on their phone."

Proving me correct, Collin whipped out his phone and showed Colette photos of Copernicus and Galileo. "The cats are good company and they're self-sufficient, which is good for someone who never knows when their workday is going to end. But one day I'd like to get a dog to take running with me."

"The cats might have something to say about that," I teased. "We'd have to get their approval first." I had no doubt that Sawdust would welcome another pet into his home. He was a sweetie, and he'd enjoy playing with his furry, four-footed housemates. Besides, from what I'd seen, in homes with both cats and dogs, the cats ruled the roost. All it took was one swipe of the claws and the dogs bowed down to their feline overlords.

"Speaking of dogs," Collin said, "I caught a break today in a drug-related double homicide I'm working. A K9 tracked an invisible trail of powder to the plastic bag it had leaked out of. We were able to lift prints from the bag. The lab is running them now to see if we can get a match. The two victims were shot in the head execution style—"

Buck threw up his hands. "Great! Now I'm picturing a bloody crime scene."

The server returned to check on us. "How are we doing over here?"

After glaring at me and Collin, Buck turned to the waiter. "I'm going to need a whiskey. Make it a double. There's been some conversation here that I really need to forget."

CHAPTER 13

KITTY CONDOLENCES

SAWDUST

Things were not all right with Whitney. Sawdust could sense it. She lay on her bed with her arm thrown back over her face, as if she were trying to block out the world. She held him close with the other arm, and ran her thumb across his cheek again and again and again. His best friend Cleo sat at the end of the bed, watching them. She appeared concerned, too, issuing a soft chirrup and twitching her whiskers.

Sawdust heard the front door open and knew it meant their roommate Emmalee had arrived home. Emmalee called out to Whitney, and Whitney responded, but her voice was soft and warbly. Emmalee came to the door. Whitney pulled her arm back from her face and said some words. Emmalee put her hands to her mouth, covering it in horror. Cleo hopped down and walked over to her person, rubbing herself on Emmalee's calves. Emmalee picked her up and held her tight to her chest.

When Whitney let out a shuddering breath, Sawdust knew he needed to up his game. He climbed up directly onto her chest and looked her in the eye, issuing a mew to tell her everything would be okay, if not now then someday. He put his head down and kissed her cheek. When she wrapped her arms around him and buried her face in his fur, he knew he'd done his job well.

CHAPTER 14

CONDOLENCES AND CASSEROLES

WHITNEY

Colette had made a pot of her creamy mushroom risotto, and divided it in two, one portion for Gideon, the other for Macy, Holden, and Alyssa. She'd sent it along with Buck as he left for work Thursday morning, along with portions he and I could eat for lunch. He stored the dishes in the refrigerator at the fire station, and we delivered the food later that day, just before suppertime.

We went to Gideon's place first. He looked just as bad when he answered the door as he had the day before, when he'd come by the fire station to inform us of Joanna's death. In fact, on closer inspection, he looked worse—hunched and haggard and hopeless. His shoulders slumped and his skin seemed to sag from his bones, as if he were melting.

"You'll enjoy this." I held out the covered foil dish. "It's the ultimate comfort food."

Buck said, "My wife made it."

Gideon took the dish from me, but looked down at it without interest. "Thank you," he said, his voice feeble. "I don't have much appetite right now, but I'll stick this in the freezer for later."

Curious whether he had any new information, I asked, "Did the pathologist confirm whether Joanna had an aneurysm?"

Gideon's grip seemed to tighten on the dish. I couldn't blame him. The thought of his friend being sliced, diced, and dissected like a frog in a high school biology class had to be upsetting. "They haven't had a chance to complete the autopsy yet. They're short-staffed in the pathology department. We were told that a couple of the docs are out, squeezing in late-summer vacations."

Looked like Macy would have to wait a bit longer to determine whether she had a viable malpractice case.

"If there's anything we can do, please let us know." It was a trite expression, one rarely taken up on, but what else could I say?

Gideon gave a small nod and quietly closed his door.

Unlike Joanna's townhouse, which had a separate front porch from the adjoining unit, Gideon's house had a wide, shared porch. We turned and headed across it to the door on the other side. On the way, I stopped to straighten the Dad's Old Fashioned Root Beer sign that hung slightly askew. As I did, I leaned in to consult the thermometer. It had been an exceptionally hot day and, per the weather app on my phone, the temperature had hit the century mark around three in the afternoon. I'd bet it was still in the upper nineties now. I squinted and peered at the thermometer from different angles, but there was no telltale line inside the device. *It must be broken*. Not surprising, I supposed, with the sign having been manufactured decades earlier. Like Joanna, its life was over. Now, it was nothing more than a kitschy relic from a bygone era, useful for decoration only.

Buck knocked lightly on the Griffins' door. A few seconds later, Alyssa answered, looking just as despondent as her next-door neighbor. Gone was the sassy, vivacious teen from before, who'd modeled her new shoes and pleaded prissily for cash. She seemed a shadow of her former self, a ghost of the girl she'd been. I hoped that, once she had time to get through her grief, she'd return to her former carefree self. The mop-like mutt stood at her feet, but he, too, seemed sad. While his tail had wagged when he'd seen us before, today it hung limply behind him.

The scent of something savory came from inside. Anyone would recognize the aroma of garlic, but having lived with a cook, I also recognized the scents of cumin and turmeric.

"Hi, Alyssa," I said. "We brought y'all some risotto. Buck's wife made it. She's a professional chef." I held out a hand to indicate my cousin, who offered her the dish. As she took the food from him, I noticed a yellow adhesive bandage on her left index finger. Colorful unicorns were printed across it, cute and playful. *Who knew bandages could be a fashion statement?* "Did you hurt your finger?"

She looked down at the bandage. "I got a splinter from the porch swing at my friend's house. I've tried to get it out but it's too deep."

"Been there." Splinters were an occupational hazard for a carpenter. Luckily, no matter how deep a splinter went, it would eventually work its way to the surface through the natural skin-shedding process. "It'll work itself out over time."

Having heard us at the door, Holden stepped up

behind his daughter and their dog. Though his demeanor was solemn, he showed no express signs of being affected by Joanna's death on a physical level. His posture was good, his eyes dry, his voice steady. "Thanks. It was nice of you to bring this by."

I offered the same trite phrase. "If there's anything we can do . . ."

To my surprise, Holden took us up on it. "Could you help us move this Saturday?"

"Into Joanna's place?"

"Well, it's *ours* now," Holden said. "My wife's anyway," he clarified. "But Macy said she'd let me and the kid live there with her so long as we behave ourselves." He grinned and angled his head to indicate Alyssa.

I knew humor could be a coping mechanism, but it seemed a little soon to be cracking jokes. It also seemed soon to be moving into Joanna's townhouse. The woman lay in a freezer in the morgue, awaiting her autopsy. But maybe they figured there was no sense in putting things off. Maybe living in Joanna's place would help them feel closer to her, even though she was gone. Maybe returning to her childhood home would bring comfort to Macy at the time when she needed it most. Maybe they wanted to get out of the place they rented from Gideon so he could find a new tenant as soon as possible. Lots of people moved in August, and he had a better chance of finding a new tenant to take over immediately if he could get someone in now.

"We'd be happy to help," I said, volunteering my cousin as well as myself with that *we*.

Buck was on board, which reminded me that, despite his occasional grumblings, he was a nice guy at heart. It also told me that Colette was working on Saturday. Otherwise, he'd want to be home with her. Buck said,

"I'll bring my flatbed trailer in case there's anything you need hauled away."

"That would be great," Holden said. "We've got our own living room furniture, so we'll be getting rid of Joanna's. Her bedroom suite, too. We plan to leave Macy's and Lane's old bedrooms upstairs as they are, at least for now. Alyssa will move into the third one. Joanna's just been using it for storage. She was quite the pack rat. It's going to take us days to get through all the paperwork she's hung onto. Most of it's probably not needed, but we can't take a chance on throwing out something important. We'll have to go through it piece by piece, figure out what's important and what's not."

I pulled out my phone to input a reminder. "What time would you like us to be here on Saturday?"

"How about eight o'clock?" Holden said.

Buck groaned. "You making the coffee?"

While his daughter stood stricken beside him, Holden laughed. "I'll have a pot ready."

The condolence meals delivered, Buck returned to the fire station to lock up, while I proceeded to our townhouse across the street, toolbox in hand. Though I'd bought the new door handles and locks earlier in the week, I'd been in no real hurry to install them. The damage had already been done and it was doubtful that whoever had vandalized the place would return.

I donned my knee pads and was kneeling on the front porch, removing the current lock, when from behind me came a shout of "Da-ba-da!" I turned to see D-Jay, Samira, and their son headed my way. This time, Kavish held on to Samira's hand but moved on his own two feet, wobbling and staggering about like a drunken sailor—*or like Joanna had when she'd come into the fire station.*

"Hello!" Samira called out, smiling. "We saw you were here and decided to come over."

I'd been at the place for only a minute or two. *Has she been keeping watch?*

D-Jay pointed at the lock. "Can I help?"

The two had said nothing about Joanna. Their pleasant demeanors seemed to indicate that they were unaware of her passing. I stood, screwdriver in hand. "I guess you haven't heard. Joanna Hartzell passed away a couple of days ago."

"Gideon mentioned it," Samira said, her tone surprisingly nonchalant.

I was silent for a moment, waiting for one or the other of them to express some type of sadness, but they didn't. It was odd, wasn't it? They seemed more than a little heartless.

My thoughts must have been written on my face. Samira said, "We feel very bad for her family, of course. But she was lucky to have lived to nearly seventy. That's a full life."

"*A full life?*" I repeated. "She'd barely reached retirement age."

Samira appeared hurt by my implication that she'd been improperly glib. A cloud passed over her face. "I am sorry. I did not mean to sound unkind. I was only trying to focus on the positives. Of course, I am sorry Joanna has passed."

D-Jay cut a glance at his wife before turning back to me. "Samira took pots of dal and rice to the Griffins yesterday."

That must've been what I'd smelled when Alyssa had opened the door earlier. I felt a twinge of guilt in my gut. *Had I been too harsh toward Samira?* "That was very nice of you."

While I showed D-Jay how to remove the old lock, Samira stood in the yard nearby, keeping a close eye on Kavish as he bent down to pick dandelions. Once the old lock was off, I stood back and simply instructed D-Jay as he installed the new one.

When he finished, I examined his handiwork. The apparatus was flush against the metal of the door and the screws were tight. "All that's left is to program a code."

Samira looked over. "Use zero-eight-two-four," she called to her husband.

D-Jay eyed me. "That's Kavish's birthday."

For the second time since they'd arrived, I felt uncomfortable with our interaction. It was awfully presumptuous of them to assume I'd even give them the door code, let alone let them choose it. Nobody other than Buck and I should have unfettered access to the townhouse. But I didn't want to insult them. I'd let D-Jay put in the code, but I'd change it later to something else, perhaps my upcoming wedding day.

I led D-Jay inside so that we could change the lock on the kitchen door, too. Samira followed us in, carrying Kavish now. She plunked him down on the kitchen counter and played a version of patty-cake with him while D-Jay changed out the locks. Again, he'd done a good job, and again, he programmed 0824 as the access code.

I gathered up the tools and returned them to my toolbox. "That's all I'd planned to do here tonight. In fact, it'll likely be some time before Buck and I get back to work here. The fire has caused some setbacks at the fire station, some things that'll cost us more time, and we're on a bit of a time crunch. Plus, Buck and I agreed to help Holden and Macy get moved on Saturday."

"We understand," Samira said. "A delay is no problem.

That will give us more time to work out our finances and save more for the down payment. We have found a private lending service that is not so strict with credit history. We believe they will give us a loan."

I could only imagine how high the interest rate would be. Banks were charging rates of nearly eight percent for a thirty-year fixed-rate mortgage, and that was for well-qualified buyers with perfect credit. D-Jay and Samira were surely looking at a double-digit rate.

She pulled out her phone. "Let me show you something I have been working on."

She came over to stand next to me and pulled up images on her phone. She'd used pictures she'd snapped inside the townhouse and Photoshopped them to show what the rooms would look like with different colors of carpet and paint. She'd designed a dozen different mockups of the living room, bedrooms, bathrooms, and kitchen. I had to admit, the living room looked much better with the soft orange paint in the doctored image than it looked in real life with *theives* still painted on it.

"Which one do you like best?" She tilted her head and scrolled forward. "I think the blue bathroom tile is my favorite, but I have not decided on the kitchen. I like them all."

D-Jay chuckled. "Samira has been watching the HGTV channel all day and night." He reached out to ruffle his son's hair. "Poor Kavish misses his cartoons."

Again, I was feeling uncomfortable. *Was Samira expecting me to use her designs in the remodel?* Though hers were undeniably good, I'd already come up with some preliminary plans of my own. I looked from D-Jay to his wife. "Samira, I've warned you not to get your hopes up."

"But there is no harm in me having a little fun, is

there?" She gave me a broad smile, tilted her head, and raised her brows in question.

I issued a soft sigh. "I suppose not." But if there was no harm in her playing with the designs, why had my guts tied themselves into knots?

CHAPTER 15

MOVING DAY

WHITNEY

Friday morning, I waited until ten o'clock to return to the townhouse. Samira and D-Jay would be at work, and wouldn't spot me changing the code on the exterior doors. I put in the digits for my upcoming wedding date on the front door, then walked to the kitchen to reprogram the side door.

As I went back out front, a commotion on Joanna's porch next door caught my attention. Alyssa stood there, dressed in a pair of ratty sneakers, nylon athletic pants, and a windbreaker, clothing that was much too hot for the summer season. Though it wasn't raining and there wasn't a cloud in sight, she had the hood of the windbreaker pulled up over her head. What's more, she wore long rubber gloves and a disposable mask, probably one leftover from the COVID pandemic. She wrangled a big black garbage bag that appeared full and heavy.

"Hi, Alyssa."

She started and cried out before turning my way. She

must not have heard me over the sound of the items rustling around in the bag. "Gah! I didn't see you there."

"Sorry," I said. "I didn't mean to startle you. That bag looks heavy. You want some help?"

"Nah, I'm good. But thanks for offering."

I didn't press her further. I remembered how it felt to be a teenager, wanting to do things myself to prove that I was capable and self-sufficient.

She pulled down her mask. "I volunteered to clean my grandmother's place before the move, but it's crazy dusty upstairs. Grammy hasn't gone up to the second floor in years. Guess she didn't have a reason to once Mom and Uncle Lane moved out. Everything in the attic is covered in dust, too."

The dust explained the improvised hazmat suit. I could relate. After all, I wore coveralls for the same reason. "That's sweet of you to help." I dipped my head to indicate the bag. "If you need some place to ditch the trash, feel free to use our dumpster around the corner."

"Thanks. I was wondering what to do with it. My grandmother's can is nearly full."

I watched as she wrestled the bag down the steps. The hood still seemed a bit much to me, but teenage girls could be very vain. Maybe she didn't want the dust getting in her pretty hair, or maybe the hood helped to keep the airborne dust particles out of her eyes.

After she stepped off the bottom stair, she turned back to look at me. Her nose and lips wriggled as she fought to keep from crying. *Poor girl.* Losing her grandmother so suddenly had to be both shocking and heartbreaking. She issued a garbled sound as she tried to clear her emotion from her throat. "Grammy . . . when she went to the fire station . . . was she . . . *bad*? I mean,

I know she had a headache, but was she in pain? Did she get hurt when she fell?"

I didn't want to lie to the girl and, fortunately, I didn't have to. "No, Alyssa," I said softly. "She didn't seem to be in pain. Just disoriented. She didn't get hurt. I was able to lower her gently to the floor and put her head in my lap until help arrived. It just seemed like she was drifting off to sleep."

She nodded and sniffled. "Thanks. That's comforting to hear."

I was glad I could make her feel a little better. My work here done, I headed back to the fire station, leaving her to struggle with the sack.

Buck and I spent the day framing the walls that would divide the bathroom and the secondary bedroom in two. It was exciting to see our ideas taking shape, especially after the setback of the fire.

At the end of the day, we readied our dollies and heavy-duty nylon straps in the bay downstairs, where we could quickly access them for the move tomorrow. After locking up, we bade each other goodbye and aimed for our vehicles. As I went to climb in the driver's seat, a warm breeze blew by, my loose hair tickling the skin on my face. Movement caught my eye as a stronger gust lifted the sleeve of Alyssa's lightweight nylon windbreaker, which hung over the side of the bin where she'd tossed it. The sleeve rose into the air, like a ghost hand reaching out from the grave. When the wind shifted, so did the sleeve, appearing now to be waving an eerie goodbye.

My phone pinged, drawing my attention down to my screen. It was a shipping update for the wedding dress

I'd ordered online. The gown had been picked up by the carrier and was on its way. *Hooray!* I could hardly wait to try it on.

Holden was as good as his word. He greeted us at eight o'clock Saturday morning with a full pot of coffee. As Buck, Holden, and I drank the warm brew and formulated a game plan for the day, Macy lounged in a recliner in the living room. She wore a loose T-shirt, yoga pants, and slippers, comfy attire for lounging and incubating a baby. Alyssa sat cross-legged on the couch, dressed in her cute new sneakers, more seasonal shorts, and a crop-top today, ready and willing to help in any way she could. Gideon sat beside her. I wasn't sure how much he could carry given his advanced age and arthritic condition, but he could be a big help organizing cabinets and drawers. Collin, his best man Ren, and Owen, Buck's brother, were also on their way to help, though they had yet to arrive.

"Step one," Buck told Holden, "is getting Joanna's furniture out to the trailer. Once it's loaded, Whitney can drive my van over to the charity thrift shop to drop it off."

"Good," Holden agreed. "While she's doing that, we can carry the large pieces across the street." He turned to look at his daughter. "Your job is to move the smaller stuff. Dishes, lamps, clothes, books."

She gave him a thumbs-up. "Got it. Grammy still had my old Radio Flyer wagon in her garage, so I can load it up with stuff." She crooked her arm and used her elbow to give Gideon a gentle nudge in the ribs. "You're with me, buddy. Okay?"

"Whatever you say, boss." He forced a smile, but the

pain of loss remained in his eyes. I hoped he would find a new best friend soon. I hated the thought of him being lonely.

Leaving Macy behind, we rose and moved en masse to Joanna's townhouse. As we approached the porch, I noticed that there wasn't a single spider web hanging about. The window screens were dust free and the glass gleamed. Alyssa must have hosed down the porch and cleaned the windows when she worked here the day before.

"Watch your step," Holden warned. "One of the boards is loose."

Buck glowered. "I know. Stubbed my toe on it the other day."

Being oh-so-helpful, I said, "Someone should nail it down."

My cousin cast a glance my way. "Maybe that someone should be *you*."

We went inside to find the interior of Joanna's townhouse to be in immaculate condition, too. There wasn't a speck of dust anywhere, and the entire place gleamed and sparkled. How the girl could have accomplished such a detailed cleaning in a single day was beyond me. The energy of youth, I supposed.

"Wow!" Holden turned to his daughter. "The place looks spotless. Good work, Lyss."

Alyssa beamed.

Owen, Collin, and Ren pulled up to help. Being tall and blond, Owen resembled Buck, though he was thinner and cleanshaven. Ren wasn't tall, but he was beefy, a dedicated gym rat, with shoulder-length dark hair worn in a trendy, shaggy style.

"Thanks for coming to help," I told Ren.

He flexed an impressive bicep. "What good is all this muscle if I don't put it to use?"

After everyone was introduced, the group got to work. My first order of business was to put a nail in the loose board on the porch so nobody would trip over it while carrying the furniture and other items. Buck had parked his van and trailer at the curb in front, and the helpers began to load it up. Joanna's couch went onto the trailer first, then her love seat and entertainment center. While Gideon moved Joanna's knickknacks into the kitchen to be dealt with later, Alyssa and I worked together to move the coffee table and end tables outside, as well as the chairs for her dining table. By then, the trailer was full. Joanna's bedroom furniture would have to wait to be transported in a second trip.

Collin came along to help me unload the furniture at the Salvation Army drop-off location. While Joanna's furniture might not be trendy, it was well made and in good condition. Someone would surely be interested in buying it.

Once we'd off-loaded everything from the trailer, we drove back to Joanna's for the second load. Macy had made the short journey across the street, and someone brought her recliner along with her. They'd set her up in Joanna's bedroom. Alyssa sorted through Joanna's drawers and closet, holding up each item so her mother could tell her whether to keep it, toss it, or box it up to donate to charity. Occasionally, one or the other would get misty.

Alyssa held up a blue blouse with silver buttons, and choked back a sob. "Grammy wore this shirt to my last choir concert."

When Alyssa reached into the bottom of the closet

and pulled out a pair of black loafers with thick rubber heels, Macy barked a joyless laugh. "I told Mom over and over that those were the ugliest shoes I'd ever seen. She said she didn't care that they were ugly because they were comfortable." Macy heaved a shuddering sigh and pointed to a trash bag. "Toss them."

Two of the three men who'd come to the fire station to give me their two cents on drywall had taken up residence on Joanna's rockers on the porch. They proceeded to supervise our activity as we carried Joanna's bedroom furniture out to the trailer.

"That's now how I'd load it," warned one.

"Me neither," said the other, gesturing. "You want to distribute the weight evenly."

They were wrong, but I wasn't going to waste my breath arguing with them again. Buck wasn't above it, though. "It's best to place the load over the axle, with a little more weight near the front. If there's too much weight in the back, the trailer will fishtail."

The men shook their heads, their expressions saying it all. *What a bunch of idiots.*

Buck scowled. "Don't you two have something better to do?"

The men exchanged glances before turning back to Buck. "Not really."

After making the second delivery, the heat and physical labor were starting to get to me. My muscles felt strained and shaky, my skin was damp with sweat, and my throat was dry with thirst. Buck, Owen, and Holden had already moved the kitchen table over from across the street. The umarells had invited themselves in and sat at the table, sipping glasses of Joanna's lemonade. I plunked myself down in one of the chairs to rest for a moment.

Holden gestured to the refrigerator. "Help yourself to a cold drink if you'd like."

"Thanks." I stood, walked over, and pulled the door open to look inside. Sure enough, a pitcher of lemonade sat on the middle shelf next to a pitcher of tea. Canned sodas and beer filled the top shelf. I reached up and grabbed a ginger ale for myself. "Anyone else?" I called, reciting the options. Both Collin and Ren opted for lemonade, while Buck and Owen opted for tea. I removed the pitchers from the fridge and poured them each a glass.

As I went to return the pitchers to the fridge, an assortment of plastic storage containers on the bottom shelf caught my eye. I bent down to take a closer look. Joanna was methodical, having attached a sticky note to the top of each container, noting the contents and the date it was placed in the fridge. There were a couple shrimp and a dollop of red sauce left over from her shrimp cocktail from the proceeding Wednesday. A small portion of the tuna casserole Gideon had brought to Joanna on Saturday remained. She must have eaten the rest of it. One container held king mackerel. The one next to it had a small portion of grouper. Another note read "orange roughy." An alarm bell went off in my mind. Colette had specifically mentioned tuna when we'd been discussing the types of fish that were high in mercury, but hadn't she also mentioned orange roughy?

Gideon's voice came from the kitchen doorway, where he stood with one hand on the frame to support himself, watching me. "Joanna sure did love fish. She must have been a cat in a former life." He hobbled over and took a seat across from me. "She grew up in Gulfport, Mississippi, and was raised on seafood. Couldn't get enough of the stuff. She was always asking me to make some sort of fish or another. She said the food re-minded her of home."

I looked from him back to the multitude of contain-ers. *Could Joanna have gotten mercury poisoning from the seafood? Could that have been what killed her?* I didn't want to raise the possibility with Gideon. The man was elderly and frail. If he thought he'd acciden-tally poisoned his best friend, there was no telling what it might do to him. *But I have to say something, don't I? At least to Macy?* Then again, Gideon showed no signs of being sick. If Joanna had ingested too much mercury, it seemed he would have, too. Maybe he sometimes pre-pared the seafood for Joanna yet didn't eat it himself. That would explain how he'd avoided getting ill. "What about you?" I gestured to the containers in the open fridge in front of me. "You brought her a lot of seafood. Do you like it, too?"

He shrugged. "I always loved my mother's tuna casserole but, other than that, I can take it or leave it. I lean toward vegetarian fare, even more so since I lost my partner. He died of a stroke. Even with medication, his cholesterol was through the roof. I cooked healthy meals for us at home, but every chance he got he'd stop at some fast-food place or another and grab a greasy burger or two. I begged him to stop sneaking burgers and barbecue, but he wouldn't hear it." He turned his face upward to the heavens and wagged a finger. "You should've listened to me! You'd still be here if you had!"

As Gideon hobbled over to the table to take a seat, Samira and D-Jay appeared in the kitchen doorway he'd vacated. Kavish peeked over his mother's shoulder, en-joying a piggyback ride. "Ba-ba-da-ga!" he hollered. Samira winced. At close range like that, it was a wonder her eardrum hadn't burst. She turned her head to eye her son. "Use your inside voice, silly boy."

It was likely a pointless instruction. Kavish was too young to understand her.

Between the Griffins, Buck, Owen, Collin, Ren, Gideon, the meddling men, and me, the townhouse was already packed. With the addition of these three, it was virtually bursting at the seams.

Samira glanced around the crowd. "We saw everyone working over here and came to help. What can we do?"

Samira and D-Jay seemed to have a poor sense of boundaries, showing up whether they'd been invited or not. Once more, I found myself feeling intruded upon—ironic in light of the fact that I had no claim to the space where I found myself now. But I supposed they were only trying to be neighborly and helpful. *Or maybe they're being nosey.*

Before Holden could make a suggestion, Samira slid Kavish off her back and opened the pantry door in the kitchen. She ran her gaze from top to bottom. "This cupboard needs to be sorted out." She reached in and pulled out a can of tomato soup. Her nose crinkled in disgust as she consulted the label. "This soup expired in twenty nineteen."

"I'm not surprised," Holden said. "With Gideon bringing food over all the time, Joanna rarely cooked herself a meal."

Again, I felt that eerie little niggle that said Gideon might have accidentally brought about Joanna's demise with all that seafood. I looked his way to gauge his response, but he simply stared down at the table in front of him.

Samira shifted her gaze to the old man, too, her lips spreading in a broad smile. "If you would like to continue feeding someone, Mister Gideon, we would be happy to volunteer."

Gideon raised his gaze and waved a gnarled, dismissive hand. "You'd be disappointed. I tried some of that stuff you brought to the Griffins. The rice and lentil dish? It was superb. No way I could top that."

D-Jay offered a smile now, too. "My wife does know her way around the kitchen." Samira yanked a wooden spoon from a holder on the counter and handed it to her son along with a plastic bowl she found in a cabinet. While Kavish banged the spoon on the back of the bowl like a drummer in a rock 'n' roll band, Samira snatched a trash bag from the cardboard dispenser on the counter and handed it to her husband. He held it open while she emptied the pantry. She worked with the speed and efficiency of a young mother who had too much to do and not enough time to do it. She checked the date on a box of crackers before opening it to sample one. "Stale." She tossed the box into the trash bag. It hit the bottom of the bag with a muffled clunk.

She continued on, moving some things around, disposing of others, organizing the spices in the rack affixed to the inside of the door. I was nearly to the bottom of my can of ginger ale when she stood on her tiptoes to reach something at the back of an upper shelf. When she pulled it out, I recognized the signature green color on the small rectangular box immediately. It was an open carton of Newport cigarettes. As she tossed the carton into D-Jay's bag, a pack fell out and hit the floor at his feet. She quickly snatched up the pack and tossed it into the sack, as well.

Cigarettes were expensive. I'd seen the astronomical prices listed on posters in the windows of gas stations when I'd stopped for fuel, and was grateful not to be addicted to the darn things. How smokers kept from going broke was beyond me. It seemed a waste to see something so valuable being thrown away yet, at the same time, I wouldn't want anyone else to smoke them. The darn things had taken too many lives through lung cancer and emphysema, not to mention the deadly fires that had been inadvertently started with cigarettes.

When everyone finished their drinks, we rallied and resumed our work, carrying load after load across the street. There was no point in boxing things up for such a short trip. Instead, we simply carried the dresser drawers over individually with everything still inside. We loaded the dishes, pots, and pans into Alyssa's wagon and rolled them over. What wouldn't fit in the wagon we stowed in the bed of Holden's pickup, which he then drove across the street. Doing so saved us only a few steps, but when performing hard labor for hours on end, every step counted. Our legs and backs would thank us later. Some of the kitchen items were duplicates of things Joanna already had, and there wasn't enough room in the cabinets to put everything away, so we set much of it on the countertops for the Griffins to sort through later.

Eventually, everything had been moved out of the townhouse across the street and into Joanna's place—which I supposed I should now start thinking of as Macy and Holden's place. As we gathered up our dollies and straps, Alyssa came to find me in the living room. She placed her grandmother's crystal candy dish on their coffee table, and plucked out one of the candies, unwrapping it, and tossing it into her mouth. She spoke around the candy, pushing it into her cheek. "My mom wants to talk to you before you go."

I walked past the kitchen and down the hall to the master. Though the door stood ajar, I rapped quietly anyway. "Macy?" I said softly.

"Come in!" she called.

I entered to see her sitting propped up atop the bed now. A laptop computer was perched on her thighs. Her moppy little mutt lay on the bed beside her. He lazily raised his head to take a look at me before putting it back down and closing his eyes to continue his nap.

I stopped just inside the door. "Alyssa said you wanted to see me?"

"Yes." She looked around, but the only place for me to sit was on the bed. The chair was loaded down with towels for the master bath. She gestured to the foot of the bed. "Sit if you'd like."

I walked over and perched on the end of the bed, curious why she'd summoned me.

"We're having a memorial service for my mother on Tuesday evening. It won't be a full-fledged funeral. She wanted to be cremated rather than buried. We'll take care of the cremation once the autopsy is done. You are welcome to attend the service, if you'd like."

"I would." I wanted to pay my final respects to Joanna and her family. I also hoped to get some closure on this tragic event. Maybe the memorial service would help me put the matter to rest.

Moving on to related matters, Macy heaved a loud breath. "I'm pretty sure the doctor at urgent care screwed up. He should've done more than just send my mother home with headache medicine. He should've run more tests on her."

"Gideon mentioned that you were concerned."

"Concerned and angry." Her hands fisted beside her on the bedspread. "With Mom being a smoker, she had a higher risk of an aneurysm. The doctor should've known that and performed more than just a quick exam. If I pursue a case against the doctor, you'll be called to testify in court if it gets that far. You'd at least have to give a deposition before the case would be settled."

No doubt she'd been researching medical malpractice cases online. The idea of being grilled in court made me anxious, and I had no idea whether the doctor had committed malpractice or not. But I figured if I simply told the truth about what happened when Joanna came to the firehouse, the rest would be sorted out by the judge or jury. It would be *their* job to reach a conclusion, not mine. "I'll cooperate with everyone, if that's what you're asking."

"Good." She gestured to her computer. "From what I see here, it's standard procedure to issue a subpoena to witnesses, even when someone's agreed to show up. Just wanted to make you aware of that so you're not surprised if someone shows up to serve you."

The idea of being served with a subpoena, a process server tracking me down like an escaped fugitive, made me uncomfortable. Of course, the only experience I had with subpoenas was what I'd seen in legal programs on TV. If it was only a matter of someone handing paperwork over to me, perhaps it could be scheduled in advance for everyone's convenience. Of course, I was getting way ahead of myself here. So was Macy. The results of the autopsy weren't even back yet. We didn't know for certain whether Joanna had actually died of a ruptured aneurysm, though all signs seemed to point to one. The headaches she'd suffered beforehand; her age;

the fact that she smoked—even if she had cut way back. "Have you hired an attorney already?"

"I put out some feelers, and I spoke with one lawyer on the phone yesterday afternoon. She said she'd need to see what the autopsy says before she'll know if I have a case."

I hated to point a finger at Gideon, but I didn't know whether screening for mercury was standard procedure during an autopsy. Once Joanna was buried or cremated, any evidence of mercury poisoning would be lost. Macy wanted to know the truth about her mother's death, and it was only right to help her discern the facts. I kept my voice low so the others wouldn't overhear me. No sense starting rumors. "Do you think your mother could have died of mercury poisoning? Or maybe ciguatera or scombroid poisoning?"

Her head tilted and her eyes narrowed. "What now?"

"You know how pregnant women aren't supposed to eat fish?"

"Yeah?"

"Do you know why that is?"

"Not really," she said. "I figured it had something to do with bacteria from dirty water. I've heard that raw sewage is dumped directly into the ocean in some poor countries." She made a revolted face and stuck out her tongue. "Parts of the ocean are basically cesspools."

I told her what I'd learned from Colette and the internet. "Pregnant women aren't supposed to eat fish because of the risk of mercury poisoning. Seafood has mercury in it. There's not much in the small fish, but the big fish can accumulate quite a bit of it from eating the small fish. It builds up. The process is called biomagnification. I can't claim to know much about it, but I've got a friend who's pregnant, like you. She mentioned it over dinner the other night. She's a professional chef and she learned about it in cooking school." I gestured in the general direction of the kitchen. "I noticed your mother has a lot of leftover seafood in her fridge. Tuna. Shrimp. Orange roughy."

Her brows lifting, Macy put her fingers to her keyboard. "What did you say the process was called? Bio . . . ?"

"Biomagnification," I repeated.

Macy typed the word into her browser then spent a moment or two reading over the links. She pondered the results aloud. "It says here that it's sometimes called Minamata disease. A chemical company dumped mercury in Minamata Bay in Japan and a lot of people got sick afterward when they ate seafood that was harvested there." Her expression grew increasingly concerned as she clicked each successive link. "Dizziness? Numbness? Tremors? Being unsteady when walking?" She looked up at me, her eyes bright with astonishment. "This describes my mother to a T." She looked down and scrolled through a couple more links. "It says here that mercury poisoning is treatable through something called"—she leaned in to take a closer look—"chelation therapy. The patient is given a special drug that binds with the metals in their systems and carries the metal out through the urination process."

I filled her in on the other possibilities—ciguatera or scombroid poisoning. Like Buck, she was thoroughly repulsed. She put one hand over her mouth, raising the other to tell me to shut mine immediately. When she got her nausea under control, she lowered her hands. "Thanks for this information, Whitney." She looked to the partially opened door and called for her husband. "Holden! Can you come here a second?"

A moment later, the door opened farther and her husband stepped into the room.

Macy pointed to me. "Whitney thinks Mom might have been poisoned by mercury."

"Mercury?" he repeated. "Like the planet?"

She rolled her eyes. "No! Mercury like *mercury*. We learned about it in chemistry class in high school, remember? The periodic table and all that?"

Holden's lips spread in a wry smile. "I don't remember much about chemistry class other than my beautiful blonde lab partner. She was all I could think about."

She rolled her eyes again, though this time a small smile tugged at her lips before she returned her attention to me. "It's a good thing you brought this up now. The autopsy is scheduled for tomorrow morning." She reached for her cell phone on the bedside table. "I'm calling the pathologist."

CHAPTER 16

WEDDING BLUES

WHITNEY

Our work at the townhouse completed, Holden and Alyssa thanked everyone and escorted the group of volunteer movers to the door, along with the two not-so-helpful self-appointed supervisors whose main mission in life seemed to be critiquing the work of others and always finding it wanting.

The group disbanded outside. Collin, Ren, Buck, and Owen drove off in their vehicles, while the neighbors left on foot. A minute later, everyone had gone but me and Gideon. Although I'd nailed down the unlevel board on the porch that morning, I'd been in a hurry and done a quick and dirty job. I took a second look at the step now. It could use another nail or two, or maybe a screw, to better hold it in place for the long term.

Gideon remained and chatted with me while I examined the board. "It was awful nice of you and your cousins to help out here. Your fiancé, too. Y'all are good people." He paused for a beat before adding, "Not all folks are."

A frown claimed Gideon's face but, rather than an angry one, it seemed sad, wounded. I wondered what sorts of not-nice folks he had encountered over the years, what those people might have said or done to him. *People can be unbearably cruel.* Having come across several murder victims, I knew this fact from personal experience.

Gideon waited on the porch while I hustled over to the fire station to round up a screwdriver and a long screw. I was back in under two minutes, but during that time a tow truck had parked in front of Joanna's house. The cab was painted bright green. CA$H4CAR$ was printed across a backdrop of a wavy rectangle with dollar signs in each corner, purporting to represent a dollar bill. Underneath the logo in smaller letters were the words Auto Salvage and Towing.

On the porch stood a man who resembled Macy. He had her same blond hair and the same hazel eyes, but that's where their similarities ended. This man had a quiet, somber quality about him, and though he looked to be near her age, he seemed worn down, as if life had been tougher on him than it had been on her. He had to be Lane, Joanna's elusive son, the one who had stolen from Joanna, the one who'd parked his tow truck in the parking lot of the fire station shortly before the place had gone up in flames.

Gideon stood in front of the door chastising the man. "You expect to just show up here and leave with Joanna's valuables?"

"Her old record albums aren't valuable," Lane said. "There's plenty of copies of them still around."

Gideon cocked his head. "If they aren't valuable, then why do you want them?"

Lane shoved his hands into the pockets of his jeans

as if to hide the fists they'd reflexively formed. "Why should I explain myself to you? I know you and Mom were friends, but Joanna was my *mother.*"

"And you broke her heart!" Gideon's face was full of rage, but his breath hitched in grief.

"You think I don't know that?" Lane shouted back. He closed his eyes and inhaled a long breath. When he opened his eyes and spoke again, his voice was calmer. "I've been clean for six months now." He pulled his hand out of his pocket and held up a key chain. No keys hung from it. "See? I've been going to narcotics anonymous. I earned a key tag. I came by a few days back to show Mom, but she wasn't home."

He must have been referring to the day that Joanna and Gideon had come to the fire station to ask Buck and me to take a look at the Bottiglieris' townhouse.

Lane slid the key chain back into his pocket. "I've been trying to make amends for the past. I'm a new person now."

"Nobody becomes a new person so quickly." Gideon pointed at Lane's pocket. "That key tag proves nothing. You could've picked that up anywhere, or lied to the folks at your drug group so they'd give it to you. There's a reason your mother cut you out of her will."

Wow. Gideon's words seemed unnecessarily harsh. Lane had just lost his mother, for goodness' sake. He deserved a little sympathy.

Lane was quiet for a beat or two, his expression equal parts hurt and confusion. "Seriously? She cut me out?"

Gideon seemed to realize he'd taken things a little too far, and attempted to backpedal a bit. "She only did it because she didn't want to enable your drug habit. She was afraid you'd spend the money on pills." But while

Gideon might have softened his rhetoric a bit, he still wouldn't move to allow Lane inside the townhouse.

"Come on, man!" Lane pleaded, shoving fisted hands into his pockets again. "Let me by!"

Gideon backed up against the door, spread his legs to make himself even wider, and put one hand on each side of the doorframe. "I'm not budging!"

I stood, ready to intervene in case things came to blows. Luckily for us all, it didn't.

Getting nowhere with Gideon, Lane looked past him to the closed door, cupped his hands around his mouth, and hollered, "Hey, Macy! Call off the guard dog!"

Behind Gideon, the door opened. Gideon swayed and, for an instant, I feared he might fall backward into the entryway. Fortunately, he'd leveraged himself fairly tightly in the doorframe with his arms, and they helped to hold him steady.

Holden raised up on his toes to peer over the man's shoulder. "Hey, Lane." Holden's tone and face held no animosity. *Were he and his brother-in-law on good terms? What about Lane and Macy?*

Lane said, "I came to see if it would be okay with Macy if I take Mom's albums." He gestured at Gideon. "But Gideon won't get out of my way."

Holden ducked under Gideon's arm and squeezed past him to step out onto the porch. Turning back to face him, he said, "It's okay, Gideon. I got this."

Gideon scoffed. "If you say so." He lumbered forward, checking Lane with his shoulder as he passed the younger man.

Lane turned and cast an incredulous look at Gideon's back. "That geezer's got some balls, trying to start something with a guy half his age. He's also got some screws loose."

I didn't want to think about Gideon's nether regions and I wasn't sure whether Gideon had any loose screws, but the porch still had the loose board and as soon as I fixed it, I'd get the heck out of here. I didn't want to get in the middle of a family squabble if one erupted.

Holden introduced me to Lane. "Whitney and her cousin are fixing up the fire station around the corner. They're turning it into a house."

Lane's brows rose and his head bobbed slowly. He pinned me with his gaze. "I hear y'all had a fire over there."

No sense being coy and evasive. "I know the deputy fire marshal spoke with you about it."

"Sorry I couldn't help. I didn't see anything." He sounded sincere. "Did they figure out who set the fire?"

"Not yet."

He jerked his shoulders in a shrug. "Probably some punk kids from the neighborhood."

"Could be." I pointed down at the board. "I'm just here to tack this board down, then I'll get out of your hair."

Holden thanked me again, allowed Lane into the townhouse, and closed the door behind them. The sound of muted conversation came through the door, but it was impossible to make out what the men were saying. A few turns of the screwdriver and I was on my way.

On Sunday, Collin rode with me out to Lynchburg to pick up the reclaimed wood. The drive took over an hour and a half, so we decided to make the most of it. The world-famous Jack Daniel's distillery made its home in Lynchburg's Cave Spring Hollow so, before getting the wood, we took a tour. The chemical process involved in the fermentation of the mash was intriguing. We also

learned that the water used to make the whiskey came
from Cave Spring, which produced eight hundred gallons of water a minute at a constant 56-degree temperature. We learned how the whiskey barrels were
made, and that the barrel makers were called coopers.
We discovered that they also sold the old whiskey barrels that were no longer suitable for use in their whiskey-
making process.

"I'm going to buy a barrel," I said, making a detour
into the shop.

Collin followed me in. "What do you want a barrel
for? To plant flowers in?"

I slid him a grin. "You'll see."

After I paid for the barrel, we carried it out to my
SUV and loaded it into the cargo bay. We climbed in and
shut our doors to go.

"Whoa!" Collin blinked, his nose wiggling. "This car
smells like a bar at closing time."

The wood had soaked up the acrid scent of the spir-
its. I jabbed the button to roll the windows down. With
a long drive home ahead of us, we had declined the tast-
ing offered at the end of the distillery tour and were
completely sober. Still, I was concerned by the smell.
"I hope we don't get pulled over by highway patrol on
the drive home. We'd have a lot of explaining to do." I
grabbed my ponytail and held it to my nose. "My hair
has already absorbed the scent."

We left the distillery and made our way out into the
countryside, where the outfit that ran the reclamation
service stored the salvaged materials in a large barn. I
presented the receipt I'd received when I'd paid for the
wood online, and the attendant helped Collin and me
load the flooring onto the flatbed trailer I'd borrowed

from Buck. We drove back to Nashville and detached the loaded trailer, stashing it in the bay at the firehouse. After Collin and I parted ways with a warm kiss, I drove home and wrangled the whiskey barrel out of my SUV. I stored it in the garage where I could work on it during the evenings. I could hardly wait to start this new project!

Buck and I were nearly done installing the reclaimed wood flooring on Monday when my phone pinged with a text to let me know the wedding gown I'd ordered had been delivered.

"My wedding dress arrived! Mind if I head out early?" It was only a little past noon, but I was dying to try it on. I'd have a hard time focusing on my work knowing the dress was waiting for me at home.

"We've got a lot to do, but I know how you women are. You'll be of no use around here with that dress on your mind." Buck made a shooing motion with his hand. "Go on. Git!"

"Thanks, Buck!" I rushed out of the station, drove to my house, and rounded up the box. It seemed a shame to try it on alone. I wanted someone to exclaim over me, tell me what a beautiful bride I would be. My mother worked part-time in my father's medical practice, and would already be home for the day. I knew she would want to see the dress, too, so I put the box in my car and drove over to my parents' house.

As I carried the box in, my mother's black and white Boston terrier ran up and danced in circles around me, as if sensing my excitement. I bent down, ruffled the dog's ears, and gave her a kiss on the head. "Hello, Yin-Yang." The bug-eyed dog looked around, probably hoping I'd set Sawdust down somewhere. For years before moving to the cottage, I'd lived out back in my parents' converted pool house, and my sweet little fellow and Yin-Yang had enjoyed playtime together. The dog seemed to miss her old playmate. *I'll have to bring Sawdust over for a visit real soon.*

My mother stood from the couch, where she'd been curled up, reading a mystery novel. "What do you have there?"

"My wedding dress."

"Your *what*?!" she shrieked.

Uh-oh. "Um . . . my wedding dress?"

"How can you have your wedding dress? We haven't finished shopping for it yet!"

"When we didn't find one before, I looked online. I saw one that I really liked so I went ahead and ordered it."

My mother was beside herself. Apparently, I had deprived her of a rite of passage that belonged to every mother of the bride, the experience of helping their daughter find her wedding dress. She looked ready to throttle me. "I can't believe you got your dress from the internet!"

"It's a new world, Mom," I said, though the internet could hardly be called new anymore. "We spent an entire day earlier with no luck. It's easier and faster to shop online than drive around to a bunch of stores. Besides, there's a bigger selection."

"But I wanted to be part of it!"

Ugh. She'd already expressed disappointment when I'd informed her about the party favors Collin and I had decided on, a handy all-in-one tool that would fit in a pocket, purse, or glove compartment, along with a small personal alarm that could be attached to a key fob. Though I'd received some lovely party favors at weddings—candles, koozies, hand-painted wineglasses, and the like—the unusual gifts we'd chosen best reflected a carpenter and a cop. The gadgets would be both useful and memorable.

Even though my mother was making things more stressful for me, I felt guilt nipping at my gut. I figured the least I could do was bring her along when I went to try on shoes. A dress could be altered to fit perfectly, but the same didn't hold for shoes. I didn't trust ordering a pair of shoes online. I wanted to make sure they fit well and were comfortable. Collin and I were in the process of making our playlist for the reception. It was the biggest party we'd ever thrown, and we planned to dance all night. I could hardly wait! "You can go with me to pick out shoes and flowers. Okay?"

The offer appeased her a little, thank goodness. She gestured at the box. "Well, you might as well put it on and let me see it."

Sheesh. "That's the spirit."

We carried the dress into my childhood bedroom, which had a full-length mirror. My mother helped me into the dress, though it was relatively easy. When I turned to look in the mirror, I gasped in delight. My mother put her hands over her mouth for a moment, then clasped them at her chest. "Oh, Whitney!" she cried. "It's perfect!"

The dress was, indeed, perfect. The fit was exact, as if the gown had been custom-tailored just for me. The fabric was high quality. The blue sash brought out the color of my eyes, which were now getting misty.

My mother's eyes were misty, too. She ran her hand over the shoulders and tugged here and there on the sides. "I hate to say it, but I don't see how we could have done any better."

I exhaled in relief.

After taking several photos with her phone, her eyes went suddenly wide. "Wait here! I'll be right back."

As she ran out the bedroom door, I called after her. "Where would I go in this dress, anyway?"

She returned a moment later, clutching something in her closed hand. She opened her fingers to reveal a pair of earrings and a pendant. The earrings were simple, pale blue stones in a silver setting. The same went for the necklace. The blue was identical to the color of the sash on my dress. "The stones are aquamarine," said my mother. "This set belonged to my grandmother."

"Why have I never seen them before?"

Her eyes became mistier. "I was saving them for a special occasion. I just didn't know which one until now."

Emotion threatened to overwhelm me, and I fanned my hands in front of my face. "Stop! You're going to make me cry!"

My mother laughed, took one of my hands, and pressed the jewelry into them. "They're yours now."

"Oh, Mom!" I burst into tears, something that was very unlike me. Though this tender moment with my mother had instigated things, I knew deep down that this cry was also a release of the pent-up feelings I'd been trying to tamper down—the horror over Joanna's death, the tension surrounding the competition for the townhouse, the frustration with the vandalism and the fire. It felt good to cry, so I just went with it. Lest I leave tear stains on my dress, my mother quickly handed me a tissue and whisked me out of the gown. We sat on my bed and had a good cry together, my mother in her lounging clothes and me in my underwear.

After a few minutes, we were able to gather our wits. "Shoes and flowers?" I asked.

"Shoes and flowers," she agreed.

Lest we have to drag the dress with us on our quest for shoes, my mother rounded up her sewing scissors and snipped a tiny piece of fabric from the hem inside the dress, where it wouldn't be noticeable. We took the small swatch with us to the bridal shop to ensure the shoes would be the right color. I tried on several pairs, walking around to test them out, even performing some moves from the line dances the deejay would play at the reception. I finally decided on a pair of low-heeled pumps with a strap around the ankle.

Next, we hit up a florist. My mother showed the woman the photos she'd taken of me in the dress. "Any ideas?"

"I know just what you need." The florist went over to a refrigerator in which a multitude of flowers sat in plastic buckets, patiently awaiting their time to be incorporated into an arrangement, spray, or bouquet. She pulled out a single stalk, a beautiful blue hydrangea. "We could intersperse hydrangeas with white roses in your bouquet, and use a white rose and a sprig of hydrangea for the groom's boutonniere."

My mother and I both loved the idea, and placed the order. I bought a flowering peace lily as well, which I'd take to Macy at Joanna's service tomorrow.

With Colette handling the food and drinks, the officiant procured, and the playlist provided to the deejay, there was little left to do to prepare for the wedding, other than choose a flavor for the wedding cake and finish the fire station remodel. I was glad Joanna's autopsy had been completed today. Once the pathologist gave Macy the results, we'd know what, exactly, had killed the poor woman, and where things would go from here. With any luck, we could put her death behind us and focus on the future.

CHAPTER 17

MERCY AND MERCURY

WHITNEY

On Tuesday evening, Collin met Buck and me in the parking lot of the chapel where Joanna Hartzell's memorial service would be held. He parked in a spot next to Lane's tow truck, and slid out of his car. He quickly caught us up on the day's developments. "The prosecutor, Landreth, and I met with Peter Bottiglieri today. He claims Judith had her grandson torch the fire station."

Buck cocked his head. "Judith admitted it to Peter?"

"No," Collin said. "It's conjecture on Peter's part, but I think he's probably right. Judith wouldn't say anything other than 'prove it,' when we went to her door. We went to talk to her grandson next. He's sixteen and a total punk. He kept saying he didn't know anything, but he was smirking the entire time. He seems to know we've got nothing on him. The kid was smart enough not to leave prints, which tells me he's not new to crime."

I couldn't imagine a grandmother encouraging her grandson to commit a crime, especially a felony, but the Bottiglieris had acted in all sorts of ways that I found unimaginable.

"Landreth's going to keep an eye on the kid," Collin said. "She'll track his social media to see if he brags about getting away with a crime, talk with some of his friends. But unless she gets a break, the crime could go unpunished."

It wouldn't go totally unpunished, of course. The six Bottiglieris would lose the additional five-hundred dollars we had planned to pay them to put them on par with John. But the punishment seemed small compared to the crime. They'd cost us two grand in the form of our insurance deductible, not to mention the value of our lost time. I could only hope that karma would come around and bite them in the butt.

I wondered whether Peter had gotten off light. "Did the DA give Peter a plea deal?"

Collin nodded, his expression sour. "He'll have to complete ten hours of community service, but that's all."

"What about our cost for painting over the graffiti? Shouldn't he have to pay restitution for the paint and supplies?"

Collin's expression soured further. "Peter argued he didn't cost you anything since you and Buck planned to repaint the walls anyway."

Though Peter had a valid point, I gritted my teeth in frustration. Justice had not been done, in my opinion, but sometimes that's just the way it goes. Life isn't fair.

The other attendees had gone inside already and, after checking my watch and seeing that only two minutes remained before Joanna's memorial service was to start, I suggested we go in. Flowers filled the chapel with a sweet fragrance, and soft, solemn music met our ears. After I placed the peace lily among the other arrangements that flanked the podium, we took seats in a row behind all the others. Macy, Holden, Alyssa, and Lane sat in the front row. Gideon sat next to Macy. Samira, D-Jay, and Kavish sat in the second row. Various other people we didn't know sat on the benches, some by themselves, others with family or friends. The three umarells sat in the fourth row. Though they'd been neighbors of Joanna's, my guess was they were here more for the purpose of critiquing the service than paying respects to the deceased. To my surprise, Mary Ruth and Tabitha Bottiglieri were in attendance. They cast narrow-eyed glances back at Buck and me. Mary Ruth dug in her purse with both hands and, though she didn't pull out her phone, appeared to be sending a surreptitious text. *Could she be alerting her siblings that Buck and I were here? If so, to what end?*

The officiant opened with a prayer and said some preliminary words about Joanna, then invited Macy to deliver the eulogy. She was remarkably calm and in control as she delivered the speech, which she did from a tall stool. It was the closest option to bed rest the chapel could offer. While many tended to paint a perfect picture of the deceased in their eulogies, Macy was much more realistic. She looked down at her brother from the raised platform. "Lane knows as well as I do that our mother could be difficult. She was stubborn sometimes, and she didn't hold back when she thought we'd screwed up. But the consolation we find in that—the consolation we've always found—is that it showed she cared, that she wanted the best for us. No matter how much we might have let her down, we never doubted for a second that she loved us with all her heart."

At that, Lane choked out a sob and hung his head. Sitting next to her uncle, Alyssa raised her arm and draped it across his shoulders to comfort him. A bandage remained on her finger. Looked like the splinter was still stuck in her skin.

When Macy finished, Gideon got up and led the group in a recitation of Psalm 23. "The Lord is my shepherd; I shall not want. He maketh me to lie down in green pastures: he leadeth me beside the still waters. He restoreth my soul: he leadeth me in the paths of righteousness for his name's sake. Yea, though I walk through the valley of the shadow of death, I will fear no evil: for thou art with me; thy rod and thy staff they comfort me. Thou preparest a table before me in the presence of mine enemies: thou anointest my head with oil; my cup runneth over. Surely goodness and mercy shall follow me all the days of my life: and I will dwell in the house of the Lord forever."

In unison, the rest of us offered an "Amen."

After a brief closing statement, the memorial concluded and the attendees drifted out to the parking lot. Buck, Collin, and I were waiting on the sidewalk to express our final condolences and to ask about Joanna's autopsy when the umarells exited, the trio chatting among themselves. I could only imagine what they were saying. *The music was all wrong. They should've used scented candles. Psalm 23:4? That scripture is overused. They should've gone with Isaiah 57:2.*

Samira and D-Jay exited the chapel. D-Jay carried a sleeping Kavish in his arms, the boy's head on his father's shoulder. They stopped in front of us.

Samira said, "It was very nice of you to come to the service."

I felt an odd urge to take a step back, put some distance between myself and the couple. "We wanted to pay our respects to the family."

Turning to other matters, Samira said, "I went to the townhouse today to take photographs of the ceiling and to measure the walls."

D-Jay smiled. "She wants to select light fixtures now."

"The door would not open with our code." Samira pinned me with an accusatory gaze that demanded an answer.

My body stiffened. Again, they'd crossed a boundary, trying to go into our townhouse without first asking permission. *No more missus nice guy.* "The door code has been changed for security purposes." I used passive language to soften the message while still making sure it was received. "Nobody should enter without getting prior permission from me or Buck. We are the owners, after all."

Mary Ruth and Tabitha exited the chapel and headed up the walkway toward us.

"But you plan to sell the home." Samira's expression and tone were irritated. "We want to buy it. We have told you that we are making preparations."

I really didn't want to have an argument here, at Joanna's memorial service, but the couple wasn't giving me much choice. "I know you are interested in the place," I said, keeping an eye on the Bottiglieri women while repeating what I'd already told Samira ad nauseam. "But we are going to sell it to the highest bidder."

"Profit!" Samira snapped. "That is all you care about?"

By then, Mary Ruth and Tabitha were upon us and heard Samira's accusation.

"You got that right!" Mary Ruth snapped, wagging her finger to indicate Buck and me. "These two are greedy, greedy, greedy!"

"You still owe us." Tabitha gave me a cold stare that said things weren't over.

As the Bottiglieri sisters headed off, the heat of anger warmed my cheeks. Samira's turned pink as well. Seeming to realize his wife had taken things too far, D-Jay took one hand off his son's back to put it on his wife's. "We can discuss the townhouse another time." He gave me a polite nod and guided her away.

As soon as they were out of earshot, I turned to Buck. "The Bottiglieris have been bad enough without Samira getting on my last nerve, too."

"Don't blame her," Buck said. "Blame that baby in her belly."

"What do you mean?" I asked.

"She's probably nesting."

"Nesting?"

"It's something pregnant women do. They get what's called a nesting instinct. It's an urge to prepare their home for their baby. Colette's got it something fierce. She's cleaned and organized like a mad woman. You should see our place. It's spotless. She threw out any of my socks that didn't have a match, and had me clean the carpets—twice. 'Course I had to put my foot down when she tried to organize the garage."

Knowing my friend, I said, "I bet that didn't go well."

"It did not. But a man's got to have his own space."

I turned to Collin and cocked my head, acting coy. "Will you need your own space when you move in with me after we're married?" I pursed my lips and squinted, giving him a flinty glare in jest.

He played along, jerking his head to indicate Buck. "You heard him. A man's got to have his own space."

We ended our exchange when Lane walked out of the

chapel alone, looking lonely and defeated. He tugged a pack of cigarettes from the breast pocket of his dress shirt, a pack that was green and white, with a gold stripe. I recognized them as Newports, the same brand Joanna had smoked. He shook one out and slid it back into his pocket. He retrieved a lighter from his pants pocket and lit up, returning the device to his pocket as he approached.

Feeling the need to say something to the bereaved man, I offered, "The service was beautiful."

"Thanks." He took a deep drag on his cigarette, his cheeks forming hollows, and shook his head, as if in disbelief. He held the smoke in his lungs for a few seconds, then shot the stream of gray air sideways out the corner of his mouth. Staring at the smoke as it dissipated, he mused aloud. "It's funny how life goes. If someone had told me back when I was a kid that Gideon would be reading a poem at my mother's funeral, I would've asked them what they'd been smoking."

"What do you mean?" I asked. "They've been friends a long time, haven't they?"

"They have," Lane agreed, "but it didn't start out that way. When Gideon and his partner moved into the neighborhood, my mother had a fit. 'There goes the neighborhood!'" he cried in a mocking tone, waving jazz hands at his shoulders. "'It'll only be a matter of time until the gays take over!'" He lowered his hands and took another drag on his cigarette, releasing small bursts of smoke as he chuckled. "Mom told us to steer clear of them. Of course, things changed after Dad died. Over time, Mom and Gideon became best friends. It was nice to see Mom grow." His shoulders shook as he inhaled, then released, a shaky breath. "I suppose we all live and learn, huh?"

It was true. Even so, it was a shame Joanna hadn't had the chance to live longer, to learn more and grow more.

Lane took another puff on his cigarette, and flicked the ashes to the asphalt. "Gideon is far from my biggest fan, but I suppose I can't blame him. He was only protecting his friend. I only wish I could've shown my mother how far I've come. I wish she'd lived to see me get my life together. I'm not totally there yet, but I'm on my way." Seeming to realize he'd spilled his guts to virtual strangers, he stood straighter, looking a little sheepish. "That was heavy, wasn't it? I suppose I forgot I wasn't at group."

Macy, Holden, and Alyssa emerged from the chapel, Gideon trailing along behind them. Macy stopped near us and turned to Gideon. "Thanks for doing the reading, Gideon. We'll see you soon, okay?"

Her words were clearly meant to dismiss him. He cast a glance at Lane, Collin, Buck, and me. *Do I detect a hint of anxiety? Annoyance? Rejection, maybe?* Some sort of emotion was in his eyes, though I couldn't immediately identify it. "All right," he said, acquiescing. He continued on to the parking lot.

Once Gideon had gone, Lane turned to Macy. "That was a nice eulogy you gave Mom."

She responded with a curt "Thanks."

He hesitated a moment, seeming to appraise his sister. "Hey, I was thinking. The apartment I'm living in now leaves a lot to be desired. What if I move back into my bedroom at Mom's place for a few months? I could save up some cash and upgrade to a nicer apartment once we get past Christmas. Y'all don't need all three upstairs bedrooms, and I'd pay my fair share of the electric and water bills. What would you think about that?"

"What would I think about that?" Macy repeated,

her brows lifting, her tone incredulous. "I'd think you have no right asking me to help you when you left me to pick up the pieces after you started using. Mom and I hardly saw you for years. *Years*, Lane! We had no idea where you were sometimes, or if you were even still alive. When you *did* show up, you were a mess and only made things worse. Mom was torn up over it. Did you ever stop to think how hard that was for me? How it affected *my* life? *My* family?"

"I'm sorry, Macy." He scrubbed a hand over his face. "I know I wrecked things. If there was a way I could make up for it, I would."

Tears filled Macy's eyes, and she gnawed at her lip, torn. "I love you, Lane. I never stopped, and I'm trying to forgive you. I really am. It's just going to take some time. I don't think you moving in with us now is a good idea."

He dipped his head in resignation. "Understood." He stepped forward and enveloped her in a hug. She tensed at first, but then relaxed and closed her eyes, hugging him back. "For what it's worth," he said, still holding her tight, "I don't blame you one bit. But I promise I'll work to make amends in any way I can." He released her and stepped back. "Y'all take care." With that, he headed off, aiming for his tow truck.

Holden put a supportive hand on her shoulder. "I know that was hard, Macy, but it was the right thing to do."

"I hope so." Macy swiped a tear from her eye, gathered herself together, and straightened. She eyed Collin, Buck, and me, her cheeks pink. "Families. Am I right?"

"You're telling me." Buck hiked a thumb my way. "I gotta put up with this pain in the butt."

All of us shared a laugh, breaking the tension.

Macy looked me in the eye. "The pathologist issued my mother's autopsy report. You were right, Whitney. My mother didn't die of an aneurysm. She died of mercury poisoning."

I now realized why she hadn't wanted to discuss the matter in front of Gideon. She didn't want him to know that he'd inadvertently poisoned his best friend. "It was the seafood, after all?"

"Actually, no." She went on to explain that the type of mercury poisoning people got from eating seafood involved a form of mercury called methylmercury, which differed from elemental, or metallic, mercury. "The pathologist explained it to us. When mercury gets into a water source, microorganisms in the sediment transform it into methylmercury." Fish then ingested the methylmercury through their mouths as they ate or through their gills as they swam about. "The doctor said that methylmercury is also used to preserve grain that is fed to farm animals, so sometimes humans ingest it that way. He said it takes weeks or months for symptoms from methylmercury poisoning to appear, but that poisoning from elemental mercury is more immediate."

"I hadn't realized there was a distinction between the types of mercury."

Macy went on to tell us that methylmercury will show up in blood tests, but that elemental mercury normally leaves the blood quickly and moves into the kidneys and brain. "Because Mom died so quickly after her exposure, the mercury was still detectable in her blood. If the doctor at urgent care had tested my mother's blood for mercury, she could've been treated with activated charcoal or dialysis, or the chelation therapy that we talked about on Saturday. She could still be alive."

From the way she spoke, it looked like Macy was still

thinking about pursuing a malpractice case. I doubted it was routine to check for mercury in light of the fact that Joanna's symptoms could be indicative of any number of run-of-the-mill health problems, but I wasn't a medical expert. Regardless, the situation begged the question, "How would elemental mercury have gotten into Joanna's system?"

"We have no idea," Macy said. "Gideon's at her house all the time and he's fine, so we think she probably got exposed somewhere she went on her own. She still had friends from her factory days who she goes to visit. She might've picked something up when she went to see one of them. But we're not taking any chances. I've ordered a testing kit online to check for mercury in the water at my mother's house. One for the air, too. We have to let that one sit for a while, then mail it to the testing center. It takes seventy-two hours to get the results once it's submitted." She cast a grateful glance at her husband. "Holden threw out all of her remaining food, whether it was expired or not. He got rid of her fluorescent bulbs, too. The doctor mentioned that they contain mercury. I don't want to risk my baby's health. We're going to stay in our unit in Gideon's building until we get the results back. We'd already paid rent through the end of the month, and he hasn't found a new tenant yet."

Buck and I had lost a full day of work moving the Griffins on Saturday, and we could scarcely afford to lose another, but how could I not offer to help under the circumstances? "Would you like us to move your furniture back across the street?"

"No need," she said. "We bought a couple of cheap memory foam mattresses and new bedding. We can make do with that until we know my mother's place is safe. But thank you for offering."

With that, the family bade us goodbye. Collin, Buck, and I returned to our cars and headed our separate ways, as well.

CHAPTER 18
CHEMISTRY LESSONS

WHITNEY

On the drive home, I pondered not only what Macy had told me, but how she'd chosen to deliver the message. Though she hadn't asked Buck and me to keep mum about the autopsy results, it had certainly seemed like she'd intentionally left Gideon out of the conversation. *Why?* Even though the seafood had been cleared as the source of Joanna's poison, did Macy nonetheless think something Gideon had done might have brought about her mother's death? Was there some other reason? Or had I simply misinterpreted things, and she hadn't meant to be dismissive at all? She'd left Lane out of the conversation, too. *Hmm . . .*

I also considered how Joanna might have ingested mercury in a way that only she could be affected and not others. Might she have attempted to take her temperature when she'd been suffering the intense headache, and somehow inadvertently swallowed the mercury when the thermometer broke? It seemed she'd have been aware if that had happened, though. Maybe there'd simply been a small crack in the thermometer and some mercury had oozed out, and she hadn't realized it.

Curious, I made a detour to my parents' house. As an ear, nose, and throat specialist, my father probably didn't have an in-depth knowledge of poisons. Still, he'd done rotations back when he'd been in med school, and surely had learned some things about poisons then. He also golfed with his doctor buddies and might have heard things.

As I walked in the door, Yin-Yang skittered over to say hello. As before, I greeted the dog with a kiss on the head.

My parents looked up from the couch, where they'd been watching a legal drama.

My father stood and came over to give me a hug. My mother, who'd seen me just the day before, merely sat up on the couch. She grabbed the remote and tapped the button to pause their show. "Hey, hon. I didn't realize you were planning to stop by."

"I didn't, either," I said. "Not until a few minutes ago, anyway."

She ran her eyes over my dark, demure outfit. "Where have you been?"

"Memorial service for the woman who died at the fire station." I plopped down in an oversized chair and put my feet up on the ottoman. I turned to my father, who'd retaken his seat next to my mother on the couch. "What do you know about mercury poisoning, Dad?"

"Enough to fill a thimble," he replied.

"That might be all I need." I told him about Joanna, her symptoms, and what Macy had told me tonight. That she'd been poisoned by elemental mercury, not methyl-mercury. "I'm wondering if she might have tried to take her temperature when she had the bad headache the day she went to urgent care, or maybe if she tried after, before she came to the fire station. What would happen if the thermometer had broken on her and she swallowed the mercury?"

Dad sat up, looking thoughtful. "For starters, most people use digital infrared thermometers these days, not oral thermometers. Secondly, most oral thermometers these days don't contain mercury."

"They don't?"

"No. The old-fashioned mercury thermometers had a silver line, because that's the color of mercury. Today's oral thermometers generally contain alcohol, either ethanol or isopropanol. Red dye is added to make the temperature easier to read. The volume of the liquid changes with temperature, and that's how you get the reading. Heat makes the liquid expand."

Though he had a point in offering this information, he still hadn't answered my question. "But what if someone had an old mercury thermometer and happened to swallow the mercury? Would they get sick, or maybe even die?"

To my surprise, my dad said, "No. Swallowing mercury from a broken thermometer was actually a somewhat common occurrence back in the day, especially for children. Swallowing mercury poses virtually no health risk because it's not readily absorbed as it passes through the digestive system. Not by a healthy person, anyway. Ingesting mercury only poses a risk if someone has an unhealthy digestive system, such as someone who suffers from ulcerative colitis."

Did Joanna have a digestive issue? I had no idea. It wasn't exactly the type of thing normally discussed in polite company. "What if you touch mercury? Can it be absorbed through the skin and hurt you?"

"It would be unlikely," Dad said. "Only minute amounts are absorbed through healthy skin. But handling it could pose a health risk to those with a skin condition, such as psoriasis."

Had Joanna had such a condition? If such were the case, it seemed Macy might have mentioned it while we were talking earlier. I didn't recall noticing any lesions or patches on Joanna's skin.

My father went on. "You've heard the term *mad as a hatter*, haven't you?"

"Sure." I'd read *Alice in Wonderland* and *Through the Looking Glass* as a child—seen the Disney movie, too. The Mad Hatter had been an entertaining, though admittedly creepy, character. "What about it?"

"The reason hatters went mad was because they used a form of mercury to cure the felt they used to make their hats. When the mercury was heated, it released vapors that eventually affected their brains. Inhaling mercury is one of the ways it enters the body." My father picked up Yin-Yang and set her on the couch between him and my mother. "People are often exposed to poisons in their jobs. Where did the woman work?"

"She was retired," I said. "I'm not sure for how long, but judging from her age I'd guess two or three years. But she worked in manufacturing years ago."

"What kind of manufacturing?"

"I don't know."

"Places are much safer now than they used to be," Dad said. "People got exposed to all sorts of things decades ago, before the Occupational Safety and Health Administration was created. Sometimes they still do. OSHA imposes fines on companies when they find violations, but some CEOs just chalk up the penalties to the cost of doing business and don't make costly changes to ensure their workers' safety. Just look at the coal industry. Nearly every time there's a disaster, it turns out the coal company had received a series of citations but hadn't changed their practices."

I asked my father if checking for mercury poisoning was routine for someone suffering from headaches and dizziness.

"It definitely wouldn't be included in a routine preliminary test," he said. "If the symptoms persisted, a physician might eventually test for it, but there'd be any number of more common potential causes the doctor would want to rule out first."

My father went on to compare the practice of medicine to automotive repair. If the cause of a health problem wasn't immediately obvious, the doctors and mechanics had to troubleshoot, starting with the more likely causes and working their way forward step by step. It would be costly both in money and time to perform every diagnostic procedure right away. The potential causes were ruled out one by one.

In other words, it seemed that the doctor Joanna had seen at urgent care had likely followed standard protocols, and Macy might not have a case for malpractice against him. I wasn't sure how to feel. I was glad that I might not be dragged into an ugly lawsuit, but I felt terrible for Macy. It would be hard to know that the source of her mother's health problem could have been easily ascertained had the right test only been given and the correct lifesaving procedures administered.

I thanked my dad for the information and stood to go.

"Is that all you wanted from me?" my dad said, putting a hand over his heart as if I'd broken it. "Just some boring medical information?"

"Of course not," I replied. "I want a hug, too, before I go."

He gave me the hug and walked me to the door. My mother came with him and hugged me as well. I felt lucky to still have both of my parents. Macy was only a few years older than me, and she'd already lost both of hers.

When I arrived home, Sawdust and Cleo scampered to the door to greet me. I reached down to give each of them a scratch behind the ears.

Emmalee sat on a stool at the breakfast bar in the kitchen, poring over a college textbook. Her laptop sat next to it, along with a steaming mug of fresh coffee. She tossed a "hey" my way. Deep worry lines puckered the skin between her brows.

The cats followed me as I walked to the kitchen. "Cramming for your final?"

"Yes," she said on a sigh. "I don't know what I was thinking taking a summer class, especially history. Seems like we cover an entire century every day." She put her hands to her head, grabbing fistfuls of red hair in angst. "Argh! How am I supposed to remember all these dates and names and places?"

"You got this, Emmalee. You've memorized all the recipes for the café menu, right? That's a lot of details to remember."

My affirmation seemed to work. She lowered her hands and sat up straighter. The worry lines disappeared, too. "True. If I can remember to put a quarter teaspoon of onion powder in our slaw seasoning, I can remember that John Brown's raid took place in Harpers Ferry." She took a slug of coffee. "How was the memorial service?"

I gave her a rundown. Samira's accusation that Buck

and I were money-grubbers. The two Bottiglieri siblings who'd accosted us. The tense interaction between Macy and Lane. Macy's revelation that her mother had, in fact, died of mercury poisoning.

"Mercury?" Emmalee tapped her pen against her lips, thinking. "Where did it come from?"

"We don't know the source," I said. "At least, not yet." I hoped to come up with some ideas tonight.

After feeding the cats a handful of treats, I left Emmalee to her studies and went to my bedroom, where I kicked off the ballet-slipper flats and shed the simple black dress I'd worn to Joanna's memorial service. I rid myself of my bra, as well, and changed into a pair of comfy pajamas. Grabbing my laptop, I curled up on the sofa—a cat on each side of me—to do some studying of my own.

I logged on to peruse the worldwide web for more information about mercury. First, I searched for oral fever thermometers. Though the recommended models on various websites contained alcohol rather than mercury, oral thermometers containing mercury were still readily available, probably because the amount contained therein was small enough as to pose only minor risks to otherwise healthy people if swallowed. A typical mercury fever thermometer appeared to contain about 0.7 grams or 700 milligrams of mercury. Larger thermometers could contain substantially more. Scary, given that this link led me to another site that said a single gram of mercury was enough to pollute a twenty-acre lake. One site noted that advisories were commonly issued in states along the Great Lakes, warning of the high mercury content in fish.

I moved on to sites that provided information about mercury poisoning. They confirmed what my father had told me, that inhalation was a quick and effective way mercury could enter the body. I learned that it was a very bad idea to attempt to vacuum up a mercury spill, as it could break up the chemical and send it airborne, where a person might breathe it into their lungs. *Yikes.*

While I felt that I now knew quite a bit about the effects of mercury poisoning and the methods by which it could enter the body, I decided to learn more about sources of elemental mercury. If I learned about potential sources of mercury, maybe I could figure out how it had gotten into Joanna's system and help protect Macy and her baby. I also couldn't fight a niggling and growing feeling that maybe Joanna's death hadn't been accidental, that perhaps someone had slipped mercury to Joanna in one way or another.

My research provided some intriguing information. I learned that mercury is the only metal to remain in liquid form at room temperature, but that it easily vaporized. The fact that it could take several forms—solid, liquid, and vapor—made it especially difficult to manage. A pea-sized drop of liquid mercury would totally vaporize in just over a year. I also learned that mercury vapor is colorless and odorless, making it difficult to detect. What's more, mercury is heavier than water and should never be disposed of by pouring it down the drain, as it could become trapped in the pipes. One should never wash clothing that had come in contact with mercury, as doing so would release the mercury into the water and pose a health risk.

As for where mercury might be found, I discovered that it could come from any number of sources. Dental labs could be a source of mercury, as the metal comprised part of the silver amalgam used to fill cavities. Of course, just like thermometers had evolved to contain alcohol rather than mercury, fillings had evolved, too. These days a composite resin was more commonly used to fill teeth, and was preferred by many because it better matched the natural enamel and was less noticeable. Mercury was evidently an excellent conductor of electricity. The thermostats, sensors, switches, and relays in some HVAC systems contained mercury. My gut formed a hard ball when I read of an air-conditioner installer in Queens, New York, who had planted hundreds of beads of mercury in the ductwork in a family's home, after they'd made complaints. The family soon become very sick from a mysterious illness that was later identified as mercury poisoning. *Horrifying!*

But what gave me pause was a site that mentioned another potential source of mercury—switches used in cars manufactured before 2003, when mercury switches were phased out. There were even special handling procedures for mechanics to remove, store, and ship mercury switches for recycling of the metal.

You know who worked in auto salvage and might have access to old mercury switches?

Lane Hartzell, that's who.

CHAPTER 19

MEAN SCREENS

SAWDUST

The cat loved curling up on the couch with Whitney. She'd cuddle him, give him caresses and kisses. She'd been doing just that until a moment ago, when something on that bright screen she'd been looking at seemed to upset her. Then she'd taken her hand from the cat and retrieved her cell phone. Sawdust could hear the voice coming through and recognized it as belonging to Collin, the nice man who came to his and Whitney's house quite often, always smelling of Galileo and Copernicus. Sawdust wouldn't mind seeing more of those cats. He liked to have friends. He'd been lonely at home alone all day before Cleo had come along.

Sawdust sat on his haunches and stared at Whitney, attempting to will her into resuming her affectionate ministrations. When that failed, he reached out a paw and gently poked her in the arm. She didn't seem to notice. Much as he didn't want to upset the woman he adored, he'd have to escalate things to regain her attention.

Tail up, he walked across her lower thighs, between her kneecaps and the back of the open laptop computer. Leaning sideways, he rubbed along the computer. It closed part way. *Good.* He turned and was about to rub along it again, when Whitney pushed the screen back up. *He'd have to push harder this time.*

Rather than risk another failure, instead of merely rubbing along the back of the screen this time, he flopped over on it. The computer snapped shut. *Success! Hooray!*

"Sawdust!" Whitney cried, clearly unhappy with what he'd done. But when he offered a pathetic mew and rolled onto his back, exposing his belly, she couldn't resist. She reached down and scratched his chest. *Aaaah. Pure bliss.*

CHAPTER 20

FEELING NOSTALGIC

WHITNEY

On the phone with Collin late Tuesday night, I told him what my father had told me. I also told him what I'd found on the web. "I'm getting an eerie vibe. Do you think someone could have intentionally poisoned Joanna?"

Collin came back with, "Would someone have a reason to?"

"Maybe Lane killed her for the inheritance. He's admitted he was addicted to drugs, and drugs don't come cheap." In fact, people had done some pretty awful and desperate things in order to feed their addictions. Burglary. Robbery. Prostitution. Murder.

"He claimed he's clean now, right?"

"Yes," I said, "but Gideon didn't seem to believe him, and Gideon knows him much better than we do." I wondered if Macy, too, suspected he might not have kicked his habit. Maybe that's the real reason she didn't want him moving in with her and her family. "There's also several people interested in the townhouse Buck and I plan to fix up and flip. Samira and D-Jay want to buy it. Those meddling men. Gideon himself."

It was also possible one of the Bottiglieris had somehow poisoned Joanna. They were a vindictive bunch, obviously. Peter had been arrested for vandalizing our townhouse. Maybe he'd somehow put mercury in the place in the hope it would hurt or kill Buck and me, but somehow the mercury had ended up seeping into Joanna's place. We knew for a fact he'd been in the building, and the only thing separating our space from Joanna's was a few inches of boards and drywall. We hadn't spent extensive time in our townhouse since we'd bought it, so even if mercury was present there, it might not have had a chance to work its evil magic on Buck and me. But could it have somehow traveled into Joanna's place? It certainly seemed possible that, if there was mercury vapor in our place, it could have invaded her adjoining townhouse.

Collin was quiet for a moment. "I don't want to tell you you're wrong, because I've thought so before and ended up being wrong myself. So how about this? Let's wait and see what the water test and air test tell us. If they show that the source of mercury was either Joanna's tap water or the air in her townhouse, you'll let this go. If not, we'll talk about next steps."

It was hard to tell whether he'd suggested this because it was a solid, methodical approach, or because it would appease me for the time being. Maybe both. But I couldn't deny that the plan made sense. "Okay. Thanks for hearing me out."

If either the water test or air test came back positive, indicating that there was indeed mercury in Joanna's home, Buck and I would need to test our townhouse as well. Until the test results were returned, I figured it was best for us to stay out of the place. Maybe it had actually been a good thing that I'd changed the door code and prevented Samira, D-Jay, and Kavish from entering the place. I might have unwittingly protected the three of them, and Samira's unborn child, as well.

Collin and I said good night and ended the call. I put my phone down and picked my cat up, cradling him to my chest. "What do you think, Sawdust? Do you think Joanna is another murder victim?"

He issued a mew, which could be taken either way.

"You're no help, kitty." I gave him a kiss on the cheek. "But I love you anyway."

On my way to the fire station Wednesday morning, I made a quick stop at the building supply store for specialized masks rated to filter out mercury vapors. No sense taking a chance. We'd wear the masks if we had to go into the townhouse for any reason.

On Wednesday and Thursday, Buck and I finished installing the drywall on the divider walls, and started a process called mudding to fill in the seams and indentations with a wet paste to smooth it out. The mud would need some time to dry before we could sand it. While it set, Buck and I installed the new countertops in the bathrooms. Owen came by to help Buck with the new bathroom fixtures. I was glad he had time to assist us. Moving heavy fixtures could be dangerous and, while I was strong enough to do it in a pinch, I'd much rather defer to someone with bigger biceps. Besides, Owen had three young girls. He could use the extra pay we'd give him.

While the men worked upstairs, I gathered up a variety of cleaning supplies and a scrub brush. I also gathered up Sawdust, who'd mewed incessantly at the door that morning, letting me know he wanted to come to work with me today. I put his harness and leash on him, and headed down to the garage bay. Though September was rapidly approaching, it was still August and warm in the bay. I raised the roll-up garage door a couple of feet, high enough to allow for air circulation, but low enough that someone couldn't just walk in. We'd had more than enough people trespassing at our properties lately.

After attaching the end of Sawdust's leash to the fireman's pole so he couldn't roam off, I donned my knee pads, filled a bucket with warm water, and got down on my hands and knees to scrub the oil stains off the concrete. Because Collin and I would be holding our wedding ceremony in this space, I planned to paint the floors with a textured, slip-resistant decorative coating so that it would look more finished. The oil stains had likely existed for years, and this task could very well be a futile effort but, even if I could only lighten them a little bit, it could mean one less coat of paint.

I was on my knees scrubbing hard, when a male voice came from under the bay door behind me. "You trying to get rid of oil stains?"

I turned to see three sets of feet and three angled faces peering under the door. The umarells were back. *Ugh*.

Before I could even respond, one said, "That abrasive cleanser won't cut it. What you want to use is dish soap. It's made to fight grease."

His friend disagreed. "No, what she ought to use is a tea kettle of boiling water. The heat will break up the oil."

"Hydrogen peroxide," said the third. "That's the only way to go."

Behind the men, a maroon Saturn sedan cruised

slowly by on the far side of the street. The rosary hanging from the rearview mirror glinted in the sunlight. Judith Bottiglieri sat at the wheel, looking over at the men. A teenage boy with shaggy hair and a surly expression sat in the passenger seat, leaning forward to eye the fire station. *Is that her grandson? The one who allegedly torched the firehouse?*

Judith's eyes met mine and snapped wide. She turned her head back to the road and punched the gas, her tires squealing for a second or two before the car roared off. *Had she and the boy been casing the fire station, planning another act of vandalism?* I could only hope the security cameras Buck had installed on the exterior would deter them from any further attempts to destroy the property. As much as I didn't want to reward Judith or Peter after they'd damaged our property, I wondered whether Buck, Presley, and I should go ahead and pay the Bottiglieri siblings the additional five-hundred dollars they'd demanded to put them on equal footing with what we'd paid their brother John. I wondered if doing so would put an end to the conflict, get them to back off.

I barely had time to entertain the thought when the upstairs door swung open and Buck trotted down the steps. "I'm out of mud. Is there any more down here?"

"Over there." I pointed to a premixed four-and-a-half-gallon tub that sat behind the boxes of bathroom tile.

One of the men chimed in under the door. "That premixed stuff is no good. You should buy the powdered kind and mix it yourself."

Buck took one look their way, turned, and aimed for the wall. He slammed the heel of his palm on the green Start button and the alarm rang out so loud I felt it through my entire body, the sound echoing in the enclosed space. I dropped my scrub brush and grabbed

Sawdust, clutching him to my chest and putting a hand over his exposed ear to muffle the sound. The meddlers yanked their heads back, which was Buck's goal. He jabbed the button to lower the bay door before hitting the Stop button to turn off the alarm. He gave his head a hard shake, as if to clear the ringing in his ears. "If those men give us one more piece of unsolicited advice, I'm going to spackle their mouths shut."

We heard the men talking on the other side of the door.

"That was uncalled for! We were only trying to help," one voice said.

"Some people just can't take criticism," another muttered.

"Let's go over to that townhouse on Van Buren Street," said the third. "Those guys sure could use our help. I saw one of them using a carriage bolt on the fence when a simple wood screw would do. Can you believe it?"

Sheesh. They'd accused me and Buck of not being able to take criticism, but they were unable to take a hint. Their advice, however well-meaning, was insulting and annoying.

Buck grabbed the tub of drywall mud and headed back upstairs. With the bay door closed now, it would be safe to let Sawdust roam about untethered. I unclipped him from his leash, and he strode forward a few steps, his tail swishing as he stopped to survey the bay and decide which part to explore first.

As Sawdust sniffed about the edges of the room, I finished scrubbing the first oil spot and moved on to another closer to the pole. Sawdust strutted over and sat down just outside the edge of the puddle formed by the soapy water. He stretched out a paw and gently touched the bubbles along the perimeter. He held his paw up to his face to examine them for a moment, like a feline detective looking over a clue, then flicked the bubbles aside.

After cleaning the second spot, I sat back on my heels on the floor. Sawdust stood and took a few steps before stopping and staring down intently at the concrete. *What's caught his attention?* Even when I squinted, I saw nothing there but a few specks of dust that had either been tracked in on our boots or blown in under the door. He reached out a paw to gently bat at the item. It rolled a few inches toward me, visible now. It was a tiny, shiny silver ball, hardly bigger than one of the round rainbow sprinkles commonly dashed onto ice cream or cookies. I never would have noticed it myself, but with Sawdust scouting around on the floor, he'd spotted it right away.

Where did that ball bearing come from? I'd swept the garage thoroughly before we'd brought in our supplies and materials to keep everything as clean and tidy as possible. I'd hosed out the space with a high-pressure water hose attachment, too. *Hmm . . .*

Sawdust gingerly batted the shiny little ball again, and it rolled a few more inches toward me. Some power tools contained ball bearings but, to do the job they were intended to do, the ball bearings were meant to stay inside the tools. *Has one of our tools been damaged? Did the ball bearing come out of it?* It seemed unlikely. We hadn't used power tools inside the bay. We'd used our power saws to cut the reclaimed flooring boards, but we'd set up out in the parking lot to perform that task, and the tools had worked perfectly. Regardless of where the ball bearing had come from, there was no sense in leaving it on the floor, where we might accidentally paint over it, leaving a tiny bump on the surface.

Sawdust watched closely as I crawled over on my hands and knees, and reached out to pick up the ball bearing. No easy feat in latex gloves. The darn thing slipped out of my grip and rolled a few inches away. I tried again to pinch it between my thumb and forefinger to no avail. Yanking off the slick gloves, I tried a third time with my bare hand. That's when I realized why the silver sphere had been so hard to pick up. It wasn't a solid ball bearing at all. Rather, it was a malleable liquid metal. *A tiny drop of quicksilver, liquid mercury.*

My heart leapt into my throat and I scrambled backward, startling Sawdust, who skittered off to hide behind my toolbox. Though a single, tiny bead in such a large space was unlikely to cause me or my cat any harm, the scary things I'd read while researching the toxic stuff nevertheless had me in a panic.

I rounded up Sawdust, secured him in his carrier, and placed it by the door, which I opened to allow fresh air to circulate. My beloved pet now safe, I ran over to the stack of supplies and grabbed one of the respirator masks I'd purchased, the ones that could filter out mercury vapors. After ripping it from the packaging and putting it on, I returned to the spot where the bead lay on the floor and knelt down to process the situation. I stared at the shiny bead, its smooth surface reflecting the blue of my coveralls. *Where had the little bead come from?*

The oil spot I'd just scrubbed nearby reminded me that an ambulance used to park in this bay alongside the fire truck. Could one of the paramedics have dropped a thermometer? It seemed possible. Maybe it had broken and released the liquid mercury. *But how long would mercury stick around? Hadn't I read something about it vaporizing while I was researching last night?* Yes, I had. I recalled that a pea-sized drop would vaporize in just over a year. This fire station had sat empty and unused for several years. There's no way a drop of mercury from a medic's broken thermometer would still be in liquid form here. The metal must have found its way onto the floor more recently.

I glanced around. There on the floor, only a few feet away, was the butt of the cigarette that Joanna had been smoking when she'd entered the bay last week, shortly before collapsing. The butt was squashed flat from my having ground it out with my boot. The second cigarette that she'd shaken from her pack and attempted to light also lay nearby, surrounded by a scattering of dry tobacco flakes. The tobacco shouldn't have fallen out of the cigarette to that extent. Clearly, it hadn't been packed well. Someone in quality control at the cigarette factory had really dropped the ball.

Dropped the ball . . .

I stared at the eerie relics for a moment, again experiencing that niggling feeling in the back of my mind that there was something to be gleaned from this tiny, shiny sphere, as if it were an itty-bitty crystal ball. *Oh, no!* I gasped inside the mask as I had a horrifying epiphany. My father had mentioned that the mad hatters had inhaled mercury vapors, and I'd read that inhaling mercury was the most common method of mercury poisoning. While the vapor from a small bead of mercury would dissipate in a large space, if the vapor were directly sucked into a person's lungs it could probably cause real damage, even death. *Had someone inserted the tiny bead of mercury into Joanna's cigarette so that she'd inhale the colorless, odorless vapors as she smoked? If so, who?*

My first thought went back to Lane and his job at the auto salvage yard. *Could he have obtained the mercury from a pre-2003 switch?* Lane smoked Newports, the same brand of cigarettes as Joanna. It seemed it would have been easy for him to sneak an adulterated pack into her home. All he'd have had to do was stop by for a visit, and leave the pack behind somewhere. Joanna might not even realize it wasn't her own, or even if she realized the cigarettes belonged to Lane, she might smoke them anyway. But had he been in her house recently?

I'd seen Gideon with a pack of Newports, too, of course. He'd carried them from his place across the street, and left them on the table on Joanna's porch rather than turning them over to her directly. *Why would he have done that? Why wouldn't he have knocked on the door to give them to her?* After all, he saw the woman nearly every day. They regularly viewed the soap opera together. He could have returned the pack to her when he came over to watch the show with her. *Hmm . . .*

Samira and D-Jay had handled Joanna's cigarettes, too. When we'd moved Macy, Holden, Alyssa, and the moppy dog into Joanna's townhouse last Saturday, Samira and D-Jay had showed up, offering to help. They'd stuck around even after seeing that there were several others already recruited and assisting with the move. Samira had aimed straight for Joanna's pantry and started tossing things out. *Had she known that Joanna stored her cigarettes there? Had she thrown out incriminating evidence under the guise of cleaning out the pantry?*

I pulled out my cell phone and placed a call to Collin. My call was sent immediately to voicemail. *Ugh!*

The nature of his work as a homicide detective meant he was often interviewing witnesses or examining evidence, and wasn't always immediately available. Maybe he'd caught a break in his double homicide case. I left a voicemail. "Hey, Collin. Call me when you can. I've found evidence that Joanna was murdered with mercury, like I'd thought." *I really hadn't wanted to be right about this.* "Judith Bottiglieri and her grandson drove by earlier, too." *Could the two things be related somehow?*

As I sat there, drawing breath through my heavy-duty plastic mask, I mulled things over. Sitting still and doing nothing was not my style. I was a woman of action. I wanted answers about Joanna's murder, and I wanted them now. The potential suspects could possibly give me some answers, but who should I contact first?

Lane seemed to work irregular shifts for the salvage yard, and I didn't have his address. He could be anywhere in the city right now. Samira and D-Jay were at work, and I wasn't about to bother them at their places of employment when, as of yet, my suspicions were only speculative. But, as a retired man with no family, Gideon was likely to be home.

I snapped several photos of the cigarettes and the bead of mercury with my phone, and texted them to Collin. I found a hex bolt in my toolbox, removed the nut, and placed it over the drop of mercury to prevent it from rolling away. I then grabbed Sawdust's carrier and took it upstairs, where I informed Buck and Owen of my discovery, showed them the photos I'd taken, and warned them not to disturb what was very likely a crime scene. I filled them in on my findings and speculated who might have killed Joanna.

Owen gaped. Though he'd helped us before on projects where someone had been found murdered, this was the first time he'd been around when things heated up. Meanwhile, Buck set down his faucet wrench and ran his fingers over his beard. Like me, this wasn't his first rodeo when it came to suspicious deaths. "You think Gideon might have tampered with her cigarettes? Why?"

"He expressed interest in buying the townhouse after we remodel it, remember? He knew I'd given Joanna the right of first refusal. The only way he'd have the chance to buy the place was if he got her out of the way."

Buck looked doubtful. "You think he'd kill her just to buy a piece of real estate?"

"Why not?" I shrugged. "People kill for less." Besides, people who committed premeditated murder weren't generally rational. They justified their actions to themselves somehow. The rest of us would only kill in immediate self-defense or defense of another. "Remember what Lane said? That Joanna hadn't exactly welcomed Gideon and her partner to the neighborhood when they moved in? He must have sensed that she wasn't happy about a gay couple living nearby. Maybe he's harbored resentment over it."

"But that was years ago," Buck said. "Lane said his mother got over it. Joanna and Gideon were good friends."

He had a point. Even so, maybe Gideon had some other reason to kill Joanna that we weren't aware of. It certainly seemed he had the means to kill her, even if, as yet, we didn't have a compelling motive for him to do so. "That old thermometer he has on his porch? The one advertising Dad's Old Fashioned Root Beer? It's broken. The mercury is gone."

Buck's eyes narrowed. "How do you know that?"

"After we stopped at Gideon's place, while you were carrying Colette's risotto over to the Griffins' unit, I noticed it was hanging crooked and I stopped to straighten it." The large sign hadn't been askew the first time I'd spotted it. As someone who religiously used a level to make sure things were straight, I'm sure I would've noticed. It wasn't until a few days later that the promotional sign had become askew. "I looked closely at it to see what the temperature was, but there was no silver line." I went on to tell him what my father had told me, that many thermometers made today contained alcohol rather than mercury. "You can still get mercury thermometers online, though. Probably in some drugstores, too. But an online purchase can be easily traced, and a security camera in a store would record someone coming in to buy a mercury thermometer. There'd be some hard evidence pointing to the killer. It still seems that the root beer sign could have been the source."

Buck cocked his head. "You want to go talk to him?"

"I do." As I said the words, I realized I'd be repeating them here in a few months when I pledged my love and fidelity to Collin on our wedding day. Of course, when I said the words then, it would be for a happy reason, to begin my life with Collin, not to investigate the end of someone else's life.

Owen appeared uncomfortable, his face contorting in a cringe. "You two are just going to march over there and accuse the guy of killing the woman who was supposedly his best friend? What if you're wrong?"

He had a point. We'd look like a couple of major jerks if we mistakenly accused Gideon—or anyone else, for that matter.

"We need a guise," I said, "some reason to ask

Gideon about the root beer thermometer." It took only a few seconds for an idea to pop into my head. "We're going with a nostalgic feel here, right? Leaning into this building's history as a fire station? Maybe I can ask him where he got the thermometer under the guise that I want to find similar kitschy things to decorate the firehouse before we put it on the market. I can ask him when and where he got the thermometer, and how it broke. We can assess how he responds."

"Works for me," Buck said.

Owen raised his palms and took a step back. "Count me out. I got a wife and kids at home. I don't need to go around antagonizing a possible killer."

Owen remained at the station with Sawdust, while Buck and I moved quickly down the stairs and exited the building. We strode around the corner, down the block, and onto Gideon's porch. Buck stepped over to take a look at the root beer sign, while I knocked on Gideon's door.

The door opened, and Gideon stood there, looking disheveled in a wrinkled white undershirt, rumpled plaid shorts, and a pair of slippers, no socks. A couple days' growth created a salt-and-pepper shadow across his face and neck. He appeared absolutely distraught. But was it because he'd lost his best friend, or was it because he'd killed her? Was I looking at a man overcome by grief or by guilt?

In order to answer that question, I peppered him with a series of questions. "Hi, Gideon. We normally stage our properties when we put them on the market. I'd noticed your old root beer sign." I pointed down the porch, where Buck stood in front of the sign. "We'd like to find some nostalgic decorative items like that. Can you tell me where you got it?"

Leaving his door open, he took a step out onto the porch. "That sign belonged to my partner. He got it from his grandfather, who ran a full-service gas station back when there still were full-service stations in the South. Y'all are probably too young to remember that time."

We were. As far as I could recall, we'd always had to pump our own gas here in Nashville, but it sure would be nice to have an attendant pump the gas for you on a rainy, windy, or hot day like today, or when you were dressed up and didn't want to get dirty.

Buck pointed to the thermometer. "I'm not getting a reading. Is the thermometer broken?"

"Not as far as I know." A V formed on Gideon's heavy browbone as he shuffled down the porch to take a look for himself. He leaned in, squinting and bobbing his head to and fro, like a bird. "You're right, Buck. I don't think it's working. I'll be damned." He reached out and gently removed the sign from the nail it hung on. He turned it over and inspected the thermometer attached to the back of it. "The glass looks like it's been broke." He peered down at the porch as if looking for glass fragments. "I wonder when it happened."

"You don't know?" I asked.

"No." He shook his head, again visually examining the oversized thermometer. "Last I checked, it was still showing the temperature." He looked up at me now, his gaze meeting mine. "That's probably been years ago, though, now that I think about it. If I want to know the outside temperature these days, I just check my phone."

I glanced down at the porch and saw no telltale sparkle of broken glass, either. Of course, if the thermometer had broken recently, any debris could've been swept up. I prodded him further. "Did you ever come out here and find the sign off the nail? Maybe it fell off at some point and that's when it broke."

He pondered the idea for a moment, then slowly shook his head. "I don't recall this sign ever falling off the wall. I think I'd remember if it did, because my partner was very attached to this rusty old thing. He worked at his grandfather's gas station when he was young. He had some fond memories of the man, said they both loved Dad's Old Fashioned Root Beer, drank case after case of it. That's how they got the sign, from placing a large order of root beer for the gas station." Going back to our purported purpose for being here, to find out where I might find pieces of Americana for sale, Gideon said, "You can find things like this in antique shops here and there. I bet there'd be some for sale on the internet, too."

"Good ideas," I said. "Thanks, Gideon." Shifting gears, I turned to the matter of the cigarettes I'd seen him carry over to Joanna's townhouse. "By the way, I saw you take a pack of Newports to Joanna's place early last week. Do you smoke that brand, too?"

"No," he said. "I came out here to enjoy my morning coffee and spotted the pack on the porch rail there." He gestured to a spot in the center of the porch he shared with the Griffins' unit next door. "I figured Joanna must've accidentally left them there when she came over to check on her daughter. Macy won't let her smoke in their house. It was odd, though. She always carries her cigarettes and lighter together, but she'd only left the pack of cigarettes." His brows formed another V, though this one was less deep. "Why?"

I shrugged. "Just thought it was a coincidence that you two might smoke the same brand."

"Not me," he said. "I've only smoked three cigarettes

in my life and each one made me sicker than the last. I didn't like the taste, either. Might as well chew on an old whitewall tire."

I cocked my head. "Can I ask you something, Gideon?"

He issued a soft snort. "When someone says that, they're asking permission to be nosey." He wasn't wrong. He cocked his head, too, his eyes narrowing. "What is it you want to know?"

I felt uncomfortable raising the issue, but I felt that it had to be addressed. "Lane mentioned at the memorial that Joanna had concerns when you and your partner moved into the neighborhood. You must've been aware of her feelings."

Gideon straightened his head. "That's not a question. That's a statement." He and I stared at each other for a long moment before he spoke again. "I could tell she wasn't happy about it. She wasn't alone in her thinking, either. But once she realized I was a good sort, she came around. So did the others."

"You didn't harbor any ill will against her?"

"It's hard to be angry at someone who's learned their lesson." He gave me a dismissive nod, letting me know the subject was closed, and turned to Buck. "I've washed your dish." He went back to his door and reached inside to retrieve it. He held the serving dish out to Buck. "Please tell your wife I enjoyed her risotto."

"Will do," Buck said, taking the dish from him.

With that, Gideon stepped back into his townhouse and shut the door on us.

Buck and I headed back to the fire station.

"What do you think?" he asked.

"If someone intentionally poisoned Joanna with mercury, it wasn't him." The poor guy was a wreck.

"That's what I think, too. He seems so lonely now."

But if it wasn't Gideon who'd killed Joanna, then who? Could the pack of Newports Gideon found on the porch have belonged to Lane? Or might Lane have left them there, knowing whoever found them would assume they were Joanna's and take them to her?

I put my mask back on and finished scrubbing the oil stains. They refused to disappear entirely, but at least they were much less noticeable once I finished. As Sawdust and I left for the day, I cast a glance back at the nut on the floor, the one keeping the tiny drop of mercury corralled. Where had it originated? Who had sneaked it into Joanna's cigarette? *If only that drop could talk. . . .*

CHAPTER 21

BARREL OF FUN

WHITNEY

I spent Thursday evening in my garage at home. Thanks to the barrel I'd picked up at the Jack Daniel's distillery, my entire garage smelled like it had been soaked in liquor. Sawdust had followed me from the house into the garage. The whiskey barrel was something new he hadn't seen before. As curious cats are wont to do, he'd sauntered over to check it out. He stopped a few feet back, blinking his eyes against the alcohol fumes emanating from the wood. He gingerly stretched his nose forward, his whiskers twitching as he sniffed. He jerked his head back in what could best be described as a kitty cringe, turned, and skittered off, trying to put as much distance between himself and the stinky barrel as possible in the confined space.

While Sawdust perched atop a lawn chair in the corner to watch me, I sawed the whiskey barrel in half lengthwise. I set one half aside and moved the other from the sawhorses to the workbench, where I proceeded to sand the edges and interior by hand.

Tiny wood particles flew, but my eyes were protected by plastic goggles and my lungs by a mask. It was a thin paper dust mask variety rather than the heavy-duty vapor-proof one I'd worn earlier at the fire station, but the simple accessory did its job of keeping the wood dust out of my nose and mouth. As I moved my hand back and forth over the whiskey-soaked wood, sanding the rough surface down to a smooth finish, I contemplated the list of Joanna's possible killers.

I'd feel terrible if the Bottiglieris had brought about her death, because it would mean that her murder had been instigated by me and Buck buying the townhouse. After all, the Bottiglieris had ignored Joanna for years. *Or had they?* I didn't recall the exact words we'd exchanged with each of the seven siblings when Buck, Presley, and I had gone to their homes to offer them money in exchange for the quitclaim deeds, but I was nearly certain I'd mentioned to one or two of them that it was Joanna who'd initially brought the townhouse to our attention. Peter had been angry enough to paint the word *theives* on the walls and cabinets, and someone else, presumably Judith, had been behind the fire at the fire station. These were not normal, reasonable people. They might blame Joanna for what transpired, felt that they'd lost the house because of her actions. Maybe they'd wanted vengeance. The more I thought about it, the more likely it seemed that a Bottiglieri was to blame, and that the Bottiglieri was probably Peter. After all, he'd been in the building when he'd vandalized our townhouse. It wasn't a stretch to think he might have somehow been able to get a tainted pack of cigarettes into Joanna's hands.

Still, when I mentally backed off and thought of the situation in more general terms, another potential suspect came to mind. Mothers-in-law were known to be over-bearing, and Joanna had clearly been no exception. If she was willing to chastise her daughter and son-in-law right in front of us, calling Holden stupid right to his face, what other derogatory things had she said to him over the years? Besides, the Griffins' unit in Gideon's building had been quite small and cramped compared to Joanna's four-bedroom townhouse, and would have been more crowded once the baby arrived. Maybe Holden realized that, if he got rid of Joanna, his wife would inherit her unit and they could move in and live much more comfort-ably in the larger space.

Something came back to me then, something I'd heard Joanna say but to which I had given little thought at the time. When Joanna had expressed concern about the family's financial stability now that Macy would have to take time off from her work as a hairdresser, Macy had assured her mother that they were fine. Jo-anna had replied with a suspicious phrase—*that's what you think*. She hadn't elaborated, and the conversation moved on without a clarification. *What had she meant when she'd said that to Macy?*

A realization struck me. My hand froze mid-swipe inside the barrel, the coarse-grade sandpaper clutched in my fingers. I'd all but forgotten in the hubbub that followed, but when Joanna had collapsed at the fire station and I'd gone to Gideon's for help in reaching Holden, Gideon had first tried Holden's cell phone. When he'd been unable to reach Holden on his mobile device, Gideon had placed a call to the cold storage fa-cility where Holden worked, only to be told that Holden wasn't there. It had been nearly two o'clock, too late in the day for a typical lunch break. Gideon had let them know the situation was dire, an emergency. If Holden had been somewhere on the premises taking a coffee break or a bathroom break, surely they could have located him and gotten him on the phone. *Holden hadn't been there, had he?* But why not? And where had he been instead? He'd been wearing a uniform for Frozen Freight Carriers when he and Macy had come to Joanna's to inform her that Macy was expecting. Had he later left his job for one reason or another? Had he quit? Been fired? Had the job given him access to mercury?

Leaving the barrel behind, I went back into the house, my sweet kitty padding along behind me. I ran a quick search on the internet and learned that commercial freezers often contained mercury. In fact, the light switches had to be removed as potential sources of toxic chemicals before any remaining metal could be recycled. The article also mentioned the chlorofluorocarbons and hydrochlorofluorocarbons that had been traditionally used in refrigerants until it was discovered that the chemicals depleted Earth's ozone layer. While certainly worrisome, I was trying to solve a woman's murder here, not the world's climate crisis, so I focused on the parts of the post that dealt with mercury. It seemed clear that Holden had access to mercury on his job. But had he obtained mercury there? If he had, did it have something to do with why he hadn't been on site the day Joanna had collapsed and Gideon had tried to call him at work?

It was after regular business hours now, but I knew what I'd be doing the instant the clock struck eight the following morning. I'd be making a phone call to Frozen Freight Carriers.

I had a hard time sleeping Thursday night, worrying and wondering whether Holden might have murdered his mother-in-law so that he could move his family into her house. My mind was also active trying to come up with a ruse for calling the company. Fortunately, by Friday morning, I'd come up with one I figured might work.

I didn't want to catch management right when they arrived at work and would be harried, trying to catch up on late-arriving emails from the day before and getting things going for the day. Thus, I began work at the firehouse and waited until half past nine to call Frozen Freight, shushing Buck before placing the call. Unlike Gideon, who'd asked to be transferred to the warehouse, I asked to speak with human resources.

"Good morning," I said. "I'm Amana DeWalt." I'd come up with the name during the wee hours of the night. It was a combination of two major tool brands. *It sounded so much more convincing at three o'clock in the morning.* "I've got a job applicant who works for your company and I need to verify employment dates." If I was off base here and Holden was still employed by Frozen Freight, I certainly hoped my call wouldn't jeopardize his job. With Macy pregnant and Alyssa poised to head off for college in a year, they'd need the income.

The woman on the phone asked, "What's the name of the employee?"

"Holden Griffin." For good measure, I spelled it as well. "G-R-I-F-F-I-N." I put the phone on speaker, and Buck and I stared each other down as we waited for a response.

"Got it." She paused for a second or two. "A long-term employee, I see."

Did that mean he was still employed at the cold storage company? Her phrasing wasn't clear.

She gave us his beginning date, which was years

before. But then she dropped a bombshell. "His employment ended on July second."

The day that Macy and Holden had come to Joanna's place, when Buck and I had first seen them, had been August tenth, more than a month after his employment terminated, yet he'd still been wearing his Frozen Freight Carriers uniform. I suppose at that point it qualified as a costume rather than a uniform given that he was only pretending to still be employed by the company.

It took everything in me not to shout "Aha!" Instead, I threw a silent finger in the air in an aha motion. "Thank you," I said. "That's all I need."

Once the call had disconnected, I said, "Holden's been lying. To his wife. To Gideon."

"But he didn't lie to Joanna," Buck said.

"Maybe he tried, but she somehow figured it out." He must not have a new job, or there'd have been no reason for her to say *that's what you think* in response to Macy assuring her they were doing fine, monetarily speaking. I wondered if his termination could have anything to do with Joanna's death. *Could he have been caught tampering with the machinery, trying to extract mercury?*

I walked to a window, but a tree blocked my view of the Griffins' unit. I rushed downstairs and outside, circling the corner. Sure enough, Holden's pickup was nowhere to be seen. But where he'd gone each day while pretending to be at work was a mystery. What's more, with today being a Friday, the mystery couldn't be solved until Monday. *Argh!*

Collin came by the fire station later that morning, between handling paperwork at the police station and a visit to the county jail to interrogate a suspect they'd arrested in the double homicide. I was wearing my vapor-proof mask when I opened the door to let him in.

Collin took one look at me and laughed. "You look like a bug."

I frowned inside the device. "Thanks a lot."

"A *cute* bug," he clarified.

Buck was working upstairs and didn't need his vapor-proof mask at the moment, so I handed his to Collin as he walked into the bay.

Once he'd slid it on and strapped it firmly in place, I led him over and bent down next to the hex nut.

I donned a pair of disposable gloves and lifted it. "See?"

Collin leaned in so far he nearly face-planted on the cement. The mask muffled his voice when he spoke. "That tiny thing is mercury?"

"Yep." I touched the silver ball with the tip of my gloved finger to show him that it was malleable.

"And you think it fell out of Joanna's cigarette?"

"Yep," I repeated, pointing at the cigarette and loose tobacco a couple of feet away.

Crouching, he took a closer look, his gaze shifting between the bead of quicksilver, the cigarette, and the butt. "It's an intriguing theory, one definitely worth pursuing." He looked up at me. "I'm very impressed, Whitney. Not many people would have even noticed the bead of mercury, let alone put it together that it might have fallen out of the cigarette."

"Sawdust found the bead," I said, giving credit where credit was due. "I never would have noticed it myself." My kitty was quite the crime solver. "But I will take credit for putting the cigarette theory together." I beamed with pride. I'd come up with what could be a critical clue. *Woo-hoo!*

Collin stood. "Don't mention this to anyone outside of your inner circle, okay? We don't want this getting out before I have a chance to interview everyone."

"Understood." I waved my finger around, pointing at the pieces of evidence on the floor. "This isn't all, though. There's been another development." I told him about my call to Frozen Freight Carriers earlier that morning.

His brows arched ever so slightly behind the clear plastic shield. "That could mean something, maybe." He backed toward the bay door, where he removed the mask. "The double homicide is going to keep me tied up for the next few days, unfortunately. In fact, I'm going to have to cancel our date tonight. Sorry about that. There's a witness who's finally agreed to talk to us, but we have to wait until after his work hours. It's likely to be a long interrogation."

I sighed. I was disappointed, but I knew his work was important and had to come first. "We're still on for dinner at the Collection Plate tomorrow night, though, right?"

"For sure." His lips curved in a grin. "Can't let you make such a big decision without me."

Colette had asked Collin and me to dinner at her café with her and Buck. She planned to have cake samples for us to taste so that we could choose a flavor for our wedding cake. I could hardly wait to savor the various options she and Emmalee had come up with.

Collin placed the mask atop the steps that led to the upper floor. "As soon I get the double homicide wrapped up, I'll talk to Holden."

"Okay," I agreed, knowing all the while that I would never be able to wait a few days to get more information. I simply couldn't. I was like a cat, and my curiosity must be satisfied. I walked over to join him near the door. "You'll want to talk to Gideon, and Samira and D-Jay, too. Also Lane." I told him how I'd seen Gideon carry the pack of Newports over to Joanna's porch and leave them, how Samira and D-Jay had thrown out cartons of cigarettes from Joanna's pantry, and how Lane smoked the same brand and could presumably sneak an adulterated pack into Joanna's supply, perhaps by leaving a contaminated pack on Macy's porch.

His brows lifted. "Five suspects? I'll have my work cut out for me."

"That's not even including the Bottiglieris. They could've seen Joanna smoking her Newports and slipped her a tainted pack, as well."

Collin gave me a pointed look. "Be careful, Whitney. If someone murdered Joanna, they might be willing to kill again to cover it up."

"Don't worry. I'll be extra vigilant." I took his hands in mine, giving them a squeeze. "After all," I teased, "I've got those cake samples to live for."

He snorted a soft laugh, reached out, and lifted my mask, giving me a warm kiss before heading out the door.

I worked late at the fire station Friday evening, alone. Buck had gone home to be with Colette, but with Collin having to cancel our date, I had nothing better to do.

It was nearly ten o'clock and fully dark outside when I exited the building. Few cars were on the street as I made my way west toward Interstate 65. As I sat at a red light, a vehicle pulled up behind me. I hadn't paid it much mind until the driver turned on the high-beam headlights. They lit up my car, and the reflection in my rearview mirror was nearly blinding. *Had they activated the high beams by accident and not been aware of it?*

As soon as the light turned green, I started out, put on my left-turn signal, and changed lanes so that the high beams wouldn't be directly behind me. I drove slow so that the car could go past. Except it didn't. After I changed lanes, it changed lanes, too, still directly behind me and much too close for comfort. *Ugh.* I wasn't sure whether the driver might be impaired, or whether they were intentionally harassing me. *One way to find out.*

Without signaling this time, I made another quick lane change. Momentum carried the car up next to my back left fender before the driver braked and moved over behind me again. The bright beams made it impossible for me to see what type of car it was, though the fact that the headlights sat low told me it wasn't a truck or SUV.

A frisson of fear moved up my spine. Whoever was behind me now must have been casing the fire station, waiting for me to leave. *Could it be Judith in her Saturn? Maybe her grandson? One of the other Bottiglieris? Somebody else entirely?*

Not knowing their intentions, I wasn't sure what to do. If I slowed to a near crawl, would it make it easier for them to launch a personal attack or damage my car, if that was their plan? If I sped away and they pursued me at high speed, would I put innocent people—including myself—in danger?

Over the time we'd dated, Collin had shared personal safety tips with me. He'd told me that if a person suspected they were being followed, the best thing they could do was to drive to a police station if there was one around, or to a busy, well-lit area. The pursuer would be

less likely to commit a criminal act where there would
be witnesses. He said it was also a good idea to draw attention to your vehicle. If there was anything criminals
didn't like, it was attention.

Maintaining a safe speed, I activated my warning flashers and laid on my horn. Unfortunately, there
were few people around to see the lights or hear the
honking. Rather than heading on to I-65 as I'd originally intended, I made a turn to the south, aiming for the
bustling South Broadway area. As yet undeterred, the
vehicle continued to trail me with its high beams on,
though it had backed off a few feet.

Luckily, I caught most traffic lights on my way south,
and in just two minutes arrived in SoBro. The flash of
my warning lights was lost among the neon lights of
the honky-tonks. As I sat at a red light, the high beams
still on behind me, a bicycle bar passed by on the cross
street in front of my SUV. The seats were filled with
tourists in various stages of sobriety, all of them hoot-
ing and hollering and having a good old time. Lest one
of them turn and fall off their seat, I refrained from
honking my horn again.

When the light turned green, the driver of the pickup
next to me hesitated as a couple of stragglers finished
crossing the street. I whipped over into the adjacent lane,
cutting the truck off before it could get moving, and
hooked a quick turn. The truck rolled forward, preventing the car in pursuit from changing lanes and coming
after me. It also prevented me from getting a look at the
vehicle, blocking the image in my rearview mirror. But
I'd gotten away—for now, at least.

As I drove home, I debated whether to call the police to report the incident. With the car no longer behind
me, and having no description of the vehicle, I decided

it was a moot point. I had to wonder, though, what the driver's intentions had been. Had they only been trying to unnerve me? Or had they hoped to hurt me—or worse? And who had been behind the wheel?

While construction work was hardly a nine-to-five job and Buck and I often worked weekends, we'd decided to take the day off from remodeling the fire station on Saturday. Both of us had personal chores we needed to catch up on and, of course, I had my top-secret whiskey-barrel project to finish.

Sawdust prowled around the garage as I finished sanding the inside of the barrel and applied a clear sealant. Thank goodness the whiskey smell was gone now. It had been enough to make your eyes water.

The whiskey barrel contained what was known as a bunghole, a hole drilled into the side of the barrel and through which the barrel was filled with the whiskey. Once the barrel had been filled, a bung, or stopper, was inserted into the hole to hold the whiskey inside. I'd acquired four bungs when I'd bought the barrel. Each had an inscription on the outer end that read Old No. 7, one of the varieties offered by the distillery. I attached the four bungs to the lower sides of the barrel to act as feet of sorts, giving the barrel a little play to rock side to side, but not so much that it could tip over. The final step was to line the inside of the barrel with thick foam padding, and cover the pad with waterproof fabric.

Sawdust came over to investigate. He cautiously sniffed at the barrel, evidently remembering how strongly it had smelled before I'd sanded it. His whiskers twitched, but he didn't run away this time. In fact, he stretched up on his hind legs so he could see inside the barrel. Noting that it was hollow, he brought his front paws back down to the ground, then proceeded to leap into the soft, padded space. He settled in to take a nap.

The project complete, I attached an enormous yellow bow to the top of the barrel. I'd planned on putting it in my car as soon as it was finished, but Sawdust looked absolutely adorable sleeping inside it. I snapped a pic with my phone and let him be. Collin could help me load it into my SUV later.

On the drive to the Collection Plate Café that evening, I told Collin about the car that had followed me the night before.

He frowned. "We'd need definitive proof of who was driving the car to get a restraining order against them. A security camera's not likely to pick up that level of detail at night. We'd be lucky to even narrow down a make and model."

We'd gotten lucky earlier identifying Lane Hartzell's tow truck on the security camera footage recorded the night the fire was set at the station. It had been relatively easy to identify the unusual shape of the large vehicle.

Collin said, "I'll send one of the uniformed officers by to speak to each of the Bottiglieris. I don't expect any of them will admit to it but, if one of them was the person who tailed you last night, a visit from law enforcement could deter them from pulling another stunt like that. I'm going to order a dashboard camera for your car. A rear cam, too. They don't always record a clear image when there's light interference, but it can't hurt."

Buck's van was already in the parking lot when Collin and I arrived at the Collection Plate Café. With all the bad stuff that had been happening lately, I was glad to have something happy to distract us for the next couple of hours.

Collin carried the half barrel inside. The hostess knew us both and greeted us warmly, directing us to a private dining room at the back of the place. "Colette and Emmalee have your cakes ready for sampling. We've been smelling them all day. Colette said the staff can eat the leftovers."

Free food was a nice fringe benefit of working in a restaurant. Colette used to bring leftovers home when we lived together before she and Buck married, and Emmalee occasionally brought some home now. When Emmalee moved out, Collin and I would have to fend for ourselves. Neither of us were into cooking. No doubt the quality of our meals would suffer.

We maneuvered our way through the tables, careful not to bang the barrel against the chairs. When we reached the doorway of the private room, Emmalee, Buck, and Colette looked up from the table, where five plates had been prepared with a dozen cake samples, each only slightly bigger than dice. The samples were big enough that we'd be able to taste the flavors, yet small enough that we wouldn't be so full by the last sample or two that it would affect our evaluation.

Colette stood, her baby bump noticeably bigger under her chef's uniform than the last time we'd seen her, though it had only been a matter of days. She pointed at the barrel, which Collin was holding upright. From Colette's perspective it would look like a complete whiskey barrel. "What's that?"

I grinned. "An early baby gift."

She exchanged a confused look with Buck. "You brought a barrel of whiskey for our baby?"

Collin placed the barrel on the floor, and lowered it onto its side. With the padded hollow part now showing, its purpose became immediately apparent.

Colette squealed in glee. "It's a cradle!"

My chest swelled with pride as she rocked it back and forth, the bungs preventing the barrel from rolling too far to the side where it might dump the baby out.

Emmalee looked it over, too. "This explains why I smelled whiskey at the house."

Colette grabbed me in a hug, having to lean forward over her baby bump to embrace me. "I love it, Whitney. You're the best!" She pulled back and swiped away a happy tear.

Buck bent down and examined my handiwork. "This is one cool cradle." He, too, tested it out, rocking it back and forth. "I can rock the baby in here while I sing her to sleep."

"*Her*?" I repeated.

Colette smiled. "The sonogram says it'll be a girl."

Having raised two boys, my aunt Nancy and uncle Roger would be glad to welcome a granddaughter. I cut Buck a glance. "Do you even know any lullabies?"

Buck looked up in thought for a moment. "Does 'Way Too Pretty for Prison' count?"

"No!" Colette, Emmalee, and I cried in unison. I mean, we were fans of Miranda Lambert, too, but the song was all about what prison might be like if a woman killed her lover for cheating. Not exactly nursery fare.

Buck stopped rocking the cradle, bent closer, and peered inside. "Did Sawdust sleep in here?"

No sense denying it. He'd obviously shed some fur, leaving clear and convincing evidence behind.

"Someone had to try it out." I mentally chastised myself for not remembering to vacuum out the cat hair. But it would have likely been a moot point. Sawdust had been the runt of a litter of three, and one of the other two cats lived with Buck and Colette. No doubt their cat would take naps in the cradle now and then, too.

Collin and I took our seats at the table, and proceeded to taste and judge the samples. Each one was more delicious than the last, and none were typical. There was a dark chocolate almond cake. A strawberry-lemon cake. Butter pecan. My favorite, though, was the pumpkin spice, which seemed particularly fitting for a fall wedding.

I looked from Emmalee to Colette. "You two have really outdone yourselves."

Colette smiled. "It was fun developing the new recipes."

Emmalee put a hand on her belly. "I gained five pounds working on them. We're thinking of serving them at a weekly high tea."

No doubt a high tea would be very popular, and the charming café, with its adorably mismatched plates and teacups, was the perfect place for it. "That's a wonderful idea."

When we'd sampled our last bite, I turned to Collin, the taste of the soft sponge still lingering in my mouth. "My vote is the pumpkin spice."

"Mine too," he said, wiping the frosting from the corner of his mouth.

"You two made it easy," Colette said. "Some of the weddings I've catered here, the bride and groom can't agree on which one to get. It's a battle of wills. If that's how the marriage starts out, I can only imagine how quickly it's going to end."

Fortunately, Collin and I were good at compromising. I felt a tug in my gut, though, when I thought about how I hadn't told him I planned to follow Holden Griffin when he supposedly left for work Monday morning.

Emmalee drew my attention back to the business at hand. "What's your second favorite? We could use that flavor for the groom's cake."

Again, Collin and I agreed. The dark chocolate almond was our second favorite, although the strawberry-lemon was a close third.

Having essentially eaten our dessert first, we proceeded to enjoy a delicious Mediterranean pasta and salad for dinner. When we finished, Emmalee returned to her work in the kitchen, while Buck and Collin carried the cradle out to place it in Buck's van. Colette and I walked behind them.

She nudged me gently in the ribs and leaned over to whisper, "What are you going to do with the other half of the barrel?"

I shrugged. "I haven't really thought about it. Maybe I'll turn it into a bookshelf, or an end table."

"You know what you should do?" She shot me a wink. "Make yourself a cradle, too."

It was much too soon for Collin and me to be thinking about children. We hadn't even walked down the aisle yet. But there was a certain little creature who deserved a reward for bringing a critical clue to our attention, and he'd love to have a comfy new bed to sleep in.

CHAPTER 22

THE CAT'S IN THE CRADLE

SAWDUST

Whitney had taken the wooden bed away with her the evening before, but she'd spent all of today making another like it just for him. Sawdust curled up against the curve of the barrel, feeling safe and secure. It was quiet and private, the perfect place for a kitty to take a cat-nap. Cleo climbed in with him. Fortunately, the barrel was big enough to hold both of them. Sawdust sure had gotten lucky when Whitney had taken him in. He looked up at her from the confines of the barrel and thanked her for his comfy new sleeping quarters with a mew. She reached in and ruffled his ears. "Enjoy your new bed, Purrlock Holmes."

CHAPTER 23

SWITCHEROO

WHITNEY

Monday morning, I parked down the street from the Griffins' unit in Gideon's house, lying in wait on the opposite side of the street. I was afraid my red SUV would be too recognizable, so I'd swapped vehicles with Emmalee for the day. I'd also donned a pink blouse, tucked my hair up inside a floppy brown camping hat, and put on a pair of sunglasses with large, round lenses. With any luck, Holden wouldn't know it was me following him if he happened to spot me. It seemed ironic, me here, planning to follow Holden, when someone had followed me Friday night. But while whoever had followed my SUV had obviously hoped to intimidate me, I hoped that Holden would remain completely unaware of my presence.

I wasn't sure what time he normally left the house for work, but I'd mapped the route from here to the Frozen Freight warehouse. It was a thirty-minute drive in light traffic, forty-five during rush hour. Assuming his shift started at eight o'clock, I calculated that he probably left

by seven fifteen at the latest. I'd gotten in place an hour
earlier, just to make sure I didn't miss him. I'd brought
a travel mug of coffee along with me, which was proving to be a blessing *and* a curse. On one hand, the caf-
feine in the coffee kept me awake when every cell of my
body begged to snooze. On the other, the coffee filling
my bladder was beginning to demand release.

Alyssa emerged from the townhouse where they
were now basically squatting, rent paid up but without
a full set of furniture. Her backpack was slung over
her shoulder. She walked down their side of the street,
Bluetooth ear buds in her ears, not casting so much as a
glance my way as she passed. She stopped at the end of
the block, joining two other teens as they waited on the
corner. Not having children, I hadn't realized today was
the first day of the new school year. The kids waited
only a minute or two before a big yellow school bus
rolled up the side street, its brakes squeaking as the
driver brought it to a stop. A *whoosh* met my ears as
the tall door folded to the side, allowing the students
to climb aboard. Once everyone had taken a seat, the
brakes squeaked again as they were released, and the
bus rolled off to pick up more students.

I continued to wait, my bladder causing me increasing discomfort. I couldn't imagine relieving myself in a
bucket, though if I'd been in my SUV right now, I'd at
least have the option. There was always a spare bucket
in my cargo bay. They came in handy for so many
things. Cleaning. Carrying water. A place to collect odds
and ends for disposal later. And . . . you know. When I
could stand it no longer, I started the car, zipped around
the corner, and hustled into the fire station to relieve myself. I was back in the car not two minutes later, driving
back to my spying spot, when Holden's white pickup

eased away from the curb, heading toward me. *Perfect timing.*

There were no signs of recognition as I drove past him on the street. I'd seen a flash of ice blue, and knew he wore his Frozen Freight Carriers uniform, even though he was no longer employed by the company. I watched in the rearview mirror to see which way he turned onto the main artery. *Right.* I whipped a quick U-turn, thankful that Emmalee's inexpensive commuter car had a small turning radius and didn't require me to execute a three-point turn. I might've lost him.

I punched the gas, raced up to the corner, and pulled onto the road without coming to a full stop. I checked my rearview mirror and could tell my rude maneuver had annoyed the driver of an approaching vehicle, who'd had to hit their brakes. The man didn't honk, however. This was Nashville, where people were known for being nice.

I drove along, keeping close enough to Holden that I wouldn't lose him at a traffic light, but far enough back that he wouldn't notice me tailing him. I wondered where we were headed. He seemed to be aiming in the same general direction of the industrial area where the Frozen Freight warehouse was located.

As we made our way to the mystery destination, I thought about the situation. Holden had seemed relatively unaffected by Joanna's death, cracking jokes not long after she'd drawn her last breath. I wondered why Macy hadn't noticed that Holden was no longer receiving a paycheck. Then again, there'd only been a couple of paydays since he'd left his previous employment. Maybe she hadn't checked their bank balances, didn't know he hadn't been paid; or maybe Holden took care of the bills and Macy was clueless as to their money situation. I had my doubts about that, though. Macy was a hairdresser, running her own business. Seemed she'd be the type who'd stay on top of things financially. Then again, being put on bedrest might have thrown her off her game.

Holden turned in to a fast-food joint, parked, and climbed out of his car. *Is he going inside to get breakfast?* I wouldn't mind some hash browns myself.

I backed into a parking spot so I'd be able to pull out easily when he returned to his vehicle. He was inside only a minute or two when the door opened and he exited. I very nearly missed him. I'd been keeping an eye out for the ice blue shirt, but he wore a striped gray and white shirt now. His uniform shirt from Frozen Freight was rolled up in his hand to keep it from getting wrinkled. The guy was certainly a quick-change artist.

He climbed back into his car, and we motored on for another ten minutes before he pulled into the parking lot of single-story building in an industrial area. The sign above the door read Tri-State Private Security Services.

I drove slowly past, pulling over to a curb once I was out of sight to ponder this development. *Why is Holden here? Does he plan to hire a security guard for personal protection? Does he fear for his family's safety? If so, why?*

Joanna's death was purportedly just an awful accident. Only the killer would know it had been intentional. I'd been operating on the assumption that Holden might have murdered his mother-in-law, but if that was the case, then there'd be no reason for him to hire protection. He'd know his family was safe.

Did he suspect someone intentionally killed Joanna, someone who might now come after his family? Lane, perhaps? But if Holden feared for Macy's and Alyssa's safety—maybe even their moppy dog's, too—why would he have left Macy home alone this morning? The dog might bark to alert her of an intruder's presence, but the cute little beast was much too small to defend her from an attacker. Maybe Macy, too, thought Lane could be guilty of causing their mother's death. Maybe that's why she didn't want him moving in with her and her family. Maybe she also had the means to protect herself while Holden was away. Guns were easy enough to get. Then again, a gun would only protect someone from a violent attacker. Whoever had killed Joanna had taken pains to obscure the fact that she'd been poisoned, and seemed unlikely to launch an open attack on anyone else.

Could Holden have concerns about his own safety? If so, there was only one explanation I could come up with. *He thinks Macy killed her mother.* But if Macy had killed her mother, why would she have pursued an autopsy that would reveal her mother had been poisoned? Wouldn't she have just let everyone think her mother had died of an aneurysm? The pieces simply didn't fall into place. Every theory just seemed to take me back into a circle. The only thing I knew for certain right now was that Holden was putting on a ruse, pretending he was going to his old job when that was clearly not the case.

A ping sounded as a text came in on my cell. It was from Macy. *Got the test results back. Can you come over to discuss?*

A creepy feeling seeped into my bones. While going into Macy's house alone might be risky, it could give me a chance to better suss out the situation, and I wasn't about to pass up the opportunity. I sent her a return text: *Running an errand. Be there soon.*

After driving back home and swapping cars back with

Emmalee, I drove to the fire station. Buck was there, preparing the bathroom floors and backsplashes for the tile. I told him where I'd been that morning, where I was going now.

He didn't look at all surprised. He knew I'd been bit by the curiosity bug, and that there was no cure for the malady other than indulging the drive to collect clues. "Take your big wrench. Text me if you need me. Jot a quick note on the wall saying this place is all mine if you get yourself killed."

I indulged him, whipping a marking pencil from my toolbox and scribbling on the wall, offering the same verbiage that had been in the quitclaim deeds the Bottiglieris had signed, with a few modifications.

"Know all men by these presents that for and in consideration of the sum of diddly-squat in hand paid to me, Whitney Whitaker (grantor), I do hereby quitclaim to Buck Whitaker (grantee) all rights, title, interest, and claim in or to the following real estate: this fire station right here where you're standing."

Knowing we'd be painting over my scrawl, I signed the wall with a flourish and left, wrench in hand.

Macy answered the door at their unit in Gideon's building, wearing a versatile knit dress that could be an outfit in itself, or serve as a beach cover-up or a nightgown. I presumed she wore it as the latter. She was barefoot, which made me slightly more comfortable. If she'd lured me here to end my life, suspecting I knew too much and to stop me from digging further, she'd have to kill me here. No way could she chase me out onto the hot sidewalk in bare feet. Her laptop was tucked under her arm.

She stared down at the enormous wrench in my hand. "What's that for?"

"Oh, this little thing?" I said, though the wrench, being as long as my forearm, could hardly be called little. "I was tightening a pipe behind the building and didn't want to leave it outside. I was afraid I'd forget it there."

Through the open door behind her, I could see three chaise longue lawn chairs set up in the living room in front of the television, which sat on the floor. I'd expected her to invite me in, but instead she came out onto the porch, closing the door behind her.

She placed her laptop on the railing and opened it. "We got the test results on my mom's townhouse." She gestured to the screen.

Leaning in, I scanned the screen, taking in the information. "Looks like everything was in normal range. No mercury contamination. That's good."

"Is it?" she said.

"Well, it means it's safe for you and Holden and Alyssa to move back into her place. Isn't that what you wanted?"

"I suppose so." She eyed me with what looked suspiciously like suspicion. "I just wish I knew exactly what happened to my mother. How in the world did she end up with mercury in her system?"

I fought the urge to scream, *I've been trying to find out!* Instead, I said, "I don't know. Do you have any guesses?" *Could your husband have done it?* I was tempted to tell her that he'd been lying about his job, but I decided to keep mum about that until I determined why, exactly, he'd been engaged in the subterfuge.

Macy gave me an odd look. In fact, she looked nervous. She closed the laptop and backed away a step or two. "No. No guesses."

We both stood there in awkward silence before I said,

"I guess I should get back to work." I gestured back at the fire station with my wrench.

Her eyes on my tool, Macy backed up, plastering her back against the wall of her porch. "Bye!" She yanked open the door to her unit, slipped inside, and slammed it behind her. I heard the rattle of locks being engaged.

That was weird.

After my odd interaction with Macy, I was more confused than ever. I returned to the fire station and texted Collin. *Macy received the test results on Joanna's townhouse. Both air and water tested negative for mercury.*

I'd expected as much, after Sawdust discovered the little ball of mercury in the fire station. Still, the lack of a second source of mercury told us that we were likely on the right track with the cigarette theory.

I spent the rest of the day wondering when and how I could confront Holden for answers as to why he'd gone to the security firm that morning. *Should I follow him again tomorrow?* I didn't want to have to get up early again, so I decided to try to intercept him when he arrived home. As strange as Macy had acted this morning, I wasn't sure she'd let me inside. It was almost as if she thought I might have something to do with her mother's death. *Ridiculous, right?* I'm sure it would be hard to accept that your mother had somehow been poisoned, but that was no reason to project guilt onto someone who'd only been trying all along to help. I figured I'd have to catch Holden right when he pulled up.

Fortunately, fate provided me with a convenient excuse to hang out at the townhouse we'd bought from the Bottiglieris, where I could keep an eye on the Griffins' place across the street. The new water heater had arrived, and the plumber called to tell me had a cancellation in his schedule. "I can install it at four o'clock this afternoon if that works for you."

"Perfect. See you then."

I headed over to the townhouse at half past three, just to make sure I wouldn't miss the plumber. I sat inside with the lights off and the mini blinds angled ever so slightly, watching the street in case Holden came home early.

The plumber arrived right on time. I let him into the townhouse and motioned for him to follow me. "This way."

The old water heater stood in the corner of the utility closet in the hallway between the kitchen and master bedroom. I showed him where it was, and got out of his way so he could do his work. Standing so long made my feet sore, so I finally sat down on the stained carpet and continued to watch out the window.

When the plumber finished installing the water heater, I retrieved my business credit card from my purse and tapped it against his card-processing device. The machine whirred and spit out a receipt. I returned the card to my wallet and stashed the receipt in there as well. We'd need it later when we completed our taxes.

I turned, walked the man to the door, and opened it for him. "Dammit!" Holden's pickup truck sat at the curb across the street. He'd arrived home in the brief expanse of time I'd been tied up with the plumber, paying for the water heater.

"Something wrong?" the plumber asked.

I couldn't exactly tell the man I was snooping around my neighbor, trying to figure out if he'd poisoned his mother-in-law right next door. "Sorry," I said. "I just remembered something I'd forgotten to do. Thanks for coming out."

He gave me a two-finger salute and strode out to his truck. The diesel engine rumbled as he drove off. Strangely, it didn't seem to be getting quieter as he made his way down the street. That's when I realized the sound was coming from another truck, a tow truck that was easing to the curb at Joanna's place.

I hadn't ruled out Lane and he seemed like one of the most viable suspects. Lane might have killed Joanna in the hopes that he'd inherit some of her money and property. In the alternative, if what Gideon said was true—that Joanna had cut Lane out of the will—he might have murdered Joanna out of anger . . . assuming he knew what she'd done. *Had he truly only learned he'd been cut out of the will when Gideon told him?*

I trotted down the steps and met Lane as he came over to Joanna's porch.

"You going inside?" I asked.

"Yeah. Macy told me she got the test results, and that the air and water are safe." He gestured to the door. "There's a few things I left in the attic when I moved out that I've come to get."

"You've got the code to get in?"

"I do now. Macy gave it to me. She changed it to keep Gideon out. She likes the guy, for the most part, but he's been butting in a lot since Mom passed. She's tired of it."

"I can see why." I offered a congenial shake of my head before tilting it. "I don't mean to pry," I lied, totally meaning to pry, "but I thought it was out of line for him to mention that your mother had cut you out of your will. He should've let Macy be the one to tell you."

"Probably, yeah," Lane agreed.

"So, you didn't already know."

"No. Mom hadn't said anything to me about it. We really didn't talk about that stuff."

Is he telling the truth? I cringed, as if I knew what I was about to ask might be painful. "Did it hurt your feelings? To be cut out of her will?"

"Honestly?" His face transformed several times, as if he was working through his emotions right there on the spot. "Not really. I mean, I get why she'd do it. Like Gideon said, she probably worried that if she left me money, I'd spend it on pills." He snorted. "Hell, at one time, I definitely would have. But now? Nah. Besides, I'd cost her enough already, not in money, but in worry and heartache." He blinked rapidly as his eyes became wet. "I just wish I could have reassured her that I was going to be okay, that I *am* okay now. I wanted to give her peace of mind, not take any more from her."

He seemed sad that he hadn't had the chance to reconnect with his mother on solid footing before she passed. Now, he'd never have the chance. But could this all be an act? It didn't seem like one, but I figured I'd come this far, I might as well see if I could rule him out entirely. I lifted my chin to indicate his tow truck. "You enjoy working auto salvage?"

He barked a laugh. "You're kidding, right?"

I shrugged one shoulder, feigning nonchalance. "I like working with my hands, building stuff, taking it apart, seeing how things work. I figured you might enjoy being a mechanic, pulling parts and fixing cars."

"I'm not a mechanic," he said. "I wouldn't know a carburetor from a crankshaft. I only tow the cars to the salvage yard, or sometimes to repair shops. It's just a job. Pays the bills—barely."

"But, surely, you're buddies with some of the mechanics. Don't you guys love to stand around and talk shop?"

"I might, if I had the chance. I'm always on the road,

though. I go to the yard at the beginning of my shift to pick up the tow truck, go back to drop off the busted-up cars to be added to the pick-and-pull inventory, and then return the truck when my shift is over. There's not much time for conversation. Most days, I'm lucky if anyone says two words to me."

It sounded like a lonely existence. It also sounded like he wouldn't know how to dismantle a pre-2003 switch to remove the mercury. I felt like I could cross his name off my list of potential suspects.

Before we could naturally wrap up our conversation, Lane's phone pinged with an incoming text. He pulled his phone from the back pocket of his jeans and read the screen. He cast a glance at his sister's unit across the street before casting a second wary glance at me. He shoved his phone into his back pocket and abruptly ended our interaction. "Gotta get moving." With that, he turned, entered the four-digit code into the keypad, and stepped inside, closing the door on me. Just as Macy had abruptly locked her door behind her earlier, Lane did the same, the deadbolt sliding home with a loud click.

CHAPTER 24

WHERE THERE'S SMOKES . . .

WHITNEY

Collin had paid for express shipping when he'd ordered the dash and rear window cams for me. They were waiting on my doorstep when I'd arrived home Monday evening, and I'd promptly installed them.

I took my own car when I followed Holden Tuesday morning, and activated the dash cam to record the evidence that he was not going to work at Frozen Freight. He was more likely to spot me in my own vehicle, but I didn't much care if he knew I was following him at this point. My patience was gone. Things had been dragging on, and I was tired of speculating and guessing and trying to make sense of things that seemed to make no sense at all.

Again, he'd come out of his house in his ice-blue Frozen Freight Carrier uniform and, again, he'd stopped at a fast-food place to change shirts in the bathroom. To my surprise, he returned to Tri-State Private Security Services. I'd thought he'd come here the day before to talk to someone about hiring protection, but it seemed that task could have been accomplished in one visit. *Is he here for something else?*

I climbed out of my SUV and accosted him as he slid out of his truck, before he could even close his door. A pair of thick nylon gloves was tucked into the map pocket. Like the shirt he'd left his house in, they were ice blue with a snowman logo on them, undoubtedly a pair he'd used in his former job at the cold storage company. I stopped directly in front of him, blocking his way. "What are you doing here, Holden? What happened to your job at Frozen Freight?"

He blinked, shocked to find me here demanding information. When he gathered his wits, his demeanor went from shocked to enraged. He draped a hand over the top of his open truck door, grabbing the frame in a death grip. "What right do you have to follow me here and interrogate me like this? You're not a cop!"

Cop? Interesting that he'd chosen to go there. "I watched Joanna die, remember?" I spat the words as if they tasted bad. "That's what gives me the right. Mercury got into her system. I don't believe that was an accident, and I want to know who made that happen. You've lied to your wife. Maybe it was you who poisoned Joanna." After all, Gideon said he'd found the pack of Newports he'd taken over to Joanna's sitting on the railing between his unit and the Griffins. Maybe Holden had tampered with the cigarettes and left them on the railing, knowing Gideon would spot them and take them to Joanna.

"Are you kidding?" Holden barked. "I needed Joanna alive more than anyone!"

"Why?"

He hesitated a moment, snarling a curse. "If I tell you, are you going to tell Macy?"

"I suppose that depends on what you tell me."

He released a long, shuddering sigh. "Look. I was up for a promotion at work. It was my third time to apply for an assistant manager position, my third time to be interviewed, and my third time to be passed over. The guys up the chain think I'm 'too nice,' a 'pushover,' that the workers would 'walk all over me.'" His hands fisted in rage. "You have to be an asshole to move up in this world." He looked down and kicked the asphalt with the toe of his shoe before returning his attention to me. "I was pissed off and insulted. Hurt, too, if I'm being honest. I've given lots of good years to that company, and they made me feel like I'd been a fool to do it. I lost my cool, called my boss a name I shouldn't have, and told him he could take my job and shove it. I walked out." He looked up at the sky now, as if pleading with the gods. "Then I go home and have a couple beers to psych myself up to tell Macy what happened. Before I can, she drops a bombshell. She's pregnant. She'd taken an at-home test and it came back positive."

"Right after you lost your job? That's some bad timing."

"You're telling me!" He snorted. "You heard about her medical history when you were at Joanna's the day we shared the news. When Macy was pregnant with Alyssa, she had all sorts of problems. Seemed every day it was something new to worry about. It was unbelievably stressful."

I could only imagine. A pregnancy seemed difficult enough when things were going well.

Holden went on. "There was no way I could tell Macy that I'd got my jockeys in a bunch and quit my job. I was afraid it would jeopardize her health and the baby's if I told her. I called my old boss and begged for my job back, but even though I'd been a good worker for years, he refused to rehire me. He said I'd been 'irredeemably insubordinate.' That jackass never used an everyday word when a ten-dollar word would do." He rolled his eyes. "Macy makes good money in her work, but she's only part-time. Like a lot of people, we live paycheck to paycheck. We try to save, but it seems there's always some unexpected expense popping up. A car repair. A vet bill. Something Alyssa needs for school or so she can keep up with her friends. Anyway, I didn't want Macy to know I was out of work. She would've worried, and she was anxious enough with the baby coming and all. I had no choice but to grovel to Joanna, see if she'd carry us until I found a new job. She didn't know yet that Macy was pregnant, and I didn't tell her. Macy wanted to wait to tell her mother until after she'd seen the doctor."

Holden had certainly been forthcoming. But was he being honest?

"Let me get this straight," I said. "You're saying you wouldn't have killed Joanna because you needed her money to support your family?"

"That's right. Joanna agreed to transfer the exact amount of my paycheck into our bank account on my usual paydays until I found a new job. I've been trying. Put in over forty applications all over town. Problem is, my old boss won't give me a good recommendation. Nobody's going to hire me without one. Joanna suggested I apply for a position at the prison where Macy's father worked. I didn't much like the thought of that, and I knew Macy wouldn't like it, either. She blames the stress of working in the prison for bringing about her father's heart attack. But it gave me the idea of working in private security. It's a growing business and I noticed there are a lot of job listings for security guards. To work as one here in Tennessee, you have to get a license from the Private Protective Services department, and to get that license you've got to complete training and take a test. That's what I'm doing here."

His story made sense, all except the part about needing to keep Joanna alive so that she'd keep transferring money to his account. After all, now that Macy had inherited all of her mother's property—other than the record albums Lane had requested—they'd no longer need Holden's pay, or a replacement for it, at least not for some time. They wouldn't immediately need Macy's earnings, either. Joanna's death had solved their financial problems.

When I pointed this out to Holden, he appeared confused for a moment. Then he simply shrugged and shook his head. "That thought of taking Joanna's life never would've occurred to me. I didn't like the way she talked to Macy and me sometimes, especially me, but we took it in stride and just tried to ignore her when she got like that." He raised his arms out to his sides. "Look at me. I might be an unemployed idiot who should've kept his mouth shut, but I'm no killer."

I stared him down, assessing. He seemed sincere. *I hope he's not fooling me.*

He eyed the door of the building and checked the time on his sports watch. "I'd better get in there. Class is about to start."

As he went to close the door of his pickup, one of the gloves fell out of the map pocket and landed on the asphalt. He bent down to pick it up. As he lifted it, something fell out of the glove. A hard strawberry candy wrapped in red cellophane. He picked up the candy and stared at it for a long moment before tossing it into a cup holder. He tucked the glove back into the map pocket, closed the door, and squeezed the fob to lock his truck. Raising a hand in a goodbye gesture, he turned and marched toward the door.

I returned to my SUV and sat there for a moment, thinking. I'd tentatively ruled out Gideon, Lane, and now Holden as Joanna's killer. That left all seven of the Bottiglieris on my list of possible murderers, as well as Samira and D-Jay. If one of the Bottiglieris had poisoned Joanna, my money was on Peter. After all, he'd been at our townhouse. Collin had proved it with the spelling test. Peter could have found a way to slip a tainted pack of cigarettes to Joanna, maybe by prying open a window or door on her unit and sneaking inside, leaving it on the kitchen counter or coffee table while she slept. But none of the Bottiglieris would talk to me now, not after everything that had transpired. There seemed to be no way to amass evidence against them.

Would I ever know who killed Joanna, or would her killer forever remain a mystery?

Early Tuesday evening, I dragged Buck with me over to Samira and D-Jay's unit. They were the last suspects on my list, and I wanted to see what they had to say for themselves.

Samira answered the door. D-Jay stepped up behind her. Before I could even speak, she said, "I am glad that you are here, Whitney. I would like to apologize to you."

"You would?" I asked. "For what?"

Her lip trembled as she cast a glance at the townhouse across the street behind me. "I want a home of our own so bad, one here in this neighborhood, that I have been much too aggressive toward you." She put a hand on her baby bump and attempted a smile. It came out small and forced. "The pregnancy hormones sometimes turn me into a person I do not recognize."

Buck had said essentially the same thing with his comment about pregnant women and their nesting instinct—that being pregnant had a big impact on their behavior.

"No worries," I said. "My cousin's wife is pregnant, too. I know it can difficult."

"Thank you."

From inside the unit, Kavish screamed, "Ga-ga-da!"

Samira put a hand to her forehead. "I love my son, but right now he is giving me a headache."

It was ironic. Here she was complaining about a headache, while here I was trying to determine whether she'd given one to Joanna by inserting tiny drops of mercury into her cigarettes.

D-Jay looked from me to Buck and politely asked, "Why are you here? May we help you with something?"

"You can," I said. "When we moved the Griffins into Joanna's townhouse, I noticed you threw away a carton of Joanna's cigarettes. It was open. A pack fell out of it."

Samira turned and looked to her husband. After exchanging confused glances, they returned their gazes in our direction.

"Yes?" D-Jay said.

"Do you know how much cigarettes cost?" I asked.

"Not precisely," D-Jay said. "We do not smoke."

Samira added, "We do know that they are expensive."

"If you know they're expensive, why did you throw them out without checking with Macy and Holden first?"

The two exchanged another confused look before Samira said, "We did not ask because we know they do not smoke. We have had them up for dinner a few times—"

"And they have also invited us to their unit for game night," D-Jay interjected.

"They never smoked," Samira said, completing her thought. "There was no reason to keep something they would not use. I was also concerned that the cigarettes might pose a temptation to their daughter or her friends."

They had a point. If the cigarettes had remained in the pantry, the teens might have wanted to try them.

D-Jay turned the tables on me, his brown eyes narrowed. "These are very odd questions. Why do you ask?"

Although I felt more assured now that these two had not likely killed Joanna, I didn't want to reveal that the mercury in Joanna's system had been introduced via smoking. Better to hold that card close to the vest, and see if someone accidentally spilled the beans. I racked my brain, trying to come up with some reason why I would ask them these questions. "I just want to be clear that, when D-Jay comes to help us at the townhouse, we do not want him to throw anything away without first checking with one of us. Sometimes, supplies or materials may look like worthless scraps but actually be quite valuable. We keep extra materials like tile and trim in case something gets damaged and needs to be replaced."

D-Jay dipped his head. "I understand. I will always ask permission before discarding anything."

Samira's eyes gleamed. "Does this mean you will be doing more work on the townhouse soon?"

"It'll be a few more weeks at least," I said. "We've got plenty more to do at the fire station."

While Samira appeared disappointed by the news,

D-Jay looked relieved. "That will give us more time to seek a loan. We have had no luck so far with private lenders. Many require a larger down payment than we are able to make."

I wasn't surprised. Those who made loans to people with questionable credit had to take measures to protect their interests.

We bade the couple good night, then headed home ourselves. I hoped Collin would have the double homicide investigation completed soon so that he could open an official murder investigation for Joanna Hartzell. So far, the killer had continued to elude me. Maybe I'd reached the end of my skill set as an amateur investigator. Maybe this case was one for the professionals.

CHAPTER 25

FROM SUSPICIOUS TO SUSPECT

WHITNEY

On Wednesday morning, I arrived at the fire station to discover a police cruiser sitting in the parking lot. My heart jolted. *Has something happened?*

As I pulled into the lot and parked, a uniformed male officer climbed out of the driver's seat. A fiftyish female in a boring beige business suit climbed out of the passenger side. Her chestnut hair was cut in a shoulder-length bob. "Whitney Whitaker?" she asked.

"That's me," I said. "How can I help you?"

The woman came over. First, she offered me her hand and her name. "Denise Gleeson." Next, she offered me her business card. It identified her as a detective with the Metro Police Department. "I'm investigating a suspicious death."

Oh, my gosh! Has there been another? I was almost afraid to ask. *"Whose* death?"

"Joanna Hartzell's," said Detective Gleeson.

"I thought Detective Flynn was going to handle that case."

She raised her chin and looked down her nose at me. "Why would you think that?"

Because he told me so? I wasn't sure what the protocols were for which detective was assigned to which murder case. I doubted a detective could call dibs on a particular case, like Gideon had tried to call dibs on the townhouse. I recalled Collin telling me they were assigned on a rotating basis, and you got the next case that came up when your name rose to the top of the list. Still, I'd gotten the impression that he had planned to open a case himself once he had time. Looked like this woman had beaten him to it. I wondered what had instigated her investigation—or who. "Detective Flynn and I have discussed the situation. I'm his fiancée."

"You are?" She looked taken aback. So did the uniformed officer.

"Yes. I told him I suspected that Joanna might have been murdered. It was my understanding he was going to look into things once he was finished with another case he's working."

"The double homicide?"

I nodded.

"Well, I officially got to this case first." She offered a wry smile. "I have some questions I'd like to ask you."

I held out a hand to indicate the fire station. "Would you like to come inside? We don't have any furniture, but I could round up a couple of buckets for you two to sit on."

"Actually," she said, "I'd prefer to talk at the station."

It would take additional time to move this conversation elsewhere, time I didn't really have to spare. But she was in charge and I wasn't going to be rude by arguing with her. "Should I follow you there?"

The uniformed officer opened the back door of the squad car. "Climb on in. We'd be happy to give you a ride."

I froze for a moment. *What, exactly, is happening here? Are they taking me into custody?* I was utterly confused and totally alarmed, but I tried to keep my cool. Surely, there was some sort of misunderstanding. Collin could help sort it out. They hadn't handcuffed me or read my rights yet, so that was a good sign, wasn't it? If I was in big trouble, they'd be telling me I had the right to remain silent, and the right to an attorney.

Buck pulled up as I slid into the back seat of the squad car. He was out of his van in an instant. "What's going on here?"

I forced a smile. "I'm just riding down to the station with them to answer a few questions." I turned my head so that the detective and the officer couldn't see my face. *Call Collin!* I mouthed silently.

The officer closed the door on me, and I found myself in a cage of sorts, separated from the cop and the detective by a layer of metal mesh. The car had a faint unpleasant smell, like Swiss cheese, a scent that was likely part body odor and part barf. I reflexively tightened my buttocks, trying to put as little of my body in touch with the seat as possible. I fastened my seat belt but leaned forward to keep my back away from the seat, hugging my knees, trying not to panic.

I remained silent as we drove, staring out the window, turning things over in my brain. What had led to me being taken in for questioning? I had no way of knowing, at least not yet. But I had a sneaky suspicion that Macy

Griffin had something to do with it. She'd acted very strange the last time I'd seen her, almost as if she was scared of me, and I wasn't sure why.

At the station, Detective Gleeson led me to a small conference room. She pulled out a chair for me on one side of the metal table and seated herself on the other. There was a metal loop in the center of the table that I surmised was for attaching handcuffs when needed. A glance downward told me the table was bolted to the floor. I wondered briefly whether I should ask to call a lawyer, but I was innocent of any wrongdoing. *Surely, I don't need one, do I?*

Detective Gleeson offered me a cup of the most stale, bitter, lukewarm coffee I'd ever tasted, and got right down to brass tacks. "I understand that, while Joanna Hartzell's autopsy was pending, you predicted that she had died from mercury poisoning, is that correct?"

"*Predicted* is not the term I would use," I said. "I simply noticed some things that pointed to the possibility."

She held out a hand in invitation. "Such as?"

"Such as lots of leftover seafood in Joanna's refrigerator." I explained how I'd overheard Macy say that pregnant women shouldn't eat seafood, and how I'd later discussed the matter with my cousin's wife who, like Macy, was pregnant. "The information was fresh in my mind, so when I saw all the shrimp and tuna and other fish in Joanna's fridge, it gave me pause. Her symptoms seemed to be consistent with mercury poisoning, too."

"You're referring to the symptoms you witnessed when she came to the fire station?"

"That's correct," I said. "She was wobbly on her feet and disoriented, incoherent. Shaking, too."

"Are you aware that nobody else saw Joanna walk to the fire station?"

"Nobody on the street, you mean?"

"Exactly."

"That doesn't surprise me," I replied. "It was just before two in the afternoon when she came into the bay. Most people are at work at that time."

Undeterred, she said, "You were the only one who saw Joanna in her compromised state before the ambulance arrived, correct?"

"No," I said. "That's not correct. My cousin Buck saw her, too. He was working in the bay with me. He'd taken some drywall and trim upstairs when Joanna came in. When I realized she was having trouble, I called for him and he came down immediately to help."

She spoke slowly and deliberately as she paraphrased my words. "What you've just told me is that you were alone in the bay when Joanna arrived. Your cousin was upstairs."

"Yes, but it was only for a matter of seconds, and then he came right down."

"A matter of seconds," she repeated.

She was silent for several beats, during which the clock on the wall slowly tick-tick-ticked. *Amazing how long a few seconds can sound.*

I wasn't entirely sure what Detective Gleeson was getting at, but she seemed to be implying that, during the brief moment I'd been alone with Joanna, I could have harmed the woman. "The only thing I did was try to help Joanna. I was afraid she'd fall and get hurt, so I helped her down to the floor as she collapsed." I was disappointed to hear how desperate I sounded, how pleading, how nervous. *How guilty?* Maybe this interrogation was karma, a payback for me putting Gideon, Lane, Holden, Samira, and D-Jay through similar interrogations.

The woman was relentless. "If I searched your browsing history on your phone and laptop, I'm guessing I would see several searches related to mercury poisoning."

Terror gripped my throat, but I told the truth—in a squeaky voice. "Yes, you would. I performed some research after Joanna passed away."

"Some beforehand, too."

I racked my brain, thinking back. "Maybe. Like I said, I talked to my best friend about mercury poisoning from seafood—"

"A moment ago, you said you spoke with your cousin's wife about it."

"I'm referring to the same person. She's both my best friend and my cousin's wife. I'm the one who introduced them, and they later got married. She and I talked about the seafood issue prior to Joanna's collapse at the fire station. I'm fairly certain I looked up some information on my phone or computer that same night, but I couldn't swear to it. I'd have to check."

Shifting gears, she said, "Let's talk about your house-flipping business."

"Okay. What would you like to know?"

"You purchased the townhouse next to the one in which Joanna Hartzell lived, isn't that right?"

"It wasn't just me. My cousin is a part owner. We have a third silent partner, too." *Why did I feel as if I'd just thrown Buck and Presley under the bus?*

"Joanna's the one who brought the place to your attention?"

"That's right," I said. "She and Gideon Koppelman came to the fire station and asked us to take a look at it. It was deteriorating, and she was afraid her place could be at risk, too, if repairs weren't made soon."

"You're quite savvy, aren't you?" she said. "Got ownership for a song through some fancy legal maneuvering."

"I certainly wouldn't say we got it for a song. We paid nearly two hundred grand for the townhouse. There's quite a bit in back taxes owed on it, and it needs a lot of work. Carpet. Paint. Light fixtures. Most of the appliances will need to be replaced, too. There's a leak in the roof. We'll have to put in new shingles and replace the damaged wood in the attic. As for 'fancy legal maneuvering,' we consulted with an attorney to see what our options were, and she suggested that the quitclaim deeds would be a relatively easy, viable option. The deeds are simple and straightforward. It wasn't like we tricked anyone. There were no smoke and mirrors."

Well, no smoke until the fire station had been set on fire. Seriously, I was a victim, not a perpetrator. Why should I have to endure this demeaning inquisition?

Rather than belabor the point, Gleeson began to speculate. "It would have been nice to own the entire building, wouldn't it?"

"We wouldn't have been able to afford it," I said. "Besides, Joanna's unit wasn't for sale."

"But it could have been if she died in it and her family felt uncomfortable staying there, put it on the market."

Is she implying that I killed Joanna in the hopes of buying her townhouse as well as the one that had been owned by the Bottiglieris? I said the same thing that Holden had said to me earlier that day. "That thought would've never occurred to me. In reality, a death by anything other than natural causes can severely lower a property's value. I wouldn't want to get stuck with a property that had depreciated." *Again.*

"Another way to look at that," suggested the detective,

"is that a decline in value would make the property more affordable for you. You might get a chance to buy her townhouse at a greatly reduced rate."

I fought the urge to groan and roll my eyes. Even though she was totally off base, I had to give this woman credit. She had the ability to see many different sides to a story, to spin the facts in any number of ways. But what she was missing here was the *real* story. I knew it must be hard for her to ascertain the truth if she'd been told things from different perspectives. Maybe the best thing I could do here was to say as little as possible. Seemed anything I said got spun around and came back to bite me in the butt.

A knock sounded on the door and Collin's voice came from the other side. "Detective Gleeson? May I come in?"

The woman rose and stepped over to the door. Rather than allow Collin inside, she blocked the door with her body. All I could see was the top of his head and part of one leg. It was like the time I'd been standing behind Joanna and Gideon when Macy had announced she was pregnant. *Macy. She has to be the reason I'm here. How had my helpful suggestion about the possibility of mercury poisoning been twisted into an implication of guilt?*

"I'm interviewing Whitney Whitaker," Gleeson told Collin at the door. "I understand she's your fiancée."

"She is," Collin said. "I can tell you right now she had nothing to do with whatever happened to Joanna Hartzell."

"You're not exactly a disinterested party now, are you, Detective Flynn?" She tilted her head. "It's probably best you recuse yourself. You don't want to do anything that could appear biased and improper."

Collin was quiet for a long moment, probably debating how best to handle this insanely awkward situation. Finally, he said, "You're right, Detective Gleeson. I should recuse myself. Carry on."

Carry on? My innards were squirming like a barrel of worms at a bait shop. *How could Collin abandon me when I needed him most?* Then again, I'd always admired him for his ethics. He lived by a strict moral code. Recusing himself was the right thing to do. I'd unwittingly put Collin in an untenable situation, risked his reputation at work. I felt horrible about that, my stomach now queasy. But he knew I was innocent, and he likely had faith I could prove it on my own, without his help. Since the things I'd said earlier only seemed to get me in more trouble, I remained mum despite that fact that every cell of my body wanted to scream in frustration.

I did my best to try to remain strong as the detective resumed the interrogation, bombarding me with more questions I answered as succinctly as possible, carefully choosing my words. I knew she was only doing her job, and doing it quite well, so I tried not to take it personally. *Not an easy task.*

It was clear that my guilt had been inferred by my seeming to know Joanna had died of mercury poisoning before the pathologist confirmed it. But the autopsy might never have confirmed it had I not mentioned the possibility to Macy. I doubted that mercury was something screened for in a routine autopsy. Without me, the family wouldn't have answers. *I'm a hero, not a villain!* Though I'd just decided it was best for me to say as little as possible, and I realized that providing the information could further implicate me, I knew that I could not in good conscience fail to inform the detective about the tiny bead of mercury on the floor of the bay at the fire station. "I think I know how the killer got the mercury into Joanna's system."

She arched a brow. "Do you, now?"

I gave up the goods, even showed her the pics I'd snapped on my phone. I hoped that my doing so wouldn't further jeopardize Collin's standing with the department. It might appear as if he'd sat on critical information when, in reality, he'd planned to get to it as soon as he was able.

After I shared these new details and photos with Detective Gleeson, she whipped out her phone and ordered a crime scene team to the firehouse. "Take precautions. Mercury is toxic. It'll require special handling."

Eventually, she ran out of things to ask me, and directed the police officer to drive me back to the fire station. The crime scene van sat in the parking lot. The bay door had been raised, and two techs in full hazmat suits worked inside, one of them using a pair of tweezers to try to lift the tiny bead of liquid mercury so that it could be secured in a small airtight canister.

I thanked the officer for the ride as I climbed out.

I'd had my own dwindling list of suspects, and now it seemed I was at the top of the police department's list. I could see why. I'd been the last person, other than the EMTs, to see Joanna alive. I'd correctly deduced that her symptoms were consistent with mercury poisoning, a relatively rare occurrence, and even identified that the delivery mechanism had been mercury vapor via tainted cigarettes. I'd been in contact with the victim several times, and could have easily slipped her a poisoned pack. Heck, if I were in Gleeson's shoes, I'd think I was guilty, too. But I was simply an inquisitive and perceptive person, not a criminal. Lest I end up reciting my wedding vows from a jail cell, I'd better identify the true killer, and fast. The problem was, I was out of suspects.

Who had I missed?

CHAPTER 26

SHE KNEADS ME

SAWDUST

Collin came to their house that night. Whitney was upset again. Sawdust could tell because her voice did all sorts of things. First it was low, then it was high. It was soft, then it was loud. He sat on her lap and, though she occasionally ran a hand over his back, she also flapped her hands around, gesticulating, and more than once put her hands over her face as if she was trying to block out the world.

Sawdust often found comfort in kneading his paws on a blanket or a soft cushion. Maybe Whitney would find the action comforting, too. He placed his paws on her belly and began working his claws. Rather than find the practice to be a comfort, she issued cries of pain, picked him up, and put him down on the floor. He'd only been trying to help! Couldn't she understand that?

CHAPTER 27

THE BUS STOPS HERE

WHITNEY

On Thursday, Buck and I continued to lay the tile in the bathrooms at the fire station. It was hard, physical work, requiring precision and concentration. One misplaced tile could have a chain reaction, and you could find a layout looking totally off-kilter. It was the perfect job for me today, when I needed something to take my mind off Joanna Hartzell's murder.

I'd racked my brain over and over and over again, all through the night, but couldn't think of a suspect—other than Macy herself. *Had she killed her own mother?* Maybe she'd grown tired of her mother berating her and her husband, second-guessing her decisions, making her feel like a disappointment. Surely if I'd had this thought, Detective Gleeson would, too. Part of me would love to see Macy put through the wringer. After all, she had to be the person who'd gotten me dragged down to the police station yesterday. But another part of me hoped she wouldn't be subject to an interrogation. In her condition, she might not be up for it. I didn't want her or her baby's health to be jeopardized. There'd been enough suffering already.

I forced the murder from my mind, and instead focused on our flip projects. My mind went back to Samira, her apology, her nesting instincts, her obsession with the townhouse, wanting it to become a happy home for herself, her husband, and their children. I'd want exactly the same thing in her situation. Though her tactics had rubbed me the wrong way, especially the question about whether profit was the only thing I cared about, her apology had gone a long way with me. *Is there some way I can help them afford the townhouse?*

While Buck, Presley, and I would need the money from the sale to continue our house-flipping business, there was someone else who'd expressed interest in the property who might be willing to help out. After all, he'd proven to be the best of friends to Joanna, a nice guy with a big, generous heart.

At half past three, my back and knees needed a break. I decided to go talk to Gideon in person, see if he'd be amenable to my suggestion. I told Buck about the idea I'd come up with. "I'm going to see whether Gideon might be willing to go along. I'll be back in a bit."

I removed my knee pads, went down the stairs, and headed outside. It was a bright late-summer day, partly cloudy, warm but not excessively hot. In other words, perfect. *Could the weather be a good omen?* I certainly hoped so.

I walked down the sidewalk, keeping my gaze straight ahead to avoid glancing over at the Griffins' former unit or Joanna's townhouse. I had no idea which one Macy might be resting in now. With the air and water having been tested and cleared, maybe the family had moved back into Joanna's place. Last time I'd seen Macy, though, she'd still been in their unit in Gideon's building.

I turned down the walkway and made my way up onto Gideon's porch, knocking softly in case Macy was napping next door. My ears detected a shuffling sound inside, and Gideon pulled the door open, but only an inch or two. *Does he suspect me, too?*

"Hi, Gideon," I said. "I have a proposition for you. It involves the townhouse."

"Yeah?" He opened the door another inch.

"I know you expressed an interest in buying it to use as a rental, but it would be wonderful to see a family be able to own it. Samira and D-Jay are interested." I told him how Samira had shown me her designs, how she'd put some real time and thought into them, how she hoped to make the townhouse her family's home. "They really want the place. I'd like to make it happen if I can. Our house-flipping business isn't only our livelihood. It's our passion. We enjoy providing homes for people."

Gideon opened his door a little farther. "Where do I come in?"

"What if we sold the place to you, and then you immediately resold it to Samira and D-Jay on an owner-finance arrangement? You'd earn interest income on your funds, and they'd be able to buy their dream home. It would be a win for everyone."

His face brightened, and he opened the door fully now. "That's not a bad idea. I like those folks. They've always paid their rent on time, never been a problem, don't complain. Their boy's a little loud, though." Gideon chuckled, then eyed me intently. "Macy thinks you might have killed her mother but, for the record, I don't believe it. You're good people. You coming up with this plan proves it."

Though I'd assumed Macy had been the one to suggest my guilt to Detective Gleeson, learning that I'd been right, that she believed I could have killed her mother, made me heartsick. I'd never felt so misjudged. It was frustrating, humiliating, demoralizing. My chest felt tight with emotion. "Thanks, Gideon," I managed. "That means a lot." Especially coming from someone I'd once considered a suspect myself. "Why don't I come back later, once Samira and D-Jay are home from work, and we'll propose the plan to them, see what they think."

He dipped his head in agreement. "It's a date."

I turned to step off the porch, and he closed the door behind me. As I made my way down the steps, the squeal of brakes drew my attention to the right. A school bus had stopped at the corner. The handful of teenagers filtering out told me it was the high school bus.

The last to emerge was Alyssa. She had her backpack slung over her shoulder, but the curve of her back told me she was bearing more weight than just the bag. She had a hand on the strap. A bright yellow bandage on her finger caught my eye, and my blood froze in my veins. An instant later, my feet moved on their own accord, carrying me on a route to intercept Alyssa on the sidewalk.

She looked up as she noticed me approaching, and offered a feeble smile. "Hi, Whitney."

We met directly in front of Joanna's townhouse, our gazes locking.

"Alyssa," I said softly, "show me your splinter."

She stared back at me for several long beats, her eyes first misting then filling with tears. One escaped and rolled down her cheek, leaving a trail in her makeup, exposing the skin underneath.

We didn't break eye contact as the door to the townhouse jerked open and Macy marched out, clad in a pair of soft shorts and a tank top. "What's going on out here?"

In my peripheral vision, I saw that Gideon, too, had opened his door and emerged onto his porch.

Macy walked up and shot me a glare, putting a hand on her daughter's shoulder. "Come inside, Alyssa."

Alyssa made no attempt to move. Instead, she rolled her backpack off her shoulder, letting it drop to the ground. Gideon walked up as she held out the bandaged finger, using the fingers of her other hand to slowly peel the adhesive strip back. Once she had, she held the finger out for Macy, Gideon, and me to see. No sliver of wood from a porch swing was embedded under her skin. Rather, her finger contained a tiny shard of glass. *Alyssa has been lying to us.*

Alyssa turned to look at her mother. "I did it, Mom. I killed Grammy. I didn't mean to. But I did."

"No!" Macy cried, backing away with her hands over her mouth. "No! No! No!"

Though the girl's face, like her mother's, was grief stricken, her straighter posture said that getting this information out in the open had unburdened her. "I figured if Grammy thought her age was catching up with her, she might ask us to move back in with her, like when I was little. I knew you and Dad were having money problems—"

Macy, still in shock, shook her head so hard she risked rattling her brain. "We weren't having money problems!"

"Yes, you were!" Alyssa insisted. "Dad just didn't

tell you. I figured it out when we went to Grammy's house and you told her you were pregnant. Remember when you said we were doing fine and she said 'that's what you think'? I knew something was going on. I put strawberry candies inside Dad's work gloves. I knew that if he was still going to work, he'd find them. He'd realize I'd been the one to put them there, and he'd think it was funny. But he never said anything about the candy to me. That's how I knew he wasn't wearing the gloves anymore."

It had been a clever ploy. If only Holden had seen the candies sooner, maybe he could have alleviated Alyssa's concerns.

She continued to explain. "I got on his computer and was able to look at your bank account. It looked like he was still getting his paycheck twice a month because the amount was the same, but the data was different. The money wasn't an automatic deposit from Frozen Freight. It was a transfer from another bank account. I knew the money had to be coming from Grammy."

Macy shook her head again, though less vehemently this time. "No!"

Alyssa continued. "You said something about pregnant women not eating fish and I was curious about it so I looked it up. The links I read said that mercury poisoning causes dizziness and memory loss and tremors. Those are things old people get. I thought if I could give Grammy just a little bit of mercury, she'd have the symptoms and think she needed some help. I knew there was mercury in old thermometers, so I broke the big one in the root beer sign on Gideon's porch to get the mercury out." She pointed across the street to the mustard yellow sign. "That's when I got the glass in my finger. I read that breathing in the vapor is how most people get mercury into their system, so I got the idea to put it in Grammy's cigarettes. I got a pack out of the carton in her pantry. I divided the ball of mercury into smaller balls, and I only put a tiny amount in each cigarette."

Sadly, I could verify that fact. The bead of liquid mercury Sawdust had discovered in the bay of the fire station had been nearly microscopic in proportion. Unfortunately, mercury was so highly toxic that a small amount was all it took to result in big consequences. The improvised hazmat suit Alyssa had worn when she'd cleaned out Joanna's townhouse made sense now. She'd been trying to be careful not to carry any mercury residue home to her pregnant mother. That's why she'd later disposed of the suit in the dumpster outside the fire station. I'd been right that day when I'd seen her on the porch of her grandmother's place. The girl had been dealing with much more than grief. She'd also been dealing with guilt.

"I left the pack of cigarettes on our porch," Alyssa said. "I figured Grammy would find them when she came over to check on you, or that Dad or Gideon would take them to her." Alyssa choked up and had to clear her throat before continuing. Her voice was a mere squeaky whisper now. "Grammy said she only smoked two cigarettes a day, but I think she must've lied about that." She cleared her throat again, to little avail. "Mercury poisoning is supposed to be treatable. I never meant to kill her!"

The girl completely broke down now, her knees giving way. Fortunately, just as I'd been able to break her grandmother's fall in the fire station, I was able to break hers now. I grabbed her by the upper arm and yanked her toward the yard so that her knees landed on soft grass rather than rough, hard concrete. She fell forward, collapsing completely, and put her hands over her face, sobbing and writhing with grief and guilt. Macy fell to her knees on the grass beside her, sobbing as well.

Gideon pulled out his phone. "I'd better call Holden."

"Text him," I said. "He's in a class."

Gideon's fingers hovered over the screen as he eyed me. "How do you know that?"

"I had the same epiphany as Alyssa about what Joanna said." *That's what you think.* "I followed Holden to a private security center. He's training to work as a guard."

"You were doing your own investigating?"

"Yes," I said. "I felt that I owed it to Joanna." The woman had spent her final moments in my arms, after all.

Gideon heaved a slow, ragged breath, then moved his thumbs over the screen as he drafted the text that would change Holden's life forever. Once he'd finished, he jabbed the button with his index finger to send it on its way.

I had no idea what else we were supposed to do here. Alyssa was a minor, a juvenile who'd made a mistake—a serious, horrible, fatal mistake. Though I wanted to call Collin and ask him to come here to help sort things out, I didn't want to circumvent regular protocols and get him into any more trouble. Instead, I stepped away from the mother and daughter, and phoned the police department, asking to be transferred to Detective Gleeson.

When she picked up her phone, I identified myself. "We've figured out what happened to Joanna Hartzell. Please come to her townhouse as soon as you can."

"I'll be right there."

Fifteen minutes later, Alyssa and Macy had calmed enough to move to the rockers on Joanna's porch and await Alyssa's fate. Gideon remained with them on the porch. I kept my distance, sitting on the dilapidated steps of our adjacent townhouse.

When the police cruiser pulled up, I stood and met Gleeson at the curb. I angled my head slightly to indicate the two on the porch. "It was the granddaughter," I said. "It was unintentional."

Gleeson took one look at the pathetic young girl and inhaled a deep breath, releasing it slowly to steel herself. "This is going to be a tough one."

Through my relationship with Collin, I knew police work was rarely black and white, clearly right or wrong. While those who went into law enforcement wanted to see justice done, determining what constituted justice in each set of circumstances could be extremely difficult.

Having delivered the information and set the wheels in motion, I turned and gave a solemn nod goodbye to the three on the porch.

CHAPTER 28

HOME. AGAIN.

WHITNEY

Over the following weeks, there were a number of developments.

Shortly after being taken into custody, Alyssa appeared in juvenile court to defend herself on the charge of criminally negligent homicide, a Class E felony punishable by one to six years in prison and a fine of up to $3,000. Fortunately, the prosecutor realized the girl was filled with remorse—overflowing with it, in fact. She had never intended to end her grandmother's life, and had only been trying, in a very reckless and ill-advised manner, to solve her family's dire financial situation. She'd also been meticulous in cleaning her grandmother's townhouse, done her best to keep her mother and unborn sibling from being exposed to the mercury.

Alyssa's attorney and the prosecutor reached a plea deal. She was ordered to attend therapy with a licensed psychologist to address the emotional ramifications of what she'd done. She was also put under the supervision of a juvenile probation officer. Because she was remorseful and posed no threat others, she was not remanded to a juvenile detention facility, and continued to live with her parents in what had formerly been Joanna's house. While I might have thought living there would be difficult for her, Alyssa preferred it. She said she felt close to her grandmother there, and that she could sense her presence and forgiveness.

Buck, Presley, and I offered Gideon a good price for the townhouse, one that was significantly below market value but would still yield us a reasonable return for our time and efforts. Gideon, in turn, worked out a financing arrangement with Samira and D-Jay, who were overjoyed to learn they'd get to buy the townhouse, after all. I recoded the keypad with Kavish's birthday, and gave the couple unfettered access to what would become their home once we finished remodeling it. Samira completed designs for the place, and Buck and I agreed to implement them just as she wanted, even though I thought some of the paint colors were a bit loud, especially in the master bathroom. But to each their own. This home would be hers. It should reflect her style and taste.

Even though the doctors might have been able to save Joanna's life had they realized she'd suffered from mercury poisoning, Macy decided not to pursue a malpractice case. It made sense under the circumstances. Had a lawsuit been filed, Alyssa would have had to endure depositions, possibly even testify in court. The doctor's defense lawyers would undoubtedly attempt to place as much blame as they could on the girl. Macy didn't want to put her daughter through any more trauma.

Despite all the guff the Bottiglieris had given us, Buck, Presley, and I paid a goodwill visit to each of them, and issued checks to make sure they'd all been paid precisely the same amount for their interests in the townhouse. We informed them that we'd sacrificed a significant amount of profit in order to allow a young family to buy the place. All of them seemed satisfied now. I wasn't followed again.

Colette and Emmalee threw me a lovely bridal shower at the café. It was nice to have some fun with female friends and family members before my big day. I came home with some wonderful gifts, including a beautiful pair of book ends shaped like cats, a set of copper Moscow mule mugs, and a beach towel big enough for two that would come in handy for relaxing on the shore on our honeymoon.

Buck and I finished the fire station remodel with two weeks to spare before my wedding. A death had recently upended our world, but life, in its new places and forms, was moving on.

CHAPTER 29
WEDDING BELLS

WHITNEY

With Joanna's murder solved and the townhouse re-model moving smoothly along, Collin and I could enjoy our wedding day without distractions. The fire station might have once sounded one, two, three, or even four alarms, but today it would sound wedding bells—proverbial speaking.

Collin and Ren dressed in one of the smaller bed-rooms, while my mother, Colette, and I got ready for the ceremony in the master, as Sawdust napped atop a chair. Colette looked positively radiant in her sky blue satin matron-of-honor dress, the Queen Anne neckline flattering the fuller figure she currently sported thanks to her pregnancy. A tailor had added stretchy spandex panels to the sides of the dress to accommodate her ever-expanding baby bump. My mother had chosen a scoop-neck tea-length chiffon dress in a beautiful teal color, the style perfect for her frame.

I sat at one of the tables while my stylist worked on me. She coiffed my hair into a pile of curls atop my head, leaving a twirly tendril hanging on each side to frame my cheeks. Once she'd wrangled my hair out of the way and applied hairspray to hold it all in place, she applied copious amounts of makeup to my face, finishing with a loose powder and setting spray. Grinning proudly, she held up a hand mirror so I could take a look at her handiwork.

Whoa. Is that even me in the reflection? I looked feminine and glamorous, a far cry from my usual look, which involved little to no makeup and my hair swept up into an easy ponytail to keep it out of the way while I worked with my tools.

I stood to give her a hug. "You're not a *beautician.* You're a *magician.*"

Once my stylist had gone, it was time to get me into my dress. My mother and Colette held out my gown and I carefully slipped into it. Mom zipped up the back for me. I slid my feet into the heels and put on the aquamarine earrings that my mother and grandmother had worn at their weddings, the jewelry singlehandedly constituting something old, borrowed, and blue.

I turned to look at myself in the full-length mirror. *I cleaned up well.*

My mother stepped up beside me, tears welling up in her eyes. "You look absolutely beautiful, Whitney!"

Colette whipped a tissue from the box on the table and handed it to my mother, who dabbed at her eyes. "Collin is a lucky guy." One hand on her rounded belly, Colette emitted a choking sound and grabbed a second tissue, holding it to her face to stifle her sob. "It's happening, Whitney! All of our dreams are coming true."

I couldn't help but get misty at her words. Back in college, we'd daydream over coffee or margaritas, imagining our futures, what careers we'd pursue, what type of house we'd live in, what kind of men we'd marry, whether we'd have children and how many. Those dreams were now unfolding, our questions being answered in wonderful ways we could have never imagined. Marrying a homicide detective in a fire station I'd remodeled myself? I would have never come up with such an outlandish idea. Life had certainly proven to be an adventure.

A chime on my mother's phone told her and Colette that it was time to assemble for the procession. My mother gave me a final hug and a kiss on the cheek, taking care not to muss my hair or makeup. "See you downstairs in a bit. I'll send your father in."

"Don't forget Sawdust." He looked up at me as I slid a blue bowtie over his head, dressing him for the occasion. I ruffled his ears. "You're such a handsome boy." I picked him up and handed him over to my mother.

Colette reached out and gave my hand a squeeze before following my mother out the door. It had just closed behind them when it opened again and my father stepped in, dressed in his best gray suit and a tie that matched the blue sash on my dress.

"Who are you?" he exclaimed. "And what have you done with my little girl?"

"I know, right?" I turned to take another look in the mirror. I'd never felt so beautiful. Or so excited. The butterflies in my belly were all aflutter.

Dad gave me a kiss on the cheek. We stepped over to the door, which he opened just a crack so we'd know when it was our turn to head down the spiral staircase. I peeked through to watch.

The soft piano music that had been coming from downstairs changed, louder now, and the murmur of voices ceased as the guests realized the ceremony was

starting. First, Buck escorted my mother, who cradled
Sawdust in her arms, down the stairs. Collin, who had
his back to the door Dad and I were peeking through,
went next. Fortunately, by the time the staircase circled around, he'd descended far enough down that he
wouldn't catch a glimpse of me. There'd been enough
bad luck recently. No sense tempting fate by having him
see his bride in her wedding dress before we met under
the floral arch downstairs.

As Collin's best man, Ren went down next, his
muscles filling out the sleeves of his tux. Ren was followed by Colette, who held onto her bouquet of hydrangeas with one hand and the railing with the other, her
grip tight, as if her life—and that of the baby in her
belly—depended on it. Clearly, she'd be a protective
mother. Next down the stairs were Collin's eight-year-
old nephew and six-year-old niece, our ring bearer and
flower girl. Both had freckled faces and gap-toothed
smiles. *Cute kids.*

The music changed once again, and the first few notes
of the traditional wedding march wafted up the staircase.

My dad slid me a smile. "It's hard to give away my
little girl, but at least I'll be handing her over to a man
who comes as close to deserving her as any ever could."

My mouth curved up in a smile. "I got a good one,
didn't I?"

Dad crooked his elbow and I took hold of his arm.
He led me to the top of the staircase. There was a scrap-
ing of chairs and rustling as the guests stood. I took a
big breath and down we went, around and around and
around the spiral staircase, circling the fireman's pole,
until our feet finally landed on the freshly painted concrete of the fire station's garage. Not as spectacular an

entrance as sliding down the pole in my wedding gown would have been, but much more refined.

My father proceeded to escort me down the aisle. I passed the smiling faces of friends and family, happy they could share in our special day. Wanda and Marv Hartley. Emmalee. Buck. Owen, his wife, and their three little girls. Aunt Nancy and Uncle Roger. Collin's extended family, several of his running buddies, coworkers of various ranks from the Metro Police Department.

As we passed the front row, Sawdust looked up from where he lay on my mother's lap, his tail softly swishing in excitement. Galileo and Copernicus were also in attendance, lounging on the laps of Collin's two aunts in the front row. Dad led me over to where Collin waited under the colorful floral arch, and released my arm.

Collin's face lit up when our eyes met. He looked me up and down, and mouthed the word *Wow!* He looked great himself, the black tuxedo a nice complement to his dark hair and green eyes. For someone whose job often took him to seedy places, he had no problem pulling off a look of refinement and elegance.

A fresh smile claimed my lips as he took my arm and we turned to face the officiate, a local criminal court judge before whom Collin had testified in several cases throughout his law enforcement career. The woman wore her black judicial robe and a pleasant demeanor as she gave us a smile and addressed our guests. "Welcome, everyone. I was so pleased when Detective Flynn asked if I would be willing to officiate his wedding ceremony. Usually, when I'm giving someone a life sentence, I'm sending them off to jail. It warms my heart that the life sentence I'll bestow upon Collin and Whitney today will instead be a willing and happy destiny."

Chuckles came from the crowd.

The judge spent a moment or two pattering on about marriage and love, and recited a poem Collin and I had chosen that we thought best reflected our feelings about marriage, "The Art of Marriage" by Wilferd Arlan Peterson. Then, she asked us to recite our vows.

As was tradition, Collin went first, his confident "I do" paired with a gentle squeeze of my hands, a warm smile, and a direct look into my eyes that said he had no reservations about the commitment he was making to me today.

I'd been doubtful about many things in my life, most recently whether it had been a mistake to buy the townhouse around the corner from where we now stood. Thank goodness the purchase ended up having nothing to do with Joanna Hartzell's death. But one thing I had never doubted was my love for Collin. He was an intelligent and handsome man, with a strong moral code and work ethic. He worked hard every day to make the world a safer place, to fight for justice. I respected him as much as I loved him, and I knew he felt the same way about me. We didn't always see eye to eye—what couple did?—but we always managed to disagree civilly and to reach mutually agreeable solutions to any issues that arose. Whatever came our way, I had no doubt we could face it together.

When it came time for me to say "I do," my voice didn't waver, as loud and strong as his had been. As if he, too, had been asked to make a commitment today, Sawdust stood up on my mother's lap and issued a loud *meow*, much to the amusement of our guests. Collin and I exchanged rings, sliding them onto each other's fingers to seal our solemn vows.

When the ceremony concluded, the judge introduced

us for the first time as husband and wife. "Mr. and Mrs. Flynn, folks!" After collecting Sawdust from my mother, I headed back up the spiral staircase to raucous applause, this time on my husband's arm rather than my father's. Below us, the judge invited everyone up to the rooftop for pre-dinner cocktails.

The reception was both a blast and a blur, seeming to be over nearly as soon as it started. We had cocktails and a fabulous dinner prepared by Colette's staff. We danced, bringing the cats onto the dance floor with us as we performed the "Cha-Cha Slide." We drank champagne. We enjoyed wedding cake baked by Emmalee with a custom-made topper Colette had fashioned out of fondant icing—a couple resembling Collin and me, as well as three cats at our feet that looked exactly like Sawdust, Copernicus, and Galileo. *So that's why Colette had asked to see photos of Collin's cats when we'd all gone to dinner.*

We departed the fire station at the end of the night in the back of a clean and detailed police cruiser driven by Officer Hogarty, who was both a wedding guest and Collin's former field training officer. Our chauffer switched on the flashing lights and siren to announce our departure, and off we went to enjoy our honeymoon.

North Carolina was the perfect place to enjoy our first days as husband and wife. While we left Galileo and Copernicus at home with a pet sitter, Sawdust was well-behaved enough to come along with us. There were seemingly endless sites to see, but we enjoyed them at a pleasant, leisurely pace. We visited a dozen cascades in the area known as the Land of Waterfalls in the southwestern part of the state. Whitewater Falls, the tallest waterfall east of the Rockies, was nothing short of spectacular. We hiked in the mountains, including a trail to the top of Mount Mitchell which, at over 6,600 feet, was the highest point east of the Mississippi River. We especially enjoyed the Balsam Nature Trail, with its fragrant fir trees. We drove the Blue Ridge Parkway, stopping at the overlooks to enjoy the gorgeous scenery. Sawdust enjoyed it all from the safety of the specially designed cat backpack I'd bought for him, complete with see-through mesh window panels.

Once the sun went down each evening, we'd find a dark spot and observe the stars and planets though Collin's telescope. Black Balsam Knob provided an excellent, unobstructed view of the night sky. We also attended a viewing at the Pisgah Astronomical Research Institute, a former NASA operations site that now offered programs for the public, one of only two Dark Sky Parks in the state.

After several fun-filled days in the mountains, we traveled farther east, and enjoyed some time in the Outer Banks. We toured the site of the Wright Brothers' first flight in Kitty Hawk, climbed the tall sand dunes at Jockey's Ridge, saw wild horses on the beach in Corolla, and visited the iconic Cape Hatteras Lighthouse, known for its bright red base. We stayed at a lovely inn on the beach, and fell asleep to the shush of the ocean.

On our last morning, we stood at the waterline, watching the sunrise over the Atlantic Ocean. The horizon was the perfect metaphor for marriage. We had no idea what might lay beyond it, but whatever came our way, we'd go through it together.

When we returned home from our honeymoon, Buck and Owen helped us move Emmalee's things to her new place, and Collin's furniture and belongings into the cottage we'd now share as husband and wife. Sawdust would miss spending time with Cleo, though Emmalee promised to bring the lively kitty over for playdates as often as she could. We'd expected the transition might take some time, but Copernicus and Galileo settled quickly into their new home, the three cats becoming fast friends. Sawdust was more than happy to share his house, his bed, and his cat trees, though he became a little jealous when he'd discover one of the other cats in my lap, which he considered his sacred space.

Collin rolled out of bed one morning, hiked a thumb at the stack of his clothing that had been draped over a chair for the past month, and put his hands on his hips. "When am I getting that closet you promised me?"

"Nag, nag, nag," I teased, pulling the sheet up to cover my head.

"What if I bring you coffee in bed?"

I flung the sheet back. "I'll have it built by the end of the day."

RECIPES

CHICKPEA-OF-THE-SEA
MOCK TUNA SALAD

Ingredients
1 can garbanzo beans
1½ cups plant-based, egg-free mayonnaise such as Vegenaise (No cholesterol, gluten, or preservatives! Yay!)
1 tablespoon lemon juice
1 teaspoon garlic powder or garlic salt
¼ cup chopped celery (optional)
¼ cup chopped green, white, or red onion (optional)

Directions
Using a potato masher, mash the beans in a large bowl until the skins separate and the beans are reduced to a lumpy paste. You may use a food processor instead if you prefer, transferring the beans to the large bowl once you've processed them. Add the other ingredients and stir together thoroughly. The chickpea salad may be served cold or at room temperature, and is great as a

sandwich spread, on crackers, or on celery sticks. Enjoy that plant-based protein!

PUMPKIN SPICE CAKE/CAKE DONUTS

Cake/Cake Donut ingredients
1 box vanilla cake mix
15-ounce canned pumpkin
1 tablespoon pumpkin pie spice

Frosting/glaze ingredients
2 cups powdered sugar
1 teaspoon vanilla extract (You can substitute maple extract or almond if preferred)
Water (amount needed varies by desired thickness of frosting or glaze)

Optional topping variations
Shredded coconut
Chopped pecans
Slivered almonds
Sprinkle of brown sugar
Sprinkle of powdered sugar

Directions
Preheat oven to 350 degrees. Stir cake ingredients together in large bowl until well blended. Grease cake pan, donut pan, or mini Bundt pan. Fill each section until ⅔ full. Bake for approximately fourteen minutes, or until a toothpick inserted in the cake or donut comes out clean.

To prepare the frosting or glaze, stir together the powdered sugar, vanilla extract, and one tablespoon water. Add one teaspoon of water at a time, stirring afterward, until the topping is at your desired thickness. For a thick frosting, you'll use less water. For a more transparent glaze, you'll use more water. Spread or drizzle the frosting or glaze over cooled donuts. For variety, add one or more of the optional toppings. This recipe can also be made in small squares and served as dessert cakes. It's the perfect autumn treat and sooooo easy!

CREAMY MUSHROOM RISOTTO

Ingredients
6 cups vegetable broth
4 tablespoons olive oil
12 ounces sliced mushrooms of your choice
2 large cloves minced garlic
1 teaspoon dried thyme
1 teaspoon salt
1 small, diced onion
1½ cups arborio rice
½ cup dry white wine
1 teaspoon lemon juice
1 teaspoon black pepper

Optional
1 cup peas or chopped asparagus

Directions
Simmer the broth over medium heat for five minutes, then reduce to low heat. Heat a large pan over medium heat. Add two tablespoons of olive oil and a small amount of mushrooms. Spread the mushrooms in a single layer so they can brown. Allow mushrooms to brown in pan for three minutes, then turn them over

to brown for an additional three minutes. Push the browned mushrooms aside and repeat the process with the remaining mushrooms, adding more oil as needed. Reduce the heat to low and add the garlic, thyme, and salt. Sauté for about one minute until fragrant. Add onions and any remaining oil, and sauté for another minute. Add the rice and stir to coat. Allow the mixture to toast for one to two minutes. Add the wine and simmer for five minutes, stirring often. Add remaining salt and broth, one cup at a time, allowing the rice and liquid to cook down before adding more. Stir often, but not constantly, to allow rice to cook.

Continue until the broth is cooked down and the rice is tender enough to eat. You may add more broth if you prefer your rice more tender. Remove from heat, add the cooked mushrooms and optional ingredients, as well as lemon juice and black pepper to taste. Stir thoroughly so that the mushrooms are coated. Enjoy!